She had met, *known*, very handsome men.

But William Reid of Thornhallow was not what she would call handsome. He was almost closer to... Beautiful? Entrancing? When she remembered his eyes... What color had they been?

Gray? No...

They had seemed so at first, so cold, but no...

Hazel. With flecks of gold, gray and green.

Eyes that had seen too much but still retained *light*. Enchanting, rapturous light.

Mrs. Murray's shouts echoing down the corridor sharply brought Rebecca back from her reverie. Cursing under her breath, she picked up her quill and returned to the ledger. It didn't matter what she would qualify his manner to be, or what precisely she thought of his eyes. Truly, it mattered not one bit that he would never *see* her. She was glad of it, verily.

She wasn't about to jeopardize her position, her *life*, by becoming foolishly *intrigued* by the master. The Earl of Thornhallow could be the most beautiful angel to descend from heaven and it would matter not one bit. She was his housekeeper. And she would do her duty. As she always had, infallibly.

Author Note

The Housekeeper of Thornhallow Hall was born of a single image, the ominous house on the hill, and my enduring love for the great gothic novels of the nineteenth century.

The exploration of liminal spaces found in these novels, between the natural and supernatural, good and evil, love and obsession, has always fascinated me. Gothic provides a space for us to explore the darkest recesses of our souls, challenging us at every turn to believe.

The story then grew as I delved into research about soaps, servants and architecture, admittedly losing myself in the history of the fur trade, which saw a boom in the Pacific Northwest during the nineteenth century. It is a long and complicated history, and one that should always be viewed in the context of First Peoples history. It is vital to remember the impact European invasions had on the First Peoples and their land, and to constantly challenge the gaze through which we view history.

On a historical note, the poems Liam gifts Rebecca are, for those not familiar with them, by Edgar Allan Poe. *Tamerlane and Other Poems* by a Bostonian was released in 1827 and is considered to be Poe's first published work.

Thank you for reading Rebecca and Liam's story. I do hope you enjoy it.

LOTTE R. JAMES

The Housekeeper of Thornhallow Hall

HARLEQUIN®
HISTORICAL™

Recycling programs for this product may not exist in your area.

ISBN-13: 978-1-335-40730-6

The Housekeeper of Thornhallow Hall

Harlequin Enterprises ULC
22 Adelaide St. West, 40th Floor
Toronto, Ontario M5H 4E3, Canada
www.Harlequin.com

Printed in U.S.A.

Lotte R. James trained as an actor and theater director but spent most of her life working day jobs crunching numbers while dreaming up stories of love and adventure. She's thrilled to finally be writing those stories, and when she's not scribbling on tiny pieces of paper, she can usually be found wandering the countryside for inspiration or nestling with coffee and a book.

The Housekeeper of Thornhallow Hall is Lotte R. James's debut title for Harlequin Historical.

Look out for more books from Lotte R. James coming soon.

Visit the Author Profile page at Harlequin.com.

To my first readers,
Tilly and Valerie.

And to my mother, Brigitte, always.

Chapter One

Northern England, 1828

The rumbling and creaking of the cart, and the bitter grumblings of the old man Rebecca had hired in the village to help her complete the journey, had long since faded. How long she stood there—feet firmly rooted in the frozen tracks of mud, the ice-cold northern wind whistling and cutting through her many layers of wool, eyes affixed on the sight beyond the daunting wrought-iron gates—was anyone's guess.

It was only a house. A house like any other.

'Unholy house,' the old man had spat as he left, but to Rebecca it remained nothing more than another house she was to work in.

So why was passing the gates, walking up the barren drive and entering proving to be such a challenge? This was not the first house she had served, and it certainly wouldn't be the last. Why was this paragon of Jacobean English grandeur, sitting upon its isolated hill in the middle of the borderlands—imposing and dreary in the light of this cold grey September morning though it may be—suddenly filling Rebecca's heart with dread and foreboding?

Stop behaving such a complete ninny, she thought as a shiver passed through her. *You are cold, and tired. It's only a house. A house with stories.*

Yes, there were many stories about this house. Tales she knew well, having heard them whispered in many a drawing room or parlour in the late hours. Tales which were the only reason she'd been offered the position—of that she was almost entirely certain. Tales of vengeance and ghosts and disappearing earls—and, naturally, murder. Gothic tales worthy of a penny blood, by which she set no store. Though there was *something* about this place. Rebecca could feel it in her bones. Something otherworldly.

No. It's only a house.

The only thing truly threatening her composure was her return to this land. Coming back, so close to home... It was bound to be upsetting. Or rather, *unsettling*. It wasn't so much the house that troubled her, but all it represented.

A return home. Well, somewhat.

No matter. This position was perfect. *Too* perfect to resist. It was worth the risk of returning to the fells and dales so near those she had explored as a child. Worth returning to this unforgiving landscape she had always felt in the marrow of her soul, and which now gave her courage as she inhaled deep breaths of the fresh, biting autumn wind.

Independence. Autonomy. Isolation. And a rather impressive salary.

All for what—at least to Rebecca, or to any other housekeeper worth her salt—amounted to child's play. Thornhallow Hall was, to all intents and purposes, abandoned. Its master, William Reid, the Right Honourable the Earl of Thornhallow, having disappeared from society, and many believed from England, some ten years prior. Since then the house had remained occupied by a diminished army of servants. Why the master had refused to close the house entirely was anyone's guess. To be certain, it added to the tantalising mystery of it all.

Regardless, it was up to this minuscule army, and now herself, to maintain the efficient and seamless running of the house—most of which, she had been informed, was closed off on the master's orders.

Only four rooms in the main wing would require her attention. *The study, the library, the drawing room and the master's bedroom. Maintain order and cleanliness as though the Earl might return within the hour*—those were her marching orders. Orders she could certainly follow, and with alacrity.

This position offered her independence, and isolation beyond her wildest dreams. Yes, it would be hard work. But never in her life had she shied away from hard labour.

Besides, I doubt I could do any worse than the others before me...

And, after all, it wasn't as if she had many other options. It was Thornhallow or a house in London. The latter being absolutely, undisputedly, out of the question. She could not return to the city. That was looking for trouble. The last time... The last time it had all nearly ended. She had skirted too close to disaster. And here...

He would never think of looking for her here.

At least that episode in London had served some good. Served as a welcome reminder of her circumstances. Of her life and limitations. Of the need to always keep moving.

So keep moving.

'Can't turn back now,' she muttered, rubbing her wool-covered frozen hands together before grabbing hold of her portmanteau and travelling bag. 'And besides, you're well nithered now, you fool.'

With that, Rebecca slid through the creaky, rusted pedestrian gate, as instructed, and began the long walk up the gravelled drive.

* * *

Having rung the bell spiritedly, Rebecca turned from the commanding arched oak doors, set into the facade beneath a delicate portico, to admire the landscape from this vantage point. It was…stunning, and invigorating. From here she could see forever. The village, there in the dell to the west, fields, pastures and more villages punctuating the folds and curves of the wild and untamed land, all greens and greys and purples. On a clearer day perhaps she might even see her home from here. So close…

The thought sent another shiver down her spine.

'Mrs Hardwicke, I presume,' grumbled a proud-sounding voice.

Rebecca whirled around and found herself staring into a pair of bright grey eyes. Their owner was a tall, lean and elegantly liveried fellow, somewhere in his mid-sixties, though his smooth face belied his age. His greying hair was neatly swept back into a small *queue*, reminiscent of a bygone age, and his bushy eyebrows joined in a curt frown. Thin lips were tightly pressed together in disapproval, but Rebecca smiled at this man who was most certainly Thornhallow's butler.

The man who she would need make her ally if she was to succeed here.

'Mr Brown,' Rebecca said brightly, stripping off a glove and extending her hand.

At her request, the Earl's solicitor, Mr Leonards, had provided her with the staff's names; there was no better way to begin a relationship than by greeting a person properly.

'Why, I didn't even hear the creak of the door! How do you do?'

'How do you do, Mrs Hardwicke?' he drawled, clearly surprised by her informal greeting, but intently steadfast.

His handshake was strong, and assured, and Rebecca would've sworn his eyes warmed ever so slightly as she returned it with vigour.

'Do come in.'

'With pleasure, Mr Brown, for I fear I am otherwise in danger of becoming an ice sculpture,' she jested, grabbing once again her portmanteau and moving to follow.

'Mrs Hardwicke, do allow me to assist you.'

'Oh, 'tis quite under control, Mr Brown, I assure you. Why, I've handled it thus far up the drive, and for longer journeys than this.'

Defeated, but obviously unwilling to make a scene, or manhandle the luggage from her grasp, the discombobulated butler simply stepped aside and ushered her in, before soundlessly closing the door.

It was certainly warmer and more inviting inside than out, the large fire set in a hearth taller than she doing a remarkable job of chasing the chill from an impressively grand atrium. Deep blue and green diamond-shaped tiles, slightly worn but clean, contrasted with and complemented the long, carved oak-panelled walls. Despite the dark colours, the hall seemed light, and airy—thanks, in part, to the row of windows directly behind her, which flooded what little sunlight this part of England offered into the monumental antechamber, its few rays reflecting against the whitewashed walls of the first floor above.

A solid, intricately carved staircase led there, lined with a disconcertingly plush and unworn Turkish-style carpet. Portraits of long-dead ancestors stared down disapprovingly, seemingly showing the way to more distinguished and fashionable rooms upstairs. To her left, beyond the stairs, was a series of doors carved in the same patterns as the wall, all neatly tucked in, shielding the inhabitants from accidental discovery.

Well. Not so very bad at all.

When she'd first heard of her orders concerning the house, of the tiny contingent of servants, she had been concerned as to what she might find. Seeing it now had defied her expectations, and she could only hope that everything else about Thornhallow—including the rest of its occupants—would do so as well.

Perhaps you will even be happy here. For a time.

'Shall I show you to your quarters, Mrs Hardwicke?' Mr Brown offered.

'Yes, that would be delightful, thank you,' Rebecca said, stripping off her other glove, her crocheted bonnet and scarf, and stuffing them into the pockets of her very aged coat. 'And then I should like to meet everyone and tour the house.'

There were six more staff, along with the estate manager—a Mr Bradley, whom she would likely meet later, as he only occasionally visited the house.

A small contingent, indeed, but we shall ensure it is a mighty one.

'Once I have shown you to your rooms I shall allow you time to…freshen up,' he said, eyeing her bedraggled figure. 'And then I shall summon the others.'

'Excellent, Mr Brown…excellent.'

'Do, however, leave your portmanteau. Gregory will fetch it down for you.'

Smiling her most winning smile, which had gained her quick and lasting loyalty over the years, Rebecca bowed her head in assent. She could tell Mr Brown already disapproved of her—many did at first. Young, brash and entirely too friendly, compared with everyone's ideal notion of what a *proper* housekeeper should be. Rebecca had, nonetheless, always managed to vanquish even her most resolute critics.

Smoothing her ever unruly wisps of auburn hair, she followed Mr Brown through the hall to the servants' stairs.

'You've come from Birmingham, is that correct?'

Rebecca was pleased that he would not be forcing her to continue the journey in silence.

Yes, I shall win you over soon enough, Mr Brown...

'Indeed. The lady I served passed, and her children closed the house, so here I am.'

'Quite a journey, Mrs Hardwicke. Pleasant, I trust?'

'As pleasant as can be, Mr Brown,' she said diplomatically, leaving out the details of the uncomfortable, mind-numbing hours she had spent in the post-chaise. 'And I have arrived in one piece, which must be counted in my favour.'

'You are unmarried, as I understand it, Mrs Hardwicke?'

Again the note of disapproval was barely concealed beneath his lofty, unconcerned air, and Rebecca sighed inwardly, minding the narrow steps they were now descending.

'Indeed. The *Mrs*, in my case, is entirely a matter of courtesy. And you, Mr Brown? Married?'

'No.'

The butler said nothing more, and Rebecca relented, too tired to force any further conversation or joviality upon the man.

Mr Brown threw open a door, through which both he and Rebecca had to duck to pass, and led them through the servants' quarters. Down a corridor, past the servants' hall, the kitchens and what Rebecca presumed was one of the pantries. Here, too, everything was worn, but clean, bright and surprisingly spacious for a house of this age and style.

Finally, Mr Brown stopped before a darkened square room at the end of the corridor, and extracted a key from his pocket. Rebecca watched with slight apprehension as he threw open the door and gestured her inside once a cloud of dust had settled. There was just enough light streaming through the dirtied windows for her to make out the monumental mess which awaited her, though Mr Brown lost no time in lighting a lamp so she could survey her new domain properly.

Rebecca managed to contain her shock—but only just—and only because she was intent on not giving Mr Brown the satisfaction of seeing it. He was watching her like a hawk, so she forced herself to put on her best uninterested expression. She gave no outward sign of noticing the precarious and haphazard piles of papers on the desk, the chairs and floors. No sign of seeing the dust, the cobwebs, and remains of tea and tobacco in every corner and on every surface. She gave no clue whatsoever to the fact that she had noted the tatty, broken and stained furniture—those pieces which weren't upturned, at least—and the upended torn books, discarded pencils and the droppings from a variety of creatures.

She dared not even think what sight the adjoining bedroom would present.

'Well, thank you, Mr Brown,' Rebecca said with a smile.

His astonishment, though well hidden, was nonetheless apparent, and she raised her chin higher. It would take much more than this to discourage her.

'Shall I meet you and the others in the servants' hall in, say, half an hour? And perhaps someone could bring me some water?'

'Of course, Mrs Hardwicke. I shall send Lizzie along.'

A bow and he had gone, leaving her a single key on the ledge by the door, beside a large set which she presumed was the housekeeper's.

Rebecca shook her head, grabbed the desk chair—at first

glance the most solid and least soiled item of furniture—and placed it outside her door. She set her coat on it, rolled up her sleeves and returned to the room to formulate a plan. Though she should be furious and appalled by this blatant mark of disregard and very plain lack of welcome, Rebecca was not. This was a clear demonstration of the staff's disrespect for the position she now held—disrespect which she could not blame them for. There had been twenty-one housekeepers— *twenty-one*—in ten years. It was unfathomable.

No wonder, really, that they had few expectations and had made no effort. This was the housekeeper's domain, and as such it was up to her to deal with her predecessors' parting gifts. The staff had clearly given up on believing in housekeepers—just as her predecessors had, judging by the state of the room, given up on the house, the staff and themselves.

Yet in that moment, when many others would have felt defeated and dejected, Rebecca felt only pride and excitement. She would make this right, make them believe again. She'd always held the belief that there was a certain nobility to her vocation. It was up to the housekeeper to unite everyone on the staff in a shared goal and inspire them. So that was what she would do. For she was precisely where she was meant to be. Rebecca knew it in her heart. This place, these people, needed her.

I shall make a difference here if it's the last thing I do. After all, no one said this would be easy, Rebecca Merrickson.

Precisely half an hour after her arrival, Rebecca stood before a nonplussed, grumpy-looking line of servants in the hall. They all stood straight, minded their manners and bore expressions of indifferent readiness—however, there was an air of boredom and irritation about them. As if they were all thinking in unison: *Merciful heavens, not another one.*

Rebecca understood the sentiment—just as she understood why they had left the housekeeper's rooms in that horrific state. She understood their disbelief that she would last more than a day, a week or however long it was they had wagered on. And there was no doubt they had a wager going. She knew she wouldn't win them all over immediately. However, she also knew that right now she needed to lay down her rules and her plans, so that when they saw her stand by them, then perhaps she would earn their respect and trust. They would see her as a worthy, steadfast leader.

Looking between them all, Rebecca tried to match faces to the names and positions Mr Leonards had provided. If she could call them all by name it might be just the trick to wake them up. Two already she knew: Mr Brown, and Lizzie, the pretty but tough-looking maid who had brought her a basin of water. So it couldn't be *that* difficult.

The plump and comfortingly motherly-looking woman, older than her, currently sporting a scowl to disintegrate stone, was surely the cook, Mrs Murray. The girl standing by her, tiny and with the air of a ferret about her, was likely the scullery maid, Betsy. As for the gentlemen...

The older of the remaining three, with his rough brown wool breeches, jacket and worn linen shirt, had to be the head groom, Tim. With mousy hair, thick dark brows and a kind, open face, he seemed a gentle sort of fellow who would do well with horses. The young man beside him, dressed in similar attire, with big, round, innocent eyes and a perpetual smile must be the other groom, Sam. Which left Gregory to be the cheeky-looking but rather handsome blond youth in livery matching Mr Brown's.

'Good afternoon,' Rebecca began in her most commanding, assured voice. 'It is a pleasure to meet you all, and to be here in Thornhallow. As I am sure you know, I am Mrs Hardwicke, your new housekeeper.'

'Welcome to Thornhallow ma'am,' Tim said gruffly, with a tug at his forelock. 'I'm—'

'Tim?'

'Aye, ma'am,' the groom said, eyeing her as though she might prove to be a witch.

'Thank you for your warm welcome.' *Warm* was saying a lot, but then, buttering them all up a little wouldn't hurt. 'Now, you are head groom here, correct?'

'Yes, ma'am.'

'And in the stables we have two mares and the old master's horse, a thoroughbred?'

Tim nodded, looking increasingly aghast.

Rebecca felt the stares of the others; she certainly had their full attention now. 'As well as your standard duties, you and Sam,' she said, pointedly looking towards the young groom, who rewarded her with an impressed grin, 'act as gamekeepers and gardeners as well?'

'*Gardener*'s a fancy word, ma'am,' Sam laughed until Tim elbowed him in the ribs. 'Wha' I means to say is that we do wha' we can, Mrs Hardwicke, ma'am. Only, Tim and I ain't proper trained. Greggy...*Gregory*...he knows a bit about roses, and he helps out, too.'

'From what I've heard you've done very well indeed. I will enjoy a visit to the gardens when you have a moment. And, yes, Gregory,' she said, turning her attention to the footman. 'I hear you assist with the gardens—and, of course, serve alongside Mr Brown.'

'Yes, Mrs Hardwicke.'

'Excellent. And you are Mrs Murray, I presume?' Rebecca continued, turning to the cook, who managed to close her mouth just in time. 'Thornhallow's famed chef.'

'You tease, Mrs Hardwicke,' Mrs Murray said, blushing nonetheless.

'Not at all. I shared a cart with a certain Mr Hardy. Said you were the best cook in all of England.'

'Tush!'

'Well, I look forward to seeing him proved right, and to working with you. Once I am settled, perhaps you would be so kind as to take me through ordering and menus and such?'

'With pleasure, Mrs Hardwicke.'

'Betsy?'

The young scullery maid curtsied awkwardly, her eyes flitting between Rebecca and Mrs Murray.

'Lovely to meet you. I'm sure you are quite invaluable to Mrs Murray.' A terrified half-smile was her response, so Rebecca moved on to Lizzie. 'And, Lizzie, you and I have already met. I am sure you will become quite invaluable to me.'

'As you say, ma'am,' the girl said, clearly unconvinced, exchanging a glance with Gregory.

'Splendid. Now, I want you all to know I am here for whatever you need. From what I can see you have things well in hand, but once I get my bearings I'm sure we can find ways to make improvements here and there.'

They all resumed their disbelieving, unconvinced air, any ground she had gained instantly lost with the notion of *improvements*. No matter.

'Lastly, I will say this: I am here to stay. I know none of you believe that, but I will prove it, and myself, to you. I will never ask you to do a job I wouldn't do or haven't done. I will respect your opinions and trust you. I ask only that you grant me the same courtesy.'

Rebecca pointedly turned her attention to Mr Brown, at whom she had intentionally avoided looking throughout the introduction. He looked as stiff and proud as ever, but she sensed nonetheless that his feelings were increasingly conflicted. Beneath his disapproval she was sure lay a tiny, infinitesimal flicker of hope.

I will win you over yet. I will win you all over...

'Well, thank you for that...*invigorating* introduction, Mrs Hardwicke,' the butler said with a hint of condescension as he stepped out of the line. 'Now, let us allow Mrs Hardwicke to settle in; we all have plenty else to see to.'

With nods, glances and the occasional smile—Mrs Murray's being the broadest and warmest—everyone shuffled out of the servants' hall, back to their own worlds.

Mr Brown waited until they had all departed before approaching Rebecca.

'They are a lovely bunch,' she said jovially. 'And seem very dedicated.'

'Indeed they are, Mrs Hardwicke. Shall I take you on a tour?' The man looked as though he had about as much desire to do so as to visit Pandemonium.

'Actually, Mr Brown, I thought I might explore myself... get my bearings. I am sure you have much to do of more importance than showing me around.'

'As you wish. Dinner is at seven,' he said, heading for the door. 'A word to the wise, Mrs Hardwicke. Though I am sure your entrepreneurial spirit has served you well in the past, if you are to call Thornhallow home, heed this: things are as they are for a reason.'

'Thank you for your solicitude, Mr Brown. I shall certainly bear that in mind.'

The butler inclined his head politely and disappeared down the corridor.

'Things are as they are for a reason...'

Perhaps that was true. But that didn't mean things were as they *should* be. This house might be functioning, but there was something more to it… Something out of sorts that needed to be set right, and she would find out what. Rebecca was not the sort simply to leave everything as it was because it worked *well enough*—where was the fun in that?

No better place to start than a tour…

Once she had got a sense of the old house, seen what she had to work with, then she would set her own domain to rights, find out what precisely her predecessors had done with their time and make a plan.

Anything can be righted with a proper plan.

'Apologies for my tardiness,' Rebecca said hours later, returning to the servants' hall.

She was greeted by a mass of disgruntled hungry faces. *Drat.* Starving them was probably not the best way to curry favour, but her tour of the house had been, in short, a trial. Making a plan had not been so easy after all.

'Time ran away with me, I fear. Apologies, Mrs Murray,' she added, noting the cook's less than discreet tutting. 'I hope whatever delectable meal you have concocted hasn't suffered with my delay.'

''Tis mutton stew tonight,' she grumbled, signalling Betsy to fetch the pot. 'So I think it will have survived well enough.'

'Well, it smells delicious. Please, everyone, sit,' she instructed, taking her own place at the head of the table opposite Mr Brown. 'I, for one, am famished.'

The others complied as Mrs Murray and Betsy served and then sat themselves. Rebecca smiled, appreciating the fact that they all joined together at mealtimes. Considering their diminished numbers, and the irregularity of their situation, it was entirely justified.

'An instructive tour, Mrs Hardwicke?' Mr Brown asked as everyone tucked into their meal.

'*Instructive* is certainly one word for it, Mr Brown.'

Rebecca could think of many others. Disheartening, distressing, angering…a call to arms. She'd sat for an hour on a window seat in the first floor's long gallery, the family portrait gallery, digesting the sorry sights she'd witnessed whilst staring out at Thornhallow's stunning park. In turn, the proud ancestors on the walls had gazed down at her, seemingly sneering at this new arrival who was only just beginning to realise what sort of place Thornhallow truly was.

The four rooms which had been kept open were impeccable, and felt lived-in. The rooms were, as instructed, ready for the master's seemingly impossible yet forever imminent arrival. Fires roared, crystal and silver sparkled, and there was not a speck of dust to be found—even the inkwell on the Earl's desk was full and fresh.

It had only been when Rebecca had begun to explore the rest of the house that she'd seen the full extent of its abandonment. In all the rooms, the only life she'd found had been in the conservatory, Mrs Murray having taken the liberty of installing her winter garden there.

The house was, simply put, unfit for habitation. Held in a general state of decrepit splendour. Lost in time. Forlorn and falling into ruin. And there was nothing she was to do about it. It wasn't right. That was what she'd sensed wasn't right with the house. Keeping only some rooms ready and closing the rest was not unheard of. But this…

If she ever met the Disappeared Earl she would certainly have some choice words for him.

The staff all knew it; that much was clear. Being forced to live in a place half-alive, dragging itself onwards, and pretending all was well with the world…no wonder they

were all so disaffected. Between the oppressive atmosphere that permeated everything and the ghost stories,
it was hardly surprising there had been such a succession
of housekeepers.

Not that Rebecca had met any ghosts today, not even
near that one place…

Rebecca shook her head and focused on her renewed
sense of purpose. 'I have come to a decision. This house
has been left to its own devices long enough. Should it be
left so further, it will cease to exist entirely.'

Cutlery clattered against the plates and the table, and
audible gasps were heard as all faces again turned towards
her, aghast. Rebecca sat there, unaffected, quietly tucking
into Mrs Murray's delectable stew with a slice of warm
brown bread.

'Do you mean to say you intend to…to…?'

'To restore every single room in Thornhallow? Yes,
Tim,' she said, before the groom could injure himself in
seeking his words.

'Mrs Hardwicke,' Mr Brown said sharply, with a look
that had undoubtedly sent many a man running in terror.
'Perhaps the instructions you received from Mr Leonards
were unclear or have led to confusion. The house is to be
kept as it is.'

'The instructions were clear. But I am choosing not to
follow them.'

'Disobey the master?' Mrs Murray gasped. 'Well, I
never…'

'If His Lordship ever decides to grace Thornhallow
with his presence, then I shall be happy to discuss this
with him, Mrs Murray. Until that day, however, I refuse
to sit idly by and watch this house crumble.'

'Mrs Hardwicke, you have been in this house for less

than a day,' Mr Brown said, in an attempt at a conciliatory tone. 'I am not sure you quite understand—'

'It has been ten years, Mr Brown,' she retorted, feeling her ire rising. She set down her cutlery and faced them. 'If we do not do something now, there will be nothing for the master to find, should he ever deign to return. I am a housekeeper, and that is what I intend to do. You have all served with loyalty. I will not ask you to disobey. I shall see to the task myself, though I will require assistance when it comes to changing mattresses and such. There is also a leak above the second-floor gallery, and I imagine further repairs with which I will require help. Other than that, I will ask nothing of you. I, alone, will suffer any consequences.'

They all stared at her, mouths gaping, half in admiration, half in dismay. It seemed to Rebecca that even though they were appalled at the idea of disobeying, in some measure they also knew she was right. Most of them, at least. Mr Brown appeared only murderous as he fixed her with his cold grey stare.

'You are set upon this course of action, Mrs Hardwicke,' he declared more than asked. 'So be it. But tread carefully. There are some things that should not be disturbed.'

'I will certainly give that due consideration, Mr Brown, thank you,' she retorted, just as sharply. 'But you must know—you must *all* know—that this place is a tomb. A cold, empty place of unhappiness and darkness.'

The thick silence, furtive glances and bowed heads which followed that statement were assent enough for Rebecca.

'Thornhallow is a beautiful place—or at least with a little effort can be again. This house—all of you—deserve better.'

'As you say, Mrs Hardwicke, you are the housekeeper,'

the defeated butler said after a moment. 'And therefore no one here may stop you from doing as you please.'

But that doesn't mean we agree, nor will we help you, Rebecca thought, as everyone begrudgingly returned to their meals in sullen silence.

'There is another matter, Mr Brown,' she said after a long moment. 'There seem to be keys missing from the set I've been left.'

'Indeed there are not. I check it myself before each *departure*.'

'Well, I'm afraid you are mistaken, for I'm missing at least one. To the East Tower,' Rebecca said, ignoring the shudder which passed through her at the memory of the place. At the memory of the sounds coming from it…

Only the howling wind, she reminded herself, though the glances the others exchanged, and the thick, tense silence which followed, lessened her conviction slightly.

'The East Tower is closed.'

This time it was Tim who spoke, harshness and pain she would not have expected in his voice. Rebecca frowned.

'No one is ever to go there.'

'It's *her* place,' Lizzie breathed, a hint of fear in her voice.

'What Tim means is that the tower was closed off by His Lordship's father,' Mr Brown said, eyeing the groom warningly. 'The key was lost then. There is nothing there.'

Doubtful, Rebecca thought, considering their reaction at her mere mention of the place. But, whatever secrets the East Tower held, they could keep. She had bigger battles to fight. No matter what they thought, Rebecca knew what she was meant to do. Why she had come to Thornhallow. It might gain her no friends, it might cost her everything, but she knew she had to try and bring some life back into this house.

After dinner everyone disappeared, shooting Rebecca reproachful glares as they did so. She retired to her rooms and spent the better part of the night making them liveable.

She would not sit by and watch Thornhallow collapse around her.

Not if I have it in my power to save it.

No one else would. Least of all the Disappeared Earl.

I believe hell will freeze over before you return to this place. And I am glad of it.

Chapter Two

Three weeks later, the haunting figure of William Reid, Fifth Earl of Thornhallow, raced along the road leading to the accursed house he'd sworn never to set foot in again. Had anyone been about to witness such an unexpected sight they might have sworn it was in fact his ghost, returning home to keep company with the others of its ilk who dwelled there.

The sun had set nearly four hours ago, but still Liam drove on. Even if the full moon had not shone so brightly, transforming the landscape into something from a dream, he would have known the way. Time and distance had done nothing to diminish his memories of this place. Of this land—*his* land.

It felt as if he'd only left yesterday. So familiar were the rise and fall of the dales and fells against the starry expanse before him, so familiar was the fresh, clean scent of heather and wild thyme on the warning icy night wind, that Liam was instantly returned to that fateful night ten years ago, when he had ridden this same road.

Only, then he'd been running *from* Thornhallow Hall and all the terrible things that had happened there. From the memory of all that had been taken from him.

Now he was returning to the bedevilled house which he had tried for so long to banish from his thoughts and heart. To the people whom he might have called his own had he not forsaken them as he had forsaken himself. Returning for a while to take up his proper place and responsibilities in the vain hope that he might be free of them. For neither time nor distance had lessened Thornhallow's hold on him.

Yet he *would* be free. He swore it to himself now, with every heartbeat and every breath. He would find a way.

During his stay in London this past week he'd told Leonards as much, and the old man had nearly had a fainting fit. Though the shock of having the Disappeared Earl himself waltz into his office without a word of warning one fateful Tuesday afternoon probably hadn't helped. Liam had felt for the old solicitor, flapping about wordlessly, chalky white, and for a moment he might have believed himself a wraith in truth, had anyone accused him of it.

After three glasses of the cognac Liam had brought as a gift, Leonards had finally regained his composure—only to lose it again as Liam uttered the words he'd been holding in his heart for so long.

'I do not wish to be Earl. I will not be any longer. Find a way to rid me of the title. Let it go to my cousin or to Beelzebub. I care not. Just free me, Leonards.'

Another glass of cognac and then the solicitor had begun listing all the reasons why Liam's plans were fanciful, impossible and downright mad. Why the man had been surprised that should be the case, when Leonards had used exactly the same words each time he'd written in response to this or that meagre order concerning the estate, was a mystery.

'It is your decision, my lord,' he had finally conceded hours later, seeing that Liam would not be swayed. *'I will do what I can to find a way.'*

If no way could be found—well, Liam wasn't entirely sure what he would do. But he had no time to dwell on that eventuality.

The last stretch. Not long now...

Turning up the lane, he felt his stomach drop and his heart flutter. Beneath the dread lay excitement. Thornhallow Hall had been his childhood home. Despite the sorrow, the grief, there had been happy times there.

Not that he could remember them anymore. Only screams echoing in the night. Frozen figures in the water. Blood on the steps. Images from his memory and born of his nightmares. The laughter, the joy—those he could not recall. Only pain. He had sought to forget it all, to lose himself in the unknown, and so he had for a time. Until he'd been cursed with more grief. More suffering. More sorrow. And more ghosts.

All no more than he deserved, he knew.

He would have given his life for her. He would give anything to bring her back. To change her fate.

My sweet Hal... Sweet sister mine...

Hell and Heaven knew he would have given his life for any of them. If only to lessen his own agony by the sacrifice. If only to change his own fate as well as theirs.

Tugging the reins, Liam drew the gig to a halt before the wrought-iron gates.

The gates of hell... My own, personal hell...full of demons waiting for me...

Liam sat there, transfixed by the sight of his home, spectral in the moonlight, unable to move for a very long time. He could hear it calling him to it across the void, welcoming him to its unforgiving and damning embrace. He could see her there, waiting at the window.

Hal...

He should have stayed in London. Sorted it all out from

there. He should have stayed far away, across the world. But he hadn't, and now here he was.

Orpheus whinnied and struck his hooves in protest against the frozen ground.

I know precisely how you feel, old boy.

Sighing, unable to delay the inevitable any longer, Liam hopped down from the gig and went to the gate. He took out the key Leonards had given him, slid it into the lock, and with surprising ease, but a resounding creak, opened the gates to his kingdom.

He led Orpheus through, shut the gates tightly, then made his way up the drive.

'Mind you don't move, stranger,' said a gruff voice, before the familiar click of a rifle sounded loudly in the night as Liam moved to lead Orpheus through the stable doors. 'You best be going back where you come from, mister, or there'll be trouble now.'

'Steady now, Tim.' Liam chuckled, turning slowly, arms raised. 'It's only me.'

'M-my lord,' Tim stuttered, confused, hurriedly lowering the gun. Apparently the sounds of intrusion had torn him from slumber; his open coat revealed a nightshirt. 'I… That is, we wasn't expecting you. I'll find Thom— Mr Brown—'

'You shall rouse no one,' Liam said, waving the groom back as he moved to rush away and handing him the reins. 'It is late, and as you say, I was not expected. You may tell Thomas I have arrived in the morning, but for the moment, if you could attend to the gig—and Orpheus, here—I shall simply find my way to bed.'

'But, my lord—'

'Tim, I am quite capable of taking care of myself, and have done so for quite some time. Tomorrow I shall be my lord the Earl, but for this evening I wish to be solely myself.'

'Yes, my lord.' Tim nodded, unconvinced, but unwilling to disobey.

'Thank you. It is good to see you.' Liam smiled, grabbing his bag from the gig. 'You haven't changed. A little more grey, and I daresay Cook has been feeding you well.'

'Aye, my lord. She has. It is good to see you home again, master,' Tim added as Liam stepped back into the night. 'You've been missed at Thornhallow.'

With a nod, Liam left the man to his duties and made his way to the house.

If he was lucky, he might be able to steal some bread and cheese from the kitchens without alerting anyone to his presence. He did, after all, have a key to the tradesman's entrance among the set Leonards had given him.

Tonight he only wanted to be Liam, while he still could. Not the damned Earl of Thornhallow. Not the master— just a man. Tomorrow he would face them all. Face the enquiring looks, the pity, the responsibilities. Tonight he had plenty to deal with simply being here. He'd been lucky enough to be discovered only by Tim and he was not about to waste his good fortune. He would pilfer some food, then drink himself to sleep in the library.

Venturing any further—well, that was something he was not quite ready for.

A fire had been lit in the library. Even though only a dim glow emanated from the now dying embers in the hearth to illuminate the room, Liam was glad he would be able to enjoy his favourite refuge without having to lay the fire himself. It seemed his orders had been thoroughly obeyed. Not that he had doubted Leonards, nor Thomas.

Indeed, he would not have entrusted his home—well, his *inheritance*—to them for so many years if he had.

Or so he told himself.

Liam strode to the fireplace and stoked the embers, letting the warmth penetrate his sore and frozen limbs for a long moment before tossing more logs onto the growing flames. The bread and cheese he had pinched from the kitchens had restored him somewhat, though he'd been tempted to make his presence known, if only for a bowl of hot stew or soup.

Mrs Murray's mutton stew...

A low groan and quiet rustle from behind sent him whirling around, poker in hand, alert and at the ready for any attack coming his way. Standing stock-still, a statue to anyone who might have seen him, he let his eyes scan the darkness. But there was nothing there. No shadows. No masked rogues or bandits.

And no ghosts.

Only the faint outlines of the furniture and oddities his father and ancestors had collected over the centuries. Was he dreaming? Or was his mind conjuring up whispers, as it was sometimes wont to do? He was certainly near enough exhaustion for it to be a possibility. Since the crossing, his nightmares had been getting worse... It was no wonder he was ready to fall down, sleep for weeks in this very spot. He couldn't remember the last full night's rest he'd had.

Sighing, he slid the poker back into its stand and leaned against the mantelpiece, rubbing his eyes. What on earth indeed had he been thinking, returning here? If there was anywhere in the world more likely to worsen his already restless and tormented mind, it was Thornhallow Hall.

How I wish I could burn it to the ground...

Another tiny rustling. There was no mistaking it this

time. This was not something he had conjured. There was someone, or something, in this room.

Whirling around, his heart pounding, he scanned the darkness again. He was about to call out when his eyes rested on the sofa nearest the fire and found a sleeping woman.

What the Devil...?

Liam rubbed his eyes again, certain his mind was playing tricks on him. But, no, he realised, studying the figure lying before him. He had missed her when he'd first looked, but now the fire had grown he saw her clearly. Cautiously, he took a few steps towards her, intent on discovering who she was, and why the Devil she was presuming to sleep in *his* library.

Why he wasn't simply striding over there, shaking her to consciousness and demanding answers, he couldn't really say. The truth was, in that moment she looked so peaceful, so at home, as if she more than he belonged here now, that Liam could not find it within himself to rouse her.

There was something about her that was ethereal or unworldly. Spellbinding. *Bewitching.* He couldn't take his eyes off her. She wasn't conventionally beautiful, and yet she was arresting. Long tresses of rich, dark auburn hair fell around her like waves, a pillow of satin gleaming in the firelight. Her face was rather square, strong and bold, but her cheeks and nose were neatly rounded, and countered the otherwise harsh lines. He wondered what colour her eyes were beneath the long dark lashes.

And her mouth...

Thin, and yet generous, the bottom lip rounded beautifully beneath the shapely, almost perfect Cupid's bow which aligned with the tiny cleft in her chin. *Contradictions*, he thought. *In every part of her.* Her lips were parted in her repose, inviting, and for a moment he pictured himself bending over to caress them, stealing a kiss like a prince in a fairy story.

God, what was the matter with him?

Shaking his head, he sighed heavily.

Tired. Exhausted. Too long without a woman. There. That is all there is to it.

Yes, that was all there was to it—even though he didn't believe half of what he told himself.

Slightly reassured, nonetheless, he returned to his examination of the stranger. She was tall, for her head was propped against one arm of the sofa, while her legs were perched over the other, her stocking-clad feet peeking out from beneath her skirts.

At least she was respectful enough to remove her shoes—no, boots.

Sturdy leather, worn, tattered old things, they stood neatly beside the sofa. Definitely not a lady's shoe. And her dress—it would have made any woman of quality shriek in terror. Drab, faded black wool, with a high collar and devoid of any adornments. Yet it was a dress that somehow seemed to suit this creature perfectly, in no way distracting from her natural grace and the shape of her body.

Voluptuous. Strong. Restrained.

Briefly, he longed to tear it from her and liberate all that awaited him beneath it.

Drat.

He needed to focus.

Liam glanced at her hands. One rested delicately across her waist and the other hung over the side of the sofa, above a fallen book that now lay open on the floor. He approached a little closer and examined them carefully. Small, sturdy little fingers—again, a contrast to the long, graceful limbs.

And no wedding ring...

Torn, callused, bleeding. Nails worn down to their barest edge. What had she been doing to achieve such a gruesome result? Scrubbing?

And then it hit him. There was only one possibility.

The new housekeeper. But surely not?

This woman before him—well, the dress might suggest such a position, but her age? She couldn't be far from thirty on either side. Housekeepers were old, and dreary, and respectable. Not… Well, not everything *she* was. And yet it was the only rational explanation.

Mrs Hardwicke. Yes, that was the name.

He should definitely rouse her. She would want to know the master had returned, and he should want an explanation as to why she had presumed to make use of his library. Still, he could not.

And what is it you were reading then, Mrs Hardwicke?

Bending down, he picked up the book. He was close now, too close not to see the rise and fall of her breasts with every breath. Not to smell her, the rich, intoxicating blend of lavender polish, soap, lemon…and something darker that reminded him of the land. Something he knew was *her.*

Liam knew he desperately needed rest, and a bed, and not to be here, in the library, in this moment, in the warm, heady cloud that surrounded his new employee.

Glancing down, he found that the woman was reading *Frankenstein.* He chuckled softly to himself, setting the book down on the table beside her.

Light reading, then, Mrs Hardwicke.

How this woman had the countenance to read such gothic tales in this forsaken place, he knew not. No matter. What the woman wished to read was none of his business. Any insights into her character, her personality, her dreams, pleasures or desire, were categorically none of his business.

And so, with renewed fortitude and energy, Liam laid a blanket on her, then left her to her peace and slumber, making for his own chambers despite his earlier reluctance to do so, pushing away the odd feeling of longing that gnawed at him.

The cool, crisp sheets of his bed would be the perfect remedy for his weary body, and the perfect thing to cool the unwelcome stirrings of his ardour. And tomorrow, the incident would be nothing more than another unwelcome dream.

Damn this house.

Chapter Three

'Good morning, my lord,' Mr Brown said crisply, throwing open the curtains in Liam's room and setting about his routine duties as though the master had never left. 'May I say what a pleasure it is to have you back. Tim advised us of your arrival this morning, and I believe Mrs Murray is currently preparing quite a welcome feast.'

'I admit I have sorely missed her cooking.' Liam grinned, slipping out of bed and into the dressing gown the butler was holding out.

As apprehensive as he'd been about returning, somehow seeing the old butler puttering about his room felt...

Normal. Heartwarming. Like home should.

'Travelled half the world and never met her match.'

'Mind you don't tell her so, my lord. There'll be no calming her as it is.'

'Aye. It's good to see you, Thomas,' he said seriously.

It *was* good to see his all too familiar face again. He and Mrs Murray, and Tim, and Hal...his sweet Hal... They were the only things that had ever made the place remotely bearable.

'I know there is much to be said, but for now let me simply say, thank you. For staying. Despite everything.'

'No thanks are necessary, my lord. I have served Thorn-hallow for nearly fifty years. I will continue to do so until I can no longer. It is an honour.'

'Now,' Liam said, clearing his throat and reminding himself that he was now master of the house. The Earl his father had longed for him to be, and that Thomas would expect him at least to *pretend* to be. 'I suppose I must part with this, mustn't I?' he asked, rubbing the long beard he currently sported. 'Though I am dreadfully loath to.'

'Afraid so, my lord,' Thomas said with the faintest of smiles. 'You do look rather wild. Like a Pict, if I may be so bold.'

'Where I have been it has suited perfectly. So, Thomas, tell me.' He took a seat at the dressing table and leaned back, ready for the butler's ministrations. 'Mrs Hardwicke, what do you make of her? I fell upon her sleeping in the library last evening. Not what I expected, I dare say.'

'I see. Yes, well, she asked, and I thought there would be no harm in her making use of the library… It seemed a shame… She must've—'

'Come, Thomas, if that is the worst of her vices I think we are quite fortunate. What I wish to know is how she is managing, as housekeeper.'

'Well, my lord,' Mr Brown said slowly, pondering his words carefully whilst he undertook restoring his master to a gentleman. 'She is certainly…*unconventional*. Then again, since your departure, conventional housekeepers seem to have…how shall I put it…'

'Failed miserably, Thomas? Do not mince your words,' Liam ordered, glancing at the man.

Thomas hesitated. He was a proper butler, through and through, and bleak, unrestrained honesty in the face of his lord was not something the man was built for.

'Come, now, you've known me since I was a babe,'

Liam coaxed. 'Tiptoeing around matters will not do. We are alone, Thomas, so out with it.'

'My lord, since you *departed*, well, the situation has been...complicated.'

The old butler sighed and Liam winced. The overt diplomacy was an attempt to dissimulate how truly terrible things had been, and Liam cursed himself for having convinced himself they could ever be otherwise.

'None of Mrs Hardwicke's predecessors had the stomach, nor the prescience to understand what Thornhallow needed. Not only to survive, but to thrive, without your guiding hand. We all tried, best we could, my lord, however... Well... How to say this?'

'Just say it, man!'

'We are all loyal to you,' he said, gently wiping off the last specks of shaving soap from Liam's face. 'And, as such, we have followed your orders.'

Liam straightened, studying the man intently as he attempted to decipher his meaning. As Thomas busied himself cleaning and stowing away the *toilette* instruments, unwilling to meet the master's eye, understanding began to dawn.

'Are you saying that Mrs Hardwicke has not, in fact, obeyed my orders?'

The butler's silence and momentary pause were answer enough.

'Where is she?' he growled.

'I believe Mrs Hardwicke is in the West Wing this morning, my lord,' Thomas said sheepishly. 'But I pray you to understand—'

He was stopped short by a raised hand. Without another word, Liam threw on his clothes, grabbed the cravat and jacket which had been laid out, and stormed off in search of his new, disobedient employee.

Though he would never admit it, Liam was more frustrated and angry with himself than with her. He had encouraged Thomas to speak freely, and so he had. And Liam had been forced to face his own inadequacy. Thornhallow needed a firm hand, and he had abandoned it. Mrs Hardwicke, on the other hand, was apparently more than happy to take the reins.

Who is she to disobey me? he raged silently, throwing on his jacket.

Who was she to know what was best for this house? The impudence! He couldn't believe Thomas had been privy to—nay, nearly praised—such insolence! He cared not for the house—could no one understand that? He paid everyone handsomely to keep it as he commanded, without question. Their duties were minimal, compared to other estates, and they were handsomely rewarded. Was unfaltering loyalty too much to ask?

Liam cursed her as he angrily, and very messily, tied his cravat. He should have known she was trouble when he'd seen her last night, lounging in the library as though she belonged there, stirring appetites long dormant. And where was she now? The West Wing!

Doing God only knows what, he thought, marching through the corridors, searching for the traitor.

Then an unfamiliar sound caught his attention and he stopped.

Singing.

His hand clenched, and he stood there a moment, unable to move.

'Ne pars donc pas, mon amour...' the voice sang.

So don't leave me, my love...

There had not been singing in this house for ten years, and even before then it had been a very rare occasion indeed. Was this yet another ghost sent to torment him?

No, this was no ghost, but a woman.

Mrs Hardwicke, I presume...

Sighing, Liam shook his head, straightened his back and followed the melody.

'Trop longtemps j'ai attendu ton retour...'

For too long I've awaited your return...

It might not be the voice of a ghost, but Liam's heart clenched nonetheless at the sound of it, for it was no less haunting, tormenting nor generally aggravating than a spectre's might have been. Why had Leonards saddled him with such a perplexing and seditious housekeeper?

You know very well...

Even so, how could he? When he knew very well what Liam desired most? Peace, calm and a semblance of normality. Those were the things he longed for, which would already be nigh impossible to achieve here. He didn't need Mrs Hardwicke and her siren songs, and her disobedience, to further add to it.

By the time he reached the door to one of the smaller guest rooms, Liam had managed to work himself into quite a state. When he opened the door to find his new housekeeper on her hands and knees scraping at the grate, still singing merrily, giving him a rather tantalising perspective of her generous charms, he nearly started shouting. All his repressed anger, grief and lust rising up like demons inside his breast.

Taking a breath, he reminded himself what his behaviour and thoughts *should* be, and strode in.

'Ne reste pas sourd à mes prières...'

Don't be deaf to my pleas...

'You must be deaf, or blind, or dull, for it seems you have completely ignored your orders, Mrs Hardwicke,' he barked, inwardly cursing himself for balking in his resolve.

The woman shrieked, surprised, toppling over as she

swerved around to face him, her face red and her hair barely contained by what had once been a severe-looking bun. She stared up, mouth slightly gaping, blinking as she assessed him.

Brown, Liam noted despite himself. *Her eyes are brown.*

'My lord,' she said, half asking, half declaring. 'I… That is, I hadn't realised…'

'That I had returned? Yes, quite. And do not fret,' Liam said, before she could give voice to the words on her lips. 'Thomas saw to all my needs this morning.'

'My lord—'

'Yes, Mrs Hardwicke, now that we have established that I am indeed your lord and master, will you give me your hand? I cannot continue to have a conversation thus,' he said gruffly.

'Of…of course,' she stammered, bringing herself to her feet without aid.

Liam ignored the disappointment he felt at being denied the opportunity to sample her touch.

'Thank you, but I fear I am rather a mess, and I would hate to give Gregory more work this evening with your clothes.'

'How considerate, Mrs Hardwicke. If only you had been so considerate regarding your instructions for the house.'

To her credit, she did not flinch under his otherwise infallibly cold and shrinking look. Many a strong man had cowered beneath his gaze, but she had the audacity to stand taller, raise an eyebrow and put her hands on her hips, ready for a confrontation.

At the very least Liam had to admire her spunk, and somewhere in the back of his mind a voice whispered that he should admire how very fine indeed she was when ruffled.

'You mean the instructions which dictated I should leave all but four rooms to ruin, my lord,' she said calmly, though Liam could see the twinkle of outrage in her eyes. 'Forgive me, then, for it is not in my nature to be complicit in such a crime. This house has been left to itself for too long, and had it been left so any longer, there would've been no home for us to meet in. I saw no harm in tidying beyond my original mandate. Or would you perhaps have preferred I sit and drink and play games? I have it on good authority that some of my predecessors did, so perhaps I should've followed their lead.'

'Do you question all your employers thus, Mrs Hardwicke? Or is it I alone who am subject to such insubordination?'

'You will forgive me for pointing this out, my lord, but you were not here to discuss such matters. After ten years you can hardly fault me for being stunned at your return.'

'Well, I am here now, and here we are discussing it. I thank you for your initiative—however, such efforts will cease immediately,' Liam said flatly, with the air of a petulant child.

'I am a housekeeper, my lord, and that is what I shall do.'

'Are you refusing to obey my orders even *now*, Mrs Hardwicke?' he asked, both astonished and intrigued.

'If an order is wrong, it is one's duty to disobey.'

'And why is it, may I ask, that *you* are cleaning grates, Mrs Hardwicke?' Liam demanded, changing the subject as his ire rose again with the realisation of just how right she was. 'That is what maids are for, Mrs Hardwicke, not housekeepers. How, I wonder, are you to be respected if you demean yourself thus?'

This time it was Liam who was graced with a look that might have felled Hannibal. *He* nearly cowered then, as she rose to her full height, eyes flashing with unrestrained anger, cheeks flushed and arms dropping as her fists clenched.

'One gains the respect of those who work for them not by demanding it, *my lord*, but by earning it,' she seethed. 'I doubt anyone would reproach me for doing a job for which I am trained and have time. Particularly when the only two maids we have are well-enough occupied, and we cannot hire any more. For it seems, *my lord*, that no one will work in this accursed house. Besides, as you so aptly pointed out, I am the one who ignored the orders, therefore it is my responsibility.'

They stood there, locked in a silent battle of wills for a very long moment, during which time Liam noted several things.

First, he noted that she was likely one of the tallest women he'd ever met, with the tip of her head coming nearly to his nose. A very disconcerting fact indeed, as it undermined his ability to, quite literally, *lord* over her as he so wished to do just now.

Secondly, he noted that she had smudges of ash on her cheeks, which he decided added to her overall resemblance to some ancient Celtic warrior.

And finally, he noted that he was, as she had so adamantly pointed out, very wrong on all counts, and for the first time in many years he felt as though he were a boy again, being chastised for having caused trouble.

His anger, frustration and aggravation at this new housekeeper's disregard for his orders, and indeed at the sheer insolence of her, had faded. Now he was simply standing there staring, unwilling to concede, but unable to find a way out of the argument.

So Liam crossed his arms and cocked his head, waiting for her to realise just how far out of bounds she was.

It wasn't much, and it wasn't in the least fair play, but it was, at that moment, his only way to preserve some semblance of authority.

He saw the dawning in her eyes, the flicker of hesitation, the understanding of just how unseemly her behaviour had been, and he would even have sworn she muttered some very choice, and very unladylike, swear words under her breath before her eyes finally turned away. Bowing her head, she took a step back, and seemed then to shrivel into the role of lowly, dutiful, subservient employee, complete with hunched shoulders and downcast eyes.

Liam decided he didn't like her this way at all, and chastised himself for having been such a proud and irrational boor.

'You will continue to do as you please, won't you, Mrs Hardwicke?' Liam asked, unable to stop an amused smile from appearing on his lips.

'I fear so, my lord,' she said matter-of-factly. 'I understand if you must dismiss me, particularly after that display. I have no excuses. I'm sure I don't know what came over me.'

'How long have you been here, Mrs Hardwicke?'

'Three weeks, my lord.'

'And do you recall, I wonder,' Liam asked casually, 'how many housekeepers have come to Thornhallow before you?'

'Twenty-one, my lord.'

'A rather impressive record, I think. Now, did Leonards tell you, perchance, how many applicants there were along with you?'

'No, my lord.'

'No, I don't suppose he would. None,' Liam mused, hoping she might dare look at him again, though sadly she did not, seemingly intent on playing her role to the letter now.

'Only one applicant this time, Mrs Hardwicke. *You.* So, you see, I shall not dismiss you—*for now.* Though you are right in that you certainly deserve nothing less.'

'Thank you, my lord,' she said softly. 'It shall not happen again.'

'Indeed, I should hope not,' he lied. 'Now, would you be so kind as to attend me in my study in half an hour? So that we might discuss the running of this accursed house civilly?'

'Yes, my lord.'

'And by the way, Mrs Hardwicke,' he said nonchalantly, turning for the door again. 'I tend to enjoy the library in the evening. Therefore if you could borrow any book you wish to, then sample it in your own quarters, I would appreciate it.'

Liam stopped to enjoy the embarrassed look that came upon her, rendering her speechless, but returning some of the life he'd so carelessly snuffed out to her eyes, and bringing a rather lovely flush to her cheeks.

'Half an hour, Mrs Hardwicke.'

Liam left her thus and strode out victorious.

He had enjoyed that little encounter much more than he should have. Despite the fact the woman was irritating, infuriating and disrespectful in every possible way, at least she'd held her own. Though he might not agree with her, or her methods, he *did* have to admit—at least to himself— that she was right. Whatever his feelings about this place, ignoring it, and letting it fall into ruin, was not the answer.

Perhaps if he had the courage he would set a match to it, but then, he knew better than to think he ever could. Besides, if he was to rid himself of the place, one way or another, tidying it wouldn't hurt. And, as she had pointed out, it was her time to do with as she pleased. If she was intent on cleaning, what business was it of his? As long as the rest of her duties were seen to, what did he care that she scraped at grates and scrubbed floors?

Except that, oddly, he did care. When he'd seen her hands last night, and then again today... The woman was quite literally working herself to the bone. No, that wouldn't do. He would tell her so. Perhaps he would hire more staff to help...

They won't come... Damn this house.

No one within fifty miles would set foot here, and that was being generous. No matter that none of the staff who *actually* lived and worked here were all alive, and had no ghastly tales to tell. No matter that the worst thing to happen here in ten years was a string of incapable housekeepers, who had most likely spread some tales themselves to excuse their ineptitude. No one would come. The house was cursed. Just as he was.

Haunted.

He was lucky Mrs Hardwicke had even applied at all. Even Leonards had advised him that, for all his money, should Mrs Hardwicke depart, there would likely never be a housekeeper at Thornhallow Hall again. So why had she come? When so many feared to even speak the name of the place?

It mattered not. She was here. And for now, Liam resolved, the quarrelsome Mrs Hardwicke could stay. Though for all her will and gumption, he doubted she would last long. Perhaps she would find a young fellow to marry. Or simply take fright, or succumb to what he suspected was an already growing hatred of him. Sooner or later, everyone left him.

Pushing open the door to his study, gazing out onto the grounds through the French doors behind his desk, he sighed, feeling the weight of it all crashing down again. Why the Devil indeed had he thought returning was a good idea? He should have left Thornhallow to the care of Mrs Hardwicke, and Thomas, and the others. Perhaps he should do so now, and return to his life of wandering beyond the horizon…

Yet even as he thought it he knew he could not.

The time had come to face the demons so that he might be free. Of this house and this land, which called him back even from the ends of the earth. Of this curse which gnawed at his soul, destroying him a little more with every passing day.

Oh, Hal…my darling, what have you done to me? Will we never have peace?

And in that moment of utter desolation, Liam bleakly registered that he was barefoot.

The flickering of the candle worsened as it neared its end, but Rebecca knew that if she intended to continue she would have to forgo lighting another. If she allowed herself to move but an inch, even if only to ease her hunched squinting with more light, she would never return and finish the task she'd set herself: reconciling ten years' worth of accounting.

Come on, Rebecca, nearly there…

Three weeks she'd been studying ledgers, half-torn payment slips and smudged invoices, barely sleeping so that now numbers swirled before her eyes together in one great jumble. Perhaps if she changed the candle she would be able to see better…

No. You know you'll find a way to distract yourself.

Rebecca desperately wanted to finish—*needed* to finish so that she could show the Earl. After this morning's embarrassing display, she needed something to redeem herself and prove her worth. When she'd met him again in the study, no reference had been made to their *discus-*

sion. He had behaved like the perfect gentleman, and she had been the most demure, contrite housekeeper the world had ever seen.

They had spoken of the arrangements made for Thornhallow, of the staff and of the weather. He had seemed content with what she'd told him, though he had offered no blatant opinion. He had asked nothing, demanded no changes, nor expressed any sort of interest whatsoever. Oddly, the only thing he *had* insisted on was that she take care of her hands. But even that had been said with such detachment. In other masters the coldness might have seemed natural, but with him it seemed…a rebuke? A reminder of his displeasure?

You really do read too much into things, you senseless ninny.

She had met the man this morning, and now she presumed to know his moods? Presumed to know the measure of his character because what? He was the sort of man to lay a blanket on a sleeping employee? At least she knew she wasn't going mad.

I knew I hadn't put the blanket on myself…

God, she was tired. It had been a trying day; surely that was why she was feeling so…out of sorts. She'd risen this morning expecting to fill the day with vigorous cleaning, to expend some of her overbrimming energy, and counter the effects of having spent too much time indoors over the past weeks. Instead, what had she done? Expended her energy shouting at the Earl. Of course she hadn't meant to, but then he had appeared and begun admonishing her and, truth be told, she might have been less surprised if Lucifer himself had waltzed in.

'*Keep the house as if the master might return at any day,*' Leonards had said.

Easily said, and easily done.

But, considering the man hadn't set foot here in a decade, it was no wonder she'd been so astonished to see him standing there. The man had given no notice of his arrival—indeed, he must have scarcely made a sound when he came in. And she had disappeared before dawn to set about her assault on the West Wing, before anyone who might have advised her of the miraculous arrival could do so.

What a hash she had made of it all.

What was truly miraculous was that she hadn't been dismissed. But then, what had the man been expecting? For her to just sit and while away the hours in idle contemplation whilst the house disappeared as he had?

Apparently so...

And what business was it of hers to argue, if that was his wish?

He had just been so...

Argh!

No, she could not be like her predecessors, but she might have told him so calmly, coolly, with some semblance of professionalism. Not scolded him as if he were her equal.

Sighing, Rebecca set down her quill and rubbed the bridge of her nose.

A mess. Of truly epic proportions.

That was what she'd made and, worse, that was what she was.

Staring down at her hands—her bloody, ink-soaked hands that she could not get clean, no matter how hard she tried—she felt...dejected. Confused and lost. She had since this morning, when she'd tried to compose herself before meeting the master again. When she had seen the mass of unruly hair and the soot all over her reddened face... A wild, lowly creature. It was no wonder the man had a low opinion of her. Her inadequacy at being what a housekeeper *should* be was plain to see, without even taking into account her behaviour.

Unprofessional, unseemly and entirely condemnable. What is the matter with you?

What, indeed? she wondered, staring down at her hands, disheartened by the fact that no amount of cleaning, tidying or rearranging would ever be enough.

For what?

To be seen, she realised suddenly.

Rebecca laughed mirthlessly, her heart sore at the discovery that she could be such a vapid fool after all. *That* was what lay beneath her frustration and shame. *That* was what had really discountenanced her. Not his words, but *him*. Of all she might have expected, none of it had been what William Reid, the Right Honourable the Earl of Thornhallow, had turned out to be.

The fact that he'd been sporting masterfully tailored, albeit dishevelled clothes, whilst barefoot, had been the first thing to catch her attention. Then there was his age. Though she knew it approximately, her mind had crafted him into some old, dissolute wastrel.

The mystery surrounding him, Thornhallow, his disappearance—all had served to obfuscate any truth that might have lain in the rare, whispered descriptions of him. Anyone who knew him before he'd quit the country—if indeed he had—was unable to remember quite what he looked like. There were no names on the portraits in the gallery. And the speculatory tales of where he'd been these past ten years only served to lend credit to the idea that he was a dark man, capable of the greatest sins, who had let himself go to the Devil.

It was, in fact, no such man who had walked in this morning.

Handsome did not quite fit properly. Yes, he had sharp, fine features, a long, strong nose and straight brows, one of which was traversed by a thin white scar. Yes, he had the most inviting generous lips. Yes, he had an unmistakably fine figure. Narrow waist, broad shoulders—very broad, in fact—long limbs and elegant, strong hands. Yes, he was tall—very much so, to have towered over her. Yes, he had the swept-back, longer-than-fashionable golden hair that seemed to gleam in the sunlight. All of those things were, when brought together to form a complete sum, the markings of a handsome man. And yet...

When she recalled that image of him as he'd stood before her, it was not *handsome* that came to mind. She had met—*known*—very handsome men. But William Reid, Earl of Thornhallow, was not what she would call handsome. He was almost closer to...beautiful? Entrancing?

Then she remembered his eyes... What colour had they been?

Grey? No...

They had seemed so at first...so cold... But, no...

Hazel. With flecks of gold, grey and green.

Eyes that had seen too much, and still retained light. Enchanting, rapturous light...

Mrs Murray's shouts echoing sharply down the corridor brought Rebecca back from her reverie. Cursing under her breath, she picked up her quill and returned to the ledger. It didn't matter what she qualified his manner to be, or what precisely she thought of his eyes. Truly, it mattered not one bit that he would never *see* her. And she was glad of it, verily.

Over the years she'd been blessed with good masters who had treated her well. She had never suffered unwelcome advances, nor had she had the terrible misfortune of developing a fondness for any of her employers, nor anyone in their circles. She wasn't about to jeopardise her position, her *life*, by becoming foolishly intrigued by this master.

The Earl of Thornhallow might be the most beautiful angel to descend from heaven; it would matter not one bit. She was his housekeeper. And she would do her duty. As she always had. Infallibly. Beginning with presenting him these accounts.

Rebecca smiled to herself, imagining his face when she did so.

The smile faded a moment later, when a knock sounded on the door. Finishing was becoming an increasingly elusive dream.

'Yes,' she sighed, rubbing her eyes so that she might focus on whoever it was needing her at this hour. 'Come in.'

'Working late again, I see, Mrs Hardwicke,' Mr Brown said as he entered. 'You will forgive me for the hour, but I wish to have a word, if I may.'

'Of course, Mr Brown. Please, do have a seat,' Rebecca said, before noticing the piles of papers strewn across the armchairs. She rose precipitately and cleared a space. 'Tea?'

'No, thank you. I will not keep you long.'

'How can I— Oh, blast,' she muttered as the candle flickered wildly. She rushed to find another, before settling down to face Mr Brown. 'Apologies. How can I assist you?'

'Nearly finished, I see. With the accounts, I mean.'

'Oh, yes, won't be long now, and I shan't lie, I will be glad to see the end of them.'

'Quite an achievement.'

'Thank you, Mr Brown, very kind of you.'

'I wish to apologise, Mrs Hardwicke,' he said, after the moment of awkward silence which had followed his compliment. 'About this morning.'

'I'm afraid I don't follow.'

'His Lordship, you see, he asked for my thoughts. On you...'

'I see. Mr Brown, please do not trouble yourself.'

'On the contrary, Mrs Hardwicke,' he said proudly. 'I meant no trouble. You and I may not have begun well— however, the opinions I expressed to His Lordship were nothing but positive. I may not have agreed with your chosen course, but I've watched you put so much care and devotion into restoring Thornhallow. I've seen how proud the others are once again to be a part of this place. To be a part of what you have started. You have not balked at any point upon realising the Herculean nature of the task you set yourself—which, in all honesty, I believed you would. I, too, wish to be a part of your worthy endeavour. Any assistance I may provide you, please do tell me.'

'I...I don't quite know what to say, Mr Brown,' Rebecca managed after a moment. The butler's kind words and the loyalty he was demonstrating were rather unsettling.

You've won him over after all...

'Thank you. I shall welcome your assistance. But, please, in regard to His Lordship, think no more of it. I could never believe you would intentionally cause trouble, whatever your opinions. I disregarded his orders knowingly; he had every right to upbraid me.'

'You must not be too hard on him, Mrs Hardwicke,' Mr Brown said with a faint smile. 'He has a rather volatile temper, but beneath the overbearing exterior, despite any tales you might have heard... He is a good man.'

'You have known him all his life, have you not, Mr Brown?'

The butler nodded, clearly slightly perplexed by the question.

'As has Mrs Murray. Tim has known him since he was

a boy. I like to think that a master capable of such things as I've heard would not inspire such devotion and loyalty.' Rebecca smiled. 'I do not set any score by gossip, Mr Brown. Or I wouldn't be here.'

Any doubts she might have harboured in the darkest recesses of her soul regarding the truth of those rumours had been quashed when she'd first set eyes on the Earl. She knew evil, and there was none in that man.

'Why are you here, Mrs Hardwicke?'

'To do what any servant does. Set this house to rights, in any way I can.'

The old butler studied her thoughtfully for a long moment, his piercing grey eyes twinkling in the candlelight. Finally he inclined his head, ever so slightly, and rose.

'You have my respect, Mrs Hardwicke, and my loyalty. Know that.'

'Goodnight, Mr Brown,' Rebecca said, swallowing the lump in her throat.

'Goodnight, Mrs Hardwicke.'

His words, not spoken lightly, had touched her. It wasn't so much that she felt she'd finally managed to pierce his thick armour of propriety, it was that she knew he respected her, and wanted to be a part of her plans. Throughout the years Rebecca had worked alongside many different people. She had served with eight butlers, most of whom had been professional and polite, but none of whom she'd felt proud to be respected by. It made her heart swell, and gave her a surge of courage. The courage to face anything.

Even these pesky numbers...

Feeling revived, and not wanting to waste the new candle, Rebecca turned her attention once again to the ledgers, the slight smile on her lips refusing to disappear.

Right, now, where was I?

Chapter Four

Over the next two weeks the weather turned even more towards winter, with gales, storms and an increasingly bitter cold slowly overthrowing the brisk but enjoyable autumn days. It somehow made the house feel warmer. More inviting than Liam had ever felt it to be. Or perhaps, it was the indomitable Mrs Hardwicke, and her seemingly mystical ability to bring warmth and light wherever she went.

He hadn't seen much of her since she had come to his study and presented him with the reconciled accounts for the past ten years. The smile of proud satisfaction on her face as she piled them high on his desk for review had nearly made him laugh. Not quite the reaction she'd expected, he sensed.

He hadn't been able to help it. Her serious, determined manner had been oddly charming, warming his heart in a strange sort of way.

However, since he had thanked her for her efforts, and commended her diligence, he had barely seen her. Which was for the best. The last thing he needed was any more *stirrings* where his employees were concerned. Luckily, he was busy enough reacquainting himself with everything, as best he could while he waited for the majority of the papers concerning the Earldom and this estate to be sent from London.

So far he had made no progress on his 'mad scheme', as Leonards called his quest for freedom from his birth-right. Which frustrated him, but he countered his sense of uselessness by taking long rides through the park and sur-rounding wilderness, and discreetly going on little tours of the house, following Mrs Hardwicke's progress.

Slowly he was making his way towards…

Somewhere he was still not ready to venture.

As the weather changed, and seemed intent on remain-ing more foul than fair, Liam knew it was time to meet with Bradley, his estate manager. Surveying the estate once more unfavourable days set in would be an added trial neither needed. Besides, he was not getting very far in assessing anything by himself, and Bradley, he was sure, could illuminate him on most matters.

It was time to face someone other than his house staff. Time to face the world again, if only partially. Time to make his plans and wishes known.

So he'd set a meeting with Bradley, knowing full well that a day away from Thornhallow was needed lest he go mad. Spending so much time indoors weighed on him. He was not accustomed to it, and quite detested it. No matter how warm and welcoming Mrs Hardwicke made the house.

'Well, aren't you a sight for sore eyes, my lord,' Brad-ley said jovially, riding up to meet Liam where he waited at the edge of the west woods. 'Welcome home.'

'Thank you. It's good to see you.' Liam smiled, leaning over Orpheus to offer his hand.

The man had aged, grey peppering the thick dark locks, and deep laughter lines marking the strong face of a man who lived his life outdoors. When Bradley had first come to Thornhallow, Liam was but a boy, and Bradley had been in his early thirties, eager, hardworking and seemingly a giant. Now it seemed they were equals, though there was a quiet wisdom about the man Liam had not recalled.

'And thank you for looking after it all these years.'

'Only doing my duty, my lord, as you well know,' Bradley said with a nod. 'Now, shall we take these fellows on a walk and discuss business?'

'Excellent.'

They rode in silence for a short while, quietly ambling through the park, heading for the tenant farms which lay beyond the ancient woodland to the north.

'He's written to you, hasn't he? Leonards? Of my "mad scheme".'

'Indeed he has,' Bradley said, with a wry smile but a hint of worry in his eyes. 'And you are quite set upon this path? Trying to relinquish the Earldom? There are other ways, you know.'

'Easier ways,' Liam corrected. 'Ways which would allow me a sense of freedom until I change my mind. Regret my choice.'

Bradley simply shrugged, and Liam sighed. He appreciated everyone's concern and well-meaning reticence, but he also wished he could make them understand.

'I am certain of my decision, and will never regret true and everlasting freedom. If indeed I can realise my dreams.'

'As long as you are certain, my lord, I will serve you in whatever course you choose. If it can be done...it will take a lot. Money, time, commitment... And your absence, I'm afraid, has been felt.'

'I know. And I know that you and Leonards, and everyone here, have done the best you could. I am grateful for it, no matter my own thoughts on the place. That is why I came back. Everything else can be sorted easily enough, but Thornhallow…'

'Quite.'

Bradley took a moment before continuing, giving Liam a moment to compose himself under the guise of leading his mount carefully onto the muddy woodland path.

'Leonards has begun making arrangements in London?'

'Yes, attempting to, at least. Much to his own dismay. He is sending on the papers regarding the estate, and once I have properly looked over everything, and we have discussed how best to proceed, I shall advise him of our plans. As for the house, he wishes for a proper surveyor to come, but I would rather my intentions remain known only to us. For now, at least.'

Liam sighed, ducking under a large overhanging branch.

'I thought, if you're up to the task, perhaps you could write up a report about the edifice? I've asked Thomas to discreetly take stock of the furnishings, the art and all the rest. With the twenty odd housekeepers he's suffered, I dare say he wasn't too confounded by the request.'

'I can manage well enough,' Bradley said thoughtfully. 'There'll be some repairs and the like, surely, but the latest of your housekeepers has already tackled some of the more pressing issues. At least, she advised she would when we met.'

'Ah, yes, the incomparable Mrs Hardwicke.'

Cannot seem to escape the wretched female, no matter how hard I try.

'So she has.'

'Haven't been up to the house but once since she arrived—'bout a week or so after she had. Everyone was in a right state, particularly Mr Brown—not that he said a word against her. Quite an enterprising sort, she seemed. Ambitious and determined. A rather pleasant, strange sort. But, well…'

Bradley let the words hang, along with their unspoken meaning. *But, well, just what Thornhallow needs.*

Et tu, Bradley?

'How are things going up there?'

'Well enough. She's won them all over with her brazen treachery,' Liam said begrudgingly, but with a hint of amusement and admiration. 'From what I can tell she's moving through the house like a whirlwind, intent on polishing every last door handle before the spring. Then, I suppose the gardens will be next.'

Liam wondered briefly if she would be able to revive his mother's work as she was reviving the house. The others had done well enough with the bones of the rose and wildflower gardens his mother had created, but for a brief moment he smiled at the thought that Mrs Hardwicke's witchcraft might restore them to the Eden he remembered.

Not that I will be here to see it if she does...

'I have to admit,' he sighed, the bitterness of that thought surprising him. 'I had no idea... I didn't mean for things to become so... Well, in any case, she's saved me a lot of trouble. So I must be thankful, I suppose.'

'Aye, I'm glad she's working out, then. Can't believe she's won over Mr Brown,' Bradley laughed. 'He's a tough one, but match enough for him, she is. Good for her.'

'Aye, match enough indeed.'

For any man or monster.

'Mrs Ffoulkes as well—mad old bat. Apparently your Mrs Hardwicke has been up to see her once a week, checking on her, bringing her treats...'

'I have not been to visit her yet, I have been remiss,' Liam said, wondering if the widow of his father's gatekeeper had changed at all.

Mrs Ffoulkes had been given a small allowance and a cottage on the estate when her husband had passed away—

one of the few selfless and generous acts his father had ever done.

But from the first time Liam had set eyes on her, and thought her a witch dwelling in the woods, to the last, a year or so before he'd left Thornhallow, Mrs Ffoulkes had not gained a single new wrinkle.

He wondered if that would still be true.

'I should do so before long, though I doubt I could live up to whatever lofty sainthood she has seen fit to bestow upon Mrs Hardwicke.'

With complicit smiles, they continued on, discussing Liam's plans and the best ways to enact them.

Soon enough I will be free. Everything will be as it should, you will see, Hal.

As Liam parted with Bradley later that afternoon, and made his way back to the stables, he wondered if she would have understood his decision. Or if she, too, would have chastised him, as she had often been wont to do, no matter that he had been her elder, her keeper, her adviser. She had always been the wisest, the kindest—the heart of Thornhallow.

And now that you are gone, sister mine, it beats no longer. I doubt it ever will again.

Rebecca awoke with a start, dread and panic churning in the pit of her stomach. She stared into the darkness, her mind attempting to make sense of her sudden awakening through the foggy mess of the remnants of her dream. Breathing deeply, she tried to think back on it. It had been pleasant enough, nothing extraordinary, at least not that she could recall.

Whereas the nightmares…

The nightmares, when her prince finally caught her

after all these years, when she could not run fast enough...
Those were impossible to forget.

She ran her hand over her forehead and cheeks. No
sweat. No temperature. Nothing abnormal.

Definitely not a nightmare, then.

And yet her heart pounded, and the awful feeling in her
stomach hadn't lessened.

Then she heard it.

A roar.

Terrible and chilling.

She sat up, and strained to listen. It seemed to echo in
her mind, but only there. There were no rushing footsteps,
no bumps or creaks, nor voices in the night. It seemed she
alone had heard it. But heard what? Echoes of a dream? A
ghost? Her imagination? Was her mind finally surrendering its reason to all the tales and gossip?

Entirely likely, Rebecca. Losing your wits at last...

Another roar.

That was it. In one fell swoop she was out of bed, had
donned her dressing robe and slippers, and had begun to
make her way through the servants' quarters as quietly as
possible, candle in hand. There would be no going back to
bed—not until she was either firmly convinced of her impending madness, or had found whoever it was who was
screaming bloody murder.

Such a vivid image you paint yourself...

Rebecca stopped at the bottom of the main servants'
staircase and listened intently. She heard only the flicker
of the candle and her own shallow, rapid breathing. That,
and her heartbeat. The dull thud of blood in her ears.

But she also heard more dull thuds—not a product of
her own fear. Those were coming from upstairs.

And then yet another scream.

Rebecca jumped, then took a deep breath and calmed

herself. Whatever—whoever—it was making them, the sounds were definitely coming from upstairs. Steeling herself, she resolved to investigate before rousing any of the others, who remained, it seemed, wholly unaware of any of this. She had yet to convince herself it wasn't all a figment of her overexhausted mind, and so on she went, slowly and carefully, dreading the sudden appearance of a spectre or masked figure with every step.

You know full well there are no ghosts here. You don't even believe in the things.

At the top of the stairs Rebecca paused, listening for any sign of life. There seemed to reign the usual silence, punctured only by the ticking of the grandfather clock. Perhaps she had been dreaming after all.

Or perhaps there are ghosts after all.

Is this how it happened? Is this what drove the others away? Screams of terror piercing through the stone walls and the heavy night? Strange towers—

Not ghosts, Rebecca realised as she moved to return to bed and another scream pierced the air, making her shudder. Not in fear, but in pain, for the sound was one of anguish, of pure suffering. It twisted her heart, and made her blood run cold.

A howl... A wolf. Or a man.

Holding out the candle, clutching her robe tightly around herself, Rebecca stepped into the corridor.

Voices, murmurs, moans...

Pricking up her ears, she tried to discern where they were coming from.

The library.

The glow of the fire was visible through the open door.

The master...

He was the only one who would be there at this time of night. Was he being attacked? Should she arm herself?

Call the men? And yet, as she cautiously approached the doorway, she knew instinctively that she alone should deal with this. In her heart, she knew there were no attackers. No rogues, and no bandits.

No ghosts.

'My lord,' she said, as calmly as she could muster, pushing the door open to peer inside. 'My lord, are you well?'

Rebecca gasped when she caught sight of the room.

It had been utterly upended. Furniture, books, even the wall hangings had been tossed and torn. And there, amidst it all, beside the fireplace, stood the master, in only his breeches and shirtsleeves. His back was to her, but she could see his laboured breathing and knew instantly that he'd done this.

'My lord,' she repeated soothingly, daring a few more steps towards him, but leaving the candle on the small table by the door. 'It's Mrs Hardwicke, my lord, I heard—'

Liam whirled around and Rebecca stopped, her breath catching. He looked like a fallen angel in the firelight. A barbaric, dangerous creature. Strands of golden hair, matted with sweat, hung limply around his tempestuous, unfocused eyes, which were full of anguish, heat and ice. His mouth was set in a tight, thin line, and his fists clenched. Every muscle in his body was tense. It wasn't difficult to see; his clothes were drenched in sweat themselves and clung tightly to him.

Every inch of him was tense, and it seemed, now focused on her. Although Rebecca knew, in that instant, that he did not see her.

She'd heard of sleepwalkers before, but never had she witnessed the phenomenon. She had heard one should not try to wake them, but neither could she leave him like this. The man was in heart-wrenching pain—not to mention he might injure himself if he continued to make his way through the house, destroying it.

'My lord, it's Mrs Hardwicke,' she repeated, as softly and reassuringly as she could manage. 'My lord, you are dreaming I think…'

Blast, Rebecca thought bleakly as he half jumped, half strode to her, throwing her to the ground before she could move an inch.

Stars shone before her eyes as her head hit the wood, her breath rushing out of her. And then he was there, his body pinning her down, and her heart was beating so fast she could almost hear it hitting her ribs like a bird flying against a cage, as blood rushed, pounding, in her ears.

Still he did not see her, she knew. Rage, anger and something far more terrifying lay there in the hazel eyes that now seemed like fire themselves as they bore down on her. She could smell the whisky on his breath, and the sweat; could feel the sticky heat clouding her. He was murmuring now, incoherent jumbled words and languages, but Rebecca understood the tone.

Accusatory. Pleading. *Murderous.*

'My lord,' Rebecca whispered, trying to push away the uneasiness growing in her belly. *This man is not a murderer.* 'Please—'

His right hand flew to her throat, immobilising, but not suffocating.

'My lord, William,' she croaked, raising her own hand, and gently sweeping her fingers across his brow before laying her palm on his cheek. 'William, please…'

And then, in an instant, she saw him return to himself.

His grip slackened, but he did not move. He gaped down in horror, the realisation of what had happened, of what he'd nearly done, dawning as he searched her face.

She saw more pain in his eyes than before. And confusion, regret, shame, disgust.

'Oh, God,' he breathed. 'What have I done?'

'Nothing, my lord,' Rebecca reassured him, stroking his cheek softly with her thumb, her hand still cradling his face. 'You have done me no harm.'

Whatever words he wished to say were drowned in the cry which escaped instead.

Crumbling into himself, he slumped back, his head coming to rest on her belly as his hands fell on her waist. And then he began to sob, his body jerking against hers, his tears soaking her nightshirt.

Rebecca felt her heart reach out to him, this tortured creature, and so what could she do but lie there and wait and hold him?

'Shh, now...' she whispered, letting her hands stroke his head comfortingly, running her fingers through his hair, cradling him as best she could. 'Everything is as it should be.'

As they lay there, for however long it may have been, Rebecca could not help but wonder what horrors, what terrors, this man had seen to bring him to such a state. His screams, the anguish she'd heard and seen in him, were beyond imagination. What terrible events could bring someone to this? Someone as strong and seemingly as impervious as this man before her? Could the stories be true after all?

No... I cannot believe that.

Finally, after what seemed hours, his crying ceased, giving way to ragged breathing.

'We should get you to bed, my lord,' Rebecca whispered.

A nod. Liam peeled away from her, bringing himself to his knees.

Rebecca lay there for a moment, a rush of cold and loss sweeping over her. Taking a deep breath, she brought herself up and slowly, carefully, so as not to frighten him, rose to her feet.

The master did not move, still curled over himself, head and shoulders hanging limply, hands resting on the floor, and Rebecca realised she would have to help him to his chambers. Unseemly, unconscionable, and yet she could not bring herself to fetch Gregory or Thomas.

No one else needed to witness the state he was in.

'My lord,' she said, placing a hand on his shoulder. 'I will help you, but I cannot carry you. Give me your hand.'

Liam did as instructed, his hand rising to meet her own, though he still refused to meet her eyes. Rebecca slid the hand that had been on his shoulder beneath his arm, and took some of his weight as he dragged himself unsteadily to his feet.

'Excellent. Now, lean on me, my lord, and we shall have you in your bed in no time.'

Sliding her hand further along his back to move it around his waist, Rebecca felt him cede, resting his arm around her shoulders. The man was all heavy muscle, but she did not demur, nor falter, simply gritted her teeth and bore it. She let his other hand drop and urged him towards the door, grabbing the candle as they left, before slowly beginning their ascent.

When they reached his chambers Rebecca led him over to the bed, then slid out from under him. He did not move, only stood limply where she had left him. Quickly, she pulled back the covers, then guided him over. Liam let himself be tucked in, his eyes fixed on a point just beyond her head. After she'd settled him she went over to the fire, stoked it and added some logs. She poured him a glass of water, then gazed down at him for a moment.

He looked so…hollow, tortured—the shadows on his face emphasised by the growing flames. He had not moved from where she'd left him, lying there pitifully, staring into a void of his own design. Rebecca felt a pang again, and wished there was more she could do to soothe him.

'Rest, my lord,' she whispered, turning to leave. 'All will be well in the morning.'

'Stay,' he pleaded, his voice barely audible.

Not in a thousand years was that a sensible, proper, acceptable idea. And yet Rebecca's feet would carry her no further.

'Please.'

She sighed, her heart twisting in her chest, and her mind reeling. Then, quieting them both, she took a chair, and carried it to his bedside. She set the candle down beside her, blew it out, and placed her hand on his. He gripped it tightly—so tightly it felt as though his life depended on it.

Perhaps it does.

'I shall stay, my lord. Now rest.'

Finally, his eyes fluttered shut. Rebecca sighed again, her heart heavy as she felt his grip slacken. She knew the moment he fell asleep, his breathing slowing and peace finally unknitting his brows.

How on earth had she managed to get herself into such a dreadful mess? She should have gone to fetch the men the moment she'd known the screams were not born of her imagination. Or walked away. Left the master to his nightmares. Not rushed in there—and all for what? What shame had she brought on herself—on him—with her reckless actions?

And yet all that notwithstanding, she couldn't convince herself that she'd done wrong. Yes, it had been reckless, and she had nearly lost her life attempting to wrench him back from his demons. But even when he had lain upon

her, his hand around her neck, she had not been afraid.
Not truly.

Why?

He could have broken her neck with a twist of his wrist.
Why had she not been afraid? Why had she not kicked and
screamed and clawed?

Because... Because what?

She thought she could bring him back? She, his housekeeper, who barely knew him? What kind of foolish nincompoop lay there whilst being throttled and somehow
still trusted the man whose hands were wrapped around
her throat?

The besotted kind.

The stupid, fairy-tale-believing, googly-eyed, foolish
girls who thought love could conquer all and that honourable, dashing creatures such as His Lordship could never
hurt them, even when they were not themselves. Girls
among whom Rebecca could never count herself again. It
had once cost her everything.

What was wrong with her?

Well, so what if she liked the master. It meant nothing.
Only that she admired him. There was...

*Something. Beneath the gruffness, and temper, and
darkness...*

That she was instinctively drawn to. That made her trust
him. There was no harm in that. It was good to like and
admire and trust the masters. And that was why she'd felt
the need to comfort, to soothe, to ease his pain.

She wasn't...*besotted.* Only someone who had never
been able to endure others' suffering without taking it
upon herself. *Empathy.* She could no sooner have left a
bird with a broken wing to die alone in the wilderness than
she could have left him to writhe in agony.

Drat, Rebecca thought, exhaustion finally creeping up

on her. Trying to sort out the Gordian knots in her mind would not fix anything. Laying her head down on the bed, she resolved to stay a little longer by his side, just in case.

Oh, what trouble you've made for yourself indeed Rebecca Merrickson.

Liam awoke as Rebecca let herself out of his room. He lay still, eyes firmly closed, until he heard the sound of her footsteps fade down the corridor, and was certain she would not return. Then, and only then, did he let them flutter open, and for a long while he simply lay there, staring blankly at the door, as though willing her to pass back through it.

Sighing, he finally pulled himself up, and sat against the headboard. Everything hurt. His body, his mind, his heart. He glanced down at his hands. Visions of what he'd done the night before were conjured in his mind at the sight of his bloodied knuckles and cut fingers. He had destroyed the library. And, God help him, he had attacked Mrs Hardwicke.

It had been a long while since the nightmares had so fully taken possession, since such an episode had occurred. But even then, no one had got hurt. Not that he could ever remember much. Only flashes, snippets of memory. Snippets of dreams. But last night… Last night had been the very worst he could recall. Even in the first days after…

God help me…

Liam raked his fingers through his hair and blinked away the tears that threatened to overcome him again. Tears of guilt and of shame. Of anger and of fear.

But not of pain, nor sorrow.

Frowning, he glanced around the room as though it, or some spectre within it, had spoken that revelation. Or as if, perhaps, it might hold the answer.

He rubbed his breast—there, over his heart—and found the tight, harrowing pain which normally lingered had gone. The weight he carried as if Atlas had lessened. In all these years not once had he felt so...

Refreshed?

Despicable, terrified, angry, yes, but somehow...

Lighter?

If he'd known it was as simple as taking his fists to the library, he might have done it years ago.

No. It was... It was the tears.

Those he'd spilled last night, those which had racked his body, and which he had shed unwillingly like pieces of his own flesh and soul. Tears he had spilled in *her* arms.

God save me.

Was there anything more shameful than attacking her and sobbing in her arms?

Pleading for her to stay, perhaps.

Yes, I did that, too.

Then why did he feel so much lighter? Was it having finally given in to his grief and sorrow as he lay with her in the midst of his destruction? Why could he not fully regret, even now, giving in to those tears he had kept firmly clutched within his breast for years? Tears for Hal and tears for...

How could he not regret having felt her beneath him, taking it all from him? He had hurt her—terrified her, most likely—and yet, it didn't hurt *him* so much anymore. And she had stayed.

Why had she stayed?

Liam threw back the covers, slipped on his dressing gown and opened the curtains before setting about pacing the room.

Not only stayed with him here, in his chamber—which, even though he, her lord and master, had asked it, was entirely improper and inconceivable—but before that. In the library.

When she had seen his state, why had she not run? Fetched the others? Or simply left him?

Foolish, reckless, careless woman.

What might have happened if she had not brought him back?

I might've killed you, so why in the name of all the saints did you not run?

And why did he feel...

Grateful. For you staying. For you bringing me back from the edge of the never-ending darkness I strayed so closely to.

He could still hear her voice calling his name.

William...

No one called him that; only his mother ever had.

He could still feel the brush of her fingers against his cheek, see the look in her eyes when he had returned to himself...

Entreaty and pleading, but no fear. Foolish, careless woman.

Why had she not feared him even as his fingers encircled her throat? As she lay there at his mercy? He hadn't even been able to look at her once he'd realised. Once he had given in to everything which had swept over him and turned him into a simpering boy.

And even then, Mrs Hardwicke, you did not recoil...

Liam strode over to the window and leaned his forehead against the cool glass. Outside, the world still lay in slumber, with the sun's first rays creeping over the horizon and casting a purplish hue over the landscape. So peaceful, so beautiful, this land of his. This place he had tried to escape, but which continued to refuse him release.

It was as if every frosted blade of grass and leaf, every

shimmer of glorious autumn delight, had been created solely to taunt him. He had seen a thousand sunrises, a hundred landscapes more breathtaking than this, and yet *this*—this was what he could not forget, no matter how hard he tried. How far he ran. This land was in his bones, in his blood, like ichor.

He should never have returned. That much was clear.

Last night had almost cost him so much more than he'd already given. If he allowed it—if he did not find a way to exorcise this place from himself soon—he might not be so fortunate. The last shred of his sanity, and any hope of redemption would be lost forever.

On that grim, unwelcome thought, Liam strode back over to his bed and rang the bell. He would dress, clean up, have breakfast and get to work within the hour. There was no more time to waste.

Thornhallow would not claim him as it had Hal, his mother and even his father.

Of that, he would make certain.

Chapter Five

Setting himself down at his desk with a heavy sigh, Liam cradled his head in his hands for a moment. The dilemma he currently faced should not, in actual fact, be one at all. He should not be devoting so much time or energy to this, having so many other more pressing and important matters to attend to. Yet he could not prevent his thoughts from returning ceaselessly to his maddening housekeeper.

Two choices now lay before him. Keep her on or dismiss her.

And yet so much more was factoring into this deceptively simple predicament. Not only did the papers Leonards had forwarded demonstrate that the woman was hiding something, but she had disobeyed his orders, behaved in a most unbecoming and unforgivable manner, and, well...

Been right to do so.

She had won over his entire staff. Brought light back into the house.

And last night...

He was grateful for what she had done, but he also feared the temptation. Of the comfort and closeness she offered. He feared the instinctual response he'd had to her from the first. It would be so much easier just to be rid of her, before anything irreversible could happen. It wasn't as if he didn't have just cause. Perhaps the papers were a godsend after all. There was so much more left for him to do, to finish, so he could be free. The very last thing he needed was to be distracted. Worried about whatever it was his housekeeper seemed to be running from. About *her*, full stop.

For there was no doubt she was running. The proof was here, lying before him on the desk.

Distractedly, he shuffled through the packet of papers Leonards had sent. No wonder she had taken the position here. She was desperate. Perhaps she had known Leonards was, too. Enough to look no further into all this. And with no master present at Thornhallow there would be fewer questions.

Yes...that must be it. Mustn't it?

Then why couldn't he resolve himself to send her away? He had to decide, and quickly. She'd be here at any moment. He'd asked Thomas to send her along when he'd met him in the library a short while ago.

That was another thing. He had gone there expecting to find the room destroyed, expecting to have to put it to rights himself. Instead he'd found Thomas, Sam and Gregory installing new chairs—the only trace of the carnage he'd wrought. No one would have been able to surmise what had passed there only hours before.

'Mrs Hardwicke said you wished for a change, my lord,' Gregory had said, slightly confused.

Which meant the enterprising Mrs Hardwicke had seen to it that the room was cleared and tidy before allowing anyone in. Then she had invented some paltry, trivial excuse to justify the need for a change of furniture, and request for help. Liam had had no doubt, looking at Thomas, that he knew nothing of the previous night's events. Something which he appreciated. He wouldn't have been able to deal with the old butler's pity and concern; he'd suffered enough of that already.

Perhaps she was merely protecting herself...

By assisting him, she had put herself in a rather compromising position, should anyone chance to discover the details. Yet even as he thought it, he knew it was not even remotely true. *How* he knew, that was what troubled him. He had a *feeling* about her. Many, in fact. None of which were remotely acceptable for a man in his position.

So be rid of her...

Easy though that may be, it was not in Liam's nature to be so callous. He owed her the benefit of the doubt, at least.

Yes. Ask her the meaning of all this. Then make a decision. A fair, objective, considered decision, based on facts, not emotion.

A compromise Liam was quite sure was the best solution, even if he half suspected his emotions would always get in the way when it concerned a certain housekeeper.

Not that he would ever admit it.

'Come in,' Liam said some time later, as the knock he'd been expecting finally sounded.

He straightened and adopted a most convincing, imperious and commanding manner. Gathering the papers concerning her, he set his gaze on them, unable quite yet, it seemed, to look her in the eye.

'Mrs Hardwicke.'

'My lord,' Rebecca said, striding over to stand before the desk. 'You asked to see me.'

'Yes, I did,' he drawled, his eyes affixed to the papers before him. 'If you would…' Liam waved his hand to beckon her, only to start slightly when he looked up and found her already before him. 'Oh.'

'Mrs Murray asked me to bring you the week's menus.'

Gingerly, Rebecca offered over the stack of papers, and his eyes flitted to her neck. He winced inwardly when he noticed the scarf she wore today.

'Thank you,' he said gruffly, tossing the menus to one side. 'About last night...'

'Did something happen, my lord?'

Rebecca stood there innocently, a polite smile on her face.

Liam frowned. 'No,' he said finally. 'Nothing of consequence, it seems.'

'If that is all my lord, I have—'

'Actually, Mrs Hardwicke,' he said, recovering his businesslike tone, and stopping her as she made to leave. 'I have here a list of your previous posts, and I find myself wondering, Mrs Hardwicke, why you seem to change households every two or so years. Rather odd, is it not? Almost a pattern, one might say.' Liam paused for effect, joining his hands before him, surveying her with idle condescension. 'Mrs Hardwicke?'

'Yes, my lord?'

'Nothing to say?'

'I did not realise there was a question, my lord.'

'Why is it, Mrs Hardwicke, that you seem to find no stability in your positions when it is rather the fashion, as far as I'm aware, for housekeepers to serve for, well, life? You, on the other hand, seem almost to be *running* from something. Why, in the past five years alone, you have served three different houses.'

Now he's asking about my suitability?

The fact that his last remark had hit rather too close to home for comfort didn't help ease Rebecca's rising anxiety.

'I have seized opportunities for advancement when they have presented themselves, my lord. With the exception of my last household, in which case I did serve until death, that of my mistress. I think you will find, however, my references irreproachable.'

'With one exception here,' he countered, perusing the papers to bring forward a particular letter. 'You remained in the Duchess of Stonehaven's London household for a mere six months before a sudden departure, which you said was due to an ailing mother. Yet I have it on good authority that you have no family, and have not for some time. Mrs Hardwicke?'

'My apologies, was there another question I failed to detect, my lord?'

'Tell me, Mrs Hardwicke, do you make a habit of lying to your employers? Or is it Thomas to whom you lied when you told him of your family, or rather, lack thereof?'

'My lord?'

'You are hiding something, Mrs Hardwicke, and I do not suffer lies nor secrets under my roof.'

The irony of that statement was lost on neither of them, but Liam forged on.

'Now, I ask again. Why so many households in so little time?'

'It is as I said, my lord. If you wish to dismiss me,' Rebecca barrelled on, her apprehension rising with every passing moment, 'you need not make a pretence of finding fault with me, for, as far as I am aware, I have given cause for none. Though I am sure many a master has been discovered in many a more compromising situation than you. You need find no excuses.'

'This is not about the events of last evening, Mrs Hardwicke,' he countered harshly. 'Enquiries were made before then, and I assure you, whatever you may think of me, I am not one to dismiss servants out of pride. What are you running from?'

'Nothing,' Rebecca said, a second too late.

Something of her fear must have shown, for she saw in his eyes a flash of triumph.

'Mrs Hardwicke, you find yourself faced with a choice. The truth, or your dismissal.'

'My secrets are my own, my lord,' Rebecca said flatly, numb and hurt beyond what she thought possible.

She did not want to leave Thornhallow—not for the world—but neither could she tell him the truth he demanded. Even if, for the first time in her life, she was sorely tempted to. Something about this man made her want to give up her secrets, to entrust them, and herself, to his strength and protection.

Dullard.

'I will not be bullied, threatened or blackmailed into relinquishing any part of myself I do not wish to give freely.'

Liam's jaw clenched, as though he was biting back some choice words, but Rebecca left him no chance to find better ones.

'I shall write an advertisement for the post immediately and find my replacement, should you wish. I would appreciate being allowed to remain until I have elsewhere to go. However, if you would prefer I quit the house immediately, I will make do.'

They stood there, eyes locked in a silent battle of wills, until finally Rebecca took his silence, indeed his entire behaviour, for what it was, and nodded sadly.

'I shall collect my things and be gone within the hour. Mr Brown will, as before, ensure things run smoothly until a replacement can be found. Good day, my lord.'

Turning on her heel, standing as proudly as she could muster despite the growing ache of her heart, Rebecca made for the door, willing the tears which were stinging her eyes, threatening to fall and humiliate her even more, to return from whence they came.

What was the matter with her? She'd been here barely over a month. Why did it feel as though she was losing the closest thing to a home she'd ever had? And why did the thought of leaving that odious, presumptuous, condescending, proud brute make her feel so…so…

Another hand was on her own before she could turn the knob and open the door. Rebecca jumped back with a squeal, bumping into a large, unmoving wall of muscle. Liam was staring down at her, a dark, menacing expression in his eyes. She took another step back, much preferring to be against the wall than to spend another second with her body in contact with his.

Rebecca tried to speak, but found she could not. She was like some hypnotised animal, with his aurous eyes affixed on her own, freezing her to the spot while at the same time heating her blood. Instead of speaking, she focused on breathing. Why was she so breathless? He was close. Too close.

Why is he so close?

Slowly his hand lifted from the door, and moved towards her neck. Then, ever so gently, without ever touching her skin, without moving his eyes from her own lest she bolt, he untied her scarf and slid it from her neck. Then and only then did his eyes wander down.

Rebecca saw his eyes darken with shame as they found the bruises. She wanted to scream, wanted to tell him it wasn't his fault, that she did not blame him, that she could never, even if she wished to, but no words came.

And then, with the lightest, feathery touch, his fingers traced the marks they had left on her skin. It wasn't even really a touch, and yet, Rebecca felt it searing through her to the bone, marking her more efficiently than any brand might have.

Unable to bear it any longer, she turned her head away and gazed at the floor. The movement was just enough to bring Liam back to the room. His hand fell, still clutching her scarf. Again Rebecca reminded herself to breathe, and found she was finally able to do so somewhat properly.

'Your tale,' he said, in a whisper that somehow filled the room. 'Does it present a danger to this house?'

'No,' Rebecca breathed, meeting his gaze again, wishing that she hadn't. Swallowing hard, she continued. 'I would never bring danger, or dishonour, to any house I served. Should there ever be a risk I would be gone in an instant.'

'You may stay, Mrs Hardwicke.' He nodded, offering her the scarf. 'And keep your secrets, if that is what you wish. Perhaps one day you might entrust me with them, or, at the very least with your true name. Tell Mrs Murray the menus are acceptable.'

How did he know?

Oh, no matter, Rebecca thought, rushing from the room as soon as Liam stepped away, caring little how much dignity she managed to maintain.

Ducking into the shadowed corner under the stairs, she leaned against the cold wood and retied the scarf.

Why was she behaving like this?

Frightened.

She had been frightened. That was it. That was why her body was flushed and her heart was beating too hard against her chest, and why she was still not wholly able to breathe.

Yes. You were terrified of losing the place.

Why shouldn't she be? It was everything she'd ever wanted, ever dreamed of.

Peace. Independence. Freedom. And you really have nowhere else to go...

Though she should be ashamed of herself, really, she thought, charging breathless down the stairs to her office. He had changed his mind, let her stay, because of guilt. All those things she valued, she now had only because he'd hurt her and felt guilty. Had she not found him last night, he would have summarily dismissed her. He'd had the papers already—he'd said as much. And yet she could only feel...

Glad. Relieved. Yes, that is all there is to it. I was frightened and now I am relieved. This has nothing to do with the master. Nothing at all.

Because if it did, *that* would be unforgivable, and an insurmountable problem.

What in God's name...?

Rebecca was momentarily distracted from the mire of her thoughts by the sight which awaited her in her office. There, neatly placed on her desk, was a large, rather ornate skeleton key.

This day just keeps getting better.

For she had a very good idea what door this key opened.

The East Tower...

She didn't know who had put it there for her, where they had found it or why they had done this now. What she did know, however, was that it was one door she wasn't going to open. Already she was on incredibly thin ice.

No chasing ghosts, Rebecca. No good'll come of it.

Thus resolved, she threw open the desk drawer, dropped in the key and slammed it closed again. Straightening, smoothing her skirts and returning to the proud, collected, unshakeable housekeeper she was, Rebecca made her way to the kitchens, to advise Mrs Murray of His Lordship's decision regarding the menus.

Menus he didn't even look at...

* * *

Meanwhile, Liam hadn't moved from the spot he seemed to have rooted to, his eyes fixed on the closed door, and the damned woman's scent still swirling in the air around him, catching in his nostrils, clouding his mind.

What on earth had he been thinking, allowing her to remain beneath his roof?

The woman was hiding something, by her own admission. Something significant enough to spend a lifetime running from. A husband? A lover? Cruel family? Perhaps she was one of those rogue gentlewomen who fled all manner of dire circumstances by posing as servants or governesses. Or a criminal.

No...

There had been fear in her eyes, a flicker—he'd seen it. Not the fear of discovery, fear of something far more dreadful. That alone should have made him send her away. And yet he hadn't. To be fair, the woman *did* have impeccable references. Every letter bemoaned her departure and sang her praises. And even he, try as he might, could find no fault with her work. Her stubbornness, her insolence and her complete disregard for orders, perhaps. But not her work.

In the short time she'd been at Thornhallow she had performed miracles and endeared herself to everyone she'd met. Perhaps she was a charlatan, slithering her way into hearts and minds the better to trick them into parting with...

With what?

Truly, he was losing his mind. That was it. He was simply going mad. That was why he'd let her stay. His reason had officially abandoned him. The sleepless nights, the torture of returning here, it was stealing away his otherwise infallible mental faculties.

If only that were true...

No, this was because of his heart, not his head. Because he pitied her, felt guilty for what he'd done, ashamed of what she'd seen...

When he had seen the marks he'd made on her, he had barely been able to restrain himself. To stop himself from throwing his fist into a wall or...or what?

Kissing it all away...

Now, where had that thought come from?

From moments ago, when he'd stood so close to her and felt an irresistible pull. A need, stirring deep within. For her. A need to give her pleasure to forget the pain. To trail butterfly kisses along her neck, to quicken the already rapid pulse fluttering there, beneath the creamy skin.

Instinct.

Yes, that was what it had been. Some primal instinct to fix what he'd broken in the same animalistic manner with which he had injured her. Yes, that was all it was. Nothing more.

God, the woman will drive me mad...

Now, where had *that* thought come from?

Was it, in fact, the woman and not the house, not the demons and ghosts which lingered in the walls, that was driving him to lose his reason altogether?

He'd outright sprinted to the door to prevent her from leaving, after declaring that that was precisely what she *should* do. What he demanded. His stomach had fallen to his boots at the thought that she might no longer haunt the house, a bewitching ghost of flesh and blood. There had been a terrible feeling of loss in his heart when she had turned from him. Abandoned him.

And when he'd looked into her eyes, those unfathomable, haunting brown pools, he had not seen fear. Confusion, anxiety, yes, but no fear, no disgust. None of the emotions she should have felt looking at *him*, the man who had nearly taken her life. She had trusted him in that moment, still as a statue and speechless, perhaps, but he had seen her trust that he would not hurt her again. If anything, she'd seemed more upset at the prospect of leaving; he was sure he'd seen the threat of tears glistening in her eyes. But when he had cornered her, prevented her leaving...

He really should have let her go. He knew that. She was a liar. Self-confessed. Full of secrets. And temptation. Yet he had not. Against his better judgement, against all reason, he had let her stay.

Now, Liam sensed, there would only be trouble.

Sighing heavily, he returned to his desk and the mounds of work which awaited him.

There would be trouble. And he would regret this.

Not nearly as much as you would've letting her go...

Drat the woman.

Damn the house.

Damn it all.

Chapter Six

During the week that followed, Rebecca was careful to avoid Liam, as careful as he seemed to be avoiding her. They each carried on with their lives in their separate spheres, moving throughout Thornhallow without ever needing to encounter the other, as if they'd come to a unified decision that neither should spend too much time in the company of the other, lest trouble be found.

She heard him sometimes, riding out across the park or speaking to Mr Bradley or Mr Brown in his study. Sometimes she would find a barely touched tray of food there, as she made her nightly rounds, or an empty decanter of whisky in the library. Other than that, and the incessant praises the others sang of the prodigal son's return, it was as if he truly was the wraith so many believed haunted the house.

As the days passed, Rebecca tried to concentrate on her duties, tried her very hardest to be nothing more than what she should. But even as she prevailed, for the most part, in chasing the master from her thoughts, she could not seem to chase away the lingering curiosity regarding the key she'd been left.

Nothing good could come of satisfying that curiosity, of

trying the key in the one locked door she inherently knew it opened. So she steadfastly continued her progress through the house. The second-floor drawing room succumbed to her invasion first, then the art room, school room, long-abandoned nursery, and finally the second-floor gallery, which had once been used for fencing and dancing, if the mats, masks and broken pianoforte were anything to go by.

But each day, as the sun's rays began to disappear, as she finished her tasks in this room or that, she invariably found herself standing before the door to the East Tower. Each evening she stood there, studying the large, medieval-looking oak door, as if one day it might simply swing open and reveal nothing but an empty, meaningless room.

Yet she knew, somehow, that behind that door lay nothing *but* meaning. It was why she knew she shouldn't give in to temptation, and why she couldn't prevent herself from doing so. Something behind that door called to her, inviting her in, until finally, a week after nearly being dismissed again, she could deny the call no longer.

Having finished in the second-floor gallery, she stood once again before the door, the key and a candle in her hand, knowing she should turn back, that this act would change everything, and knowing full well she would do no such thing.

A cold gust of wind whistled through the darkened corridor, nearly blowing out the candle, and Rebecca shivered.

No ghosts. Only wind.

Shielding the candle from any further draughts, Rebecca took a step forward, then slid the key into the lock. It took some effort to turn it, rust, cobwebs and general disuse having stiffened the mechanism.

Finally, she was able to swing open the heavy door enough to go in, albeit with a loud creak that might have awoken any dead hidden therein. Before her, a staircase, narrow and winding, barely visible at the edge of her light.

She went over and stood at the foot of it.

It was richly furnished, with a once-plush runner, now worn, its edges threadbare, and ancient tapestries lining the stone walls. This place was so very different from the rest of the house. Someone with very peculiar tastes had left their mark here.

The wind howled down the staircase from above, and for a moment Rebecca toyed with the idea of returning another day—*during* the day—when the darkness was not so enveloping, when her imagination might not run so wild with every creak, every whisper of wind, every creeping shadow. When one's rational mind might more easily dismiss the blood-soaked tales that surrounded this place.

Yet Rebecca was unable to turn away. Something was beckoning her up those stairs. She had a feeling in the pit of her stomach that, perhaps, the final piece of the dismal puzzle that was Thornhallow Hall lay there.

So, with a steady hand tightly clutching the thick ropes which served as handrails, Rebecca began her ascent.

Halfway up the tower Rebecca fell upon a landing, and another large oak door, though this one had no lock. Again, rust and disuse meant it took her a moment to open it. Lifting up the candle once she had, Rebecca let her eyes scan the contents of the circular room she now found herself in.

Once, it seemed to have been a lady's sitting room. Tastefully decorated, in delicate hues, and elegant floral patterns, it contained all manner of little areas within it.

Rebecca slowly made her way around the room, discovering all the distinct worlds which had been created, careful not to disturb them. There was something...a caution, a warning. She could look, but not touch.

She had been invited in, but was not yet trusted enough for anything more.

A richly decorated mahogany Carlton House writing desk sat beside one of the impressive and strangely large windows which surrounded the room. Papers still lay upon it, scribbled on and blotted with ink. A quill lay beside them, and dust which once had been flowers filled a miniature vase. And there, an easel, set before another window, a sketch of some nymph-like creature upon it. Paints, and a palette peppered with dried mounds of coloured material, lay beneath it, along with worn and now useless brushes. More sketches, papers and charcoal lay on the sill beside it all. There, a telescope. And beyond it, a little sitting area, with a coffee table and moth-eaten chairs.

Lifting her candle even higher, Rebecca noticed there were more sketches, notes, ceramic flowers, wooden figures, even fanions, all around the room. She felt her heart clench and tears sting at the back of her eyes. This room was unlike any of the others. Lost in time, yes. Abandoned, yes. But in a heartbreakingly different way.

This room had belonged to someone very special. She could feel her presence in everything. Every detail, every personal touch. It had all been preserved, frozen, as a reminder. There was an infinite sadness permeating through to her bones. This place was a shrine.

Hers. The Earl's sister. The one they say he murdered...

Shaking her head, taking a deep breath, she left the room, closing the door behind her as quietly as she could before continuing upstairs.

But he didn't. He isn't capable of such a thing. He's just...

Grieving.

Perhaps that was why she needed to see this place. She

was being called to see what lay at the heart of Thornhallow's distress, the master's distress.

You are the one who invited me, little one whose name I do not know. Though I declare that I still do not believe in spirits...

At the top of the tower Rebecca found another door, identical to the others. It was colder up here, and the howling of the wind as it swept around the solitary tower, creeping in through every crack, made it seem even more so. Again, Rebecca lifted her candle, mindful of its growing flickering as gusts of wind caught the flame, and entered the room.

Her bedchamber...

An elegantly carved four-poster bed with graceful hangings. A dressing table, and chairs by the window. A trunk, a wardrobe, a chest of drawers. All the very finest, most elegant furnishings, which again had been decorated with drawings, paintings and mementos.

Taking a further few steps into the room, Rebecca noticed a shawl and an old porcelain doll, shabby from use, not abandon. A lump formed in her throat and she turned away, unable to bear the reminder of life, youth and innocence too quickly taken.

The blackened, disused hearth seemed to echo her mournful thoughts, and the wind rushing down it sounded like an otherworldly lamentation. Rebecca's eyes stopped above the mantelpiece, where a striking painting had been hung in a place of honour. An unlikely subject for a young girl's bedroom, but as Rebecca peered closer, examining the free flow of brushstrokes, vivid choice of colours and haunting face peering out back at her, she noticed the signature at the bottom: *H. Reid.*

So you painted this, then, young mistress... How talented you were...

And beneath the painting, another tiny vase, surrounded by dust.

'I see now, Miss Reid, what you wished me to,' she whispered, respectfully making her way out. 'I shall return, and we shall be friends, you and I.'

For although Rebecca still did not, and never would believe in ghosts, she believed every word she spoke to the air. She believed that every house was alive. Retained memories.

And she knew, beyond a shadow of a doubt, that there was some spirit in this one which had invited her in, and somehow needed her.

Liam was, during that week, just as eager to avoid Rebecca as she suspected. He, too, heard her sometimes, carrying on upstairs, sometimes singing, subjecting more rooms to her fearsome touch. Sometimes he would notice another book missing from the library, but other than that, it was as if he *had* had the courage to send her away.

The papers Leonards had sent along with those concerning her had given him ample work and worry that week. And Leonards's attached note, warning that he was no further on in his quest, threw Liam into a foul mood.

And though the old solicitor, and Bradley, had done the best they could to keep his affairs in order over the years, there was still much to be done. He had ten years' worth of accounts, end-of-year reports, decisions, hirings, dismissals, new tenants, returns and other matters to familiarise himself with before he could even consider taking charge and imposing his will. Not only upon the Thornhallow estate, but the house in London and other assets, holdings and schemes the title was currently linked to.

It had been so easy, running away without care or concern, leaving his father and then Leonards and Bradley to handle it all whilst he sought a new life, his own fortune, far across the sea. It had been easy to forget all those who depended on the Earldom for their livelihoods, all those other responsibilities which came with the title. Now, coming back, trying to make up for lost time... It was overwhelming, to say the least.

His days he spent either knee-deep in paperwork, ensconced in legal volumes, or out on the estate, sometimes with Bradley, but most days alone. He had taken to regularly visiting those who worked and lived on Thornhallow land, speaking to them, getting to know them again, seeing first-hand what had become of them all.

Bradley had come and undertaken his discreet evaluation, taking the opportunity to once again praise Rebecca's achievements, which had only served to darken Liam's mood further. He needed no reminders of the woman's witchcraft and presence. Not when he could still feel her skin against his fingertips, and smell her scent all around him, reminding him of so many things he wished to forget.

Evenings, too, were spent mainly at his desk, until such time as he could no longer think, or see. He retired, usually to the library, where he drank and lost himself in bitter, tormenting memories. Many nights he slept there, and Thomas had taken to ensuring he had a change of clothes, and his *toilette*, ready when that occurred.

The only positive outcome of this new way of living was that he hadn't suffered any more nightmares since Rebecca had found him. Unpleasant recollections haunted him by day, but by night he slept, most often dreamlessly, and without consequence to the furniture or staff.

Though still he could not bring himself to visit the one part of the house which called to him. Every day he tried to, brought himself a little closer, but as he grew nearer, the harder his approach became.

Occasionally, when the oppression and emptiness of the house became too much to bear, Liam would ride out at breakneck speed, to exorcise the demons gnawing at him the only way he knew how. The thrill of danger, the exercise, the sweat and power of the beast beneath him, the wind whistling past, all numbed his mind—if only for a moment.

'Was gettin' worried, my lord,' Tim said, as he walked Orpheus back into the stables after one such ride. He was a strong, swift beast, and of a surprisingly gentle nature despite his breeding. 'Was going to send Sam out if you hadn't made it back before nightfall.'

'I did not see the time pass.' Liam smiled wanly. 'And I didn't mean to worry you. Oh, it's all right, Tim,' he added as the groom moved to take the reins. 'I will look after Orpheus. It will cool my blood as well as his.'

'As you wish, my lord,' Tim said, tugging at his forelock. 'I'll finish settling the others for the night, then.'

'How is he settling in with the others?' Liam asked as he began his ministrations. 'Not too much trouble with old Thackeray there?'

'Oh, no. Years ago, perhaps, when he was still a young chap. But Thack's gettin' older, just like the rest of us. Calmer now than when your father rode him. Ain't taken no issue with your young 'un yet.' The groom chuckled, making his way down the boxes, checking the horses were all comfortably set for the night ahead. 'And ol' Arty and Callie, here, they're sweet as always. Don't reckon they mind a young buck around again either.'

Artemis and Calliope.

His sister's horses, which neither he nor his father had found it in themselves to be rid of. He smiled despite himself as he brushed Orpheus, remembering the smile on

Hal's face as she proudly rode Calliope for the first time, convinced she was Boadicea herself.

And then an image of the three of them, all riding through the park, Hal, his mother and he, side by side, flashed before his eyes. It was an image born of his imagination, of a past which had never been, but might have changed everything.

So alike... You might've saved her, Mother, when I could not...

'Sure did love these horses, she did, Lady Hal,' Tim said wistfully, echoing Liam's thoughts as he patted Callie goodnight. 'And they loved her. Knew what a sweet spirit she was.'

'I miss her, Tim,' Liam blurted out, before he could stop himself, the swelling of emotion too much to contain. 'Coming back here...'

'I know, Master Reid, I know. We all do. And we all know, what happened—'

'I think I should let you see to Orpheus after all,' he said abruptly, unwilling to delve any further into the past he had ridden out to escape.

'O' course, my lord. Goodnight, then.'

'Goodnight, Tim.'

Liam fled the stables before his emotions could overwhelm him, before Tim could see the tears that had escaped and slid down his cheeks.

Please, Hal, set me free...

Chapter Seven

'I am sorry, my lord, I thought you still in your study,' Rebecca said later that evening, retreating back towards the door as soon as she spotted the master, deep in thought, far away from the crystal decanters he loomed over without seeing. The flames lanced through the glass, and sent tiny rainbows dancing across his face.

It's for noticing little useless details such as that you've exiled yourself from his presence, you goose.

'I shall leave you.'

'I would be working if I thought I could achieve anything further. Come, now, do not be absurd,' Liam growled, waving her back in as he poured himself a whisky. 'Take your pick of the books. I may have behaved rather boorishly thus far, Mrs Hardwicke, but I am not entirely tyrannical.'

'Thank you, my lord,' she said, shyly coming back in and perusing the shelves.

Yes, it's because he behaved a beast that you've steered clear. No other reason at all.

'If I may, you have not been boorish, my lord. I overstepped my bounds on many occasions, and I do not know any other master who would allow me such pleasures as books, or even a position after the way I behaved.'

'Yes, well,' Liam said, his lip curling in a sardonic smile as he watched her. 'We have both behaved badly and we have spoken enough of it, I think.'

Rebecca shot him a quizzical look and, noting his half-smile, responded in kind before hurriedly turning back to the shelves. Still, she could feel his gaze raking her, as tangible as the whisper of his fingers across her bruises that morning...

'More gothic tales for you, Mrs Hardwicke?' he continued, his nonchalance ringing false. 'Or perhaps something lighter? You were reading *Frankenstein* the night, I arrived,' he added, spotting the quizzical furrowing of her brows.

'I had not set my mind upon anything in particular,' she said distractedly. 'And I have no particular fondness for gothic tales, only *Frankenstein* is quite the masterpiece...'

'Indeed. You have read it before?'

'Yes, my lord. It is one of my favourites. It is so...' Rebecca turned and smiled broadly at him, then remembered herself, and resumed her perusal of his collection.

Silence fell over the room, though she thought she heard Liam curse himself. It was so tempting to stand there and list all the reasons why she adored the book when he'd looked at her like that and made her feel as though he was actually interested to have *her* thoughts, and everything about this entirely improper situation felt right.

But to keep the conversation going was dangerous.

'You're here to set things right, aren't you, my lord?' she asked softly, her eyes still fixed on the volumes before her. *Ninny.* 'That is why you came back after all this time?'

'Yes,' he managed, after a moment of bewildered silence.

'I apologise,' she said hurriedly. 'I spoke out of turn

again.' Flushing, she distractedly grabbed one of the nearest books and rushed to the door. 'I shall leave you.'

'Please, Mrs Hardwicke, sit with me awhile,' Liam said, half irritatedly, half sweetly. 'I will behave, I promise. I am quite starved of conversation, and company.'

'Oh, I... That is... I fear you might find me quite unsatisfactory company, my lord.'

Run away, Rebecca.

'Nonsense. Anyone who reads Wollstonecraft Shelley and Defoe is bound to be at least remotely satisfactory. I know well all the books in this library, and I recognise that one very well indeed,' he added, noting her confusion at his spot-on guess of her choice.

Cocking her head, she surveyed him for a moment, trying to decide if he was mocking. Trying to decide whether or not she could trust herself in his presence.

Liam raised an eyebrow in challenge, and sipped his whisky. Finally she relented, and he waved her to the sofa by the hearth. She thought for a moment he might offer her a whisky, but after a second's hesitation he simply settled into a nearby armchair. A good thing he hadn't, for already they were testing the bounds of propriety.

Rebecca sat on the edge of the sofa, *Robinson Crusoe* on her lap, hands grasped tightly above it.

'Do I frighten you, Mrs Hardwicke?' he asked gently.

'No, my lord,' she replied vehemently. Then, noticing her posture, she relaxed with a defeated sigh. 'No, you do not frighten me,' she said softly, with the hint of a smile.

'Nor does this house,' he said, his eyes narrowing.

'Of course not. I should not be here if it did.'

'And why *are* you here, Mrs Hardwicke?'

'I was in want of a position, my lord.'

'I am not seeking to interrogate you—that is, not again,' he said, obviously sensing her distancing herself again. 'I

am curious, that is all. As I said, you were the only applicant, and, well…'

'I don't put any stock in gossip, my lord. I prefer to
make up my own mind. In truth, I have found more decay
and terror in the cleanest, most respectable houses than I
ever have in those more apparently dark and dangerous.'

As with men, she refrained from saying, but only just.

'And what have you decided about Thornhallow, then?'

'It is, if anything, my lord, a sad house. In want of…'
She frowned, searching for words more diplomatic than
those which immediately sprang to mind.

Love. Attention. Care. Just like you.

'Warmth.'

Liam pondered Rebecca's words, and her, for a moment.
He was quite sure she'd been on the verge of saying something far more controversial but had refrained. She may
not be afraid of him, even after all that had passed, but neither did she trust him fully. Natural, yet something which
left a bitter taste in his mouth. Especially when she had
the ability to command *his* trust with her sheer presence.

When she made him despise a solitary evening for one
brief moment of her company. When she could warm him
better than whisky with only a smile. If something so small
could have such an effect, he wondered—

No. She is not for you.

Some men in his position might not be bothered by
crossing lines with their employees, but despite the black-
est marks on his soul, he wasn't a cad. And dishonouring
her, taking her fire for himself… Well, he may be selfish,
and he may be damned, but he couldn't do that to her. If he
was going to forget himself and toe the line by conversing
with her, he needed to abide by one very simple precept.

Do not touch. Keep your distance.

'I will not deny I have neglected Thornhallow,' he ceded. 'As you say, it is a sad house. Full of painful memories. But it was thus long before I left it.'

'Where did you go? I am sorry. I pry—'

'Mrs Hardwicke, do stop apologising. You pry, but I see no harm in answering you.' Telling her a little wouldn't be so terrible after all. Would it? 'Though I would ask you not to immediately run off to tell everyone of the *haut ton*,' he added wryly, before he could change his mind. 'I fear it might quite put a tarnish on my dashing mystery.'

Rebecca eyed him carefully for a moment before a slight giggle escaped her.

Liam grinned—rather stupidly, he knew—as Rebecca composed herself and mimicked locking her lips shut.

'In truth, I ran as far away from here as I could. The Continent for a while. Then the Americas, the Columbia District. The wild there, it reminded me of this place, only grander. And there was freedom to do anything. A man could be whatever he wished so long as he had the courage to face the trials of such a new country.'

'I've heard tales of it… What did you do there?' she asked eagerly.

'I worked in trade,' he said, his gaze travelling to the fire as he sipped his whisky again. 'Travelled to different posts, secured new routes…'

The memories came upon him like some fierce and drowning wave, the faces and voices of those he'd lost taunting him. He shook his head and pinched the bridge of his nose, attempting to banish them back to the dark, forgotten recesses of his soul.

'My lord?' Rebecca asked, concerned. 'Are you well?'

Torn abruptly from his demons, Liam stared at her, bewildered, almost surprised at her presence.

You were meant to share a little. Not so much. Too much. Send her away.

'Forgive me, Mrs Hardwicke,' he managed after a moment. 'I was quite lost in thought.'

'You seem tired, my lord. I should leave you now.'

'Please stay,' he pleaded before he could stop himself. *Let. Her. Leave.*

She eyed him again, measuring his request, as if she could see Liam's desire for her to remain warring with his better self. He knew if she didn't go, he would cross a line more threatening than if he simply took her to bed and buried himself within her, as he fervently wished to do. He wasn't sure what it was about her—why he continually found it impossible to do without her when he would have sworn not long ago he needed no one.

Perhaps she was some manner of enchantress after all.

'Something happened there,' Rebecca said, going against her own better judgement, too, it seemed.

There was no pity, no curiosity, only concern and openness in her expression. Things which Liam, in his current state, could not resist even if he wanted to. Besides, soon he would be gone from this place, from her, so what harm could it do?

'Yes.'

'Your…nightmares. The night…'

'Yes. Among other things.'

Rebecca nodded, and now there was only understanding in her expression.

She turned thoughtfully towards the fire, and Liam knew he could leave it there. *Should* leave it there. She was his housekeeper. Not a friend, lover or confidante. She had no right to know—no business knowing. He'd said too much already. And yet… He *wanted* to confide in her. Needed to. Needed her to know something of what tormented him, of why he had nearly…

'There was an American I worked with, and his son. He was the one who convinced me to cross the sea, to begin that new life,' he blurted out. He thought about telling Rebecca about that night, but that would mean explaining so much more… 'He'd lost his wife,' he continued, clearing his throat, determined to remain clinical in his storytelling. 'He was taking his son to start anew, and I went along. We worked together for years, and he was one of the best friends I ever had. There was a kinship, an understanding. I felt…part of his circle, part of something larger than myself, for the first time in a long while, and then…'

What words could ever describe the horror, the unspeakable that had happened?

Liam looked over to Rebecca, as if her eyes might hold the answer. They did not, though their steadfastness gave him the courage to continue.

'I left to explore another route, and when I returned to camp… It was gone, but for frozen, mangled corpses… That is, those that hadn't been picked clean by scavengers…' Liam took a steadying breath, and finished his drink, disgust and pain contorting his face into a grotesque mask. 'There had been territorial disputes, with the British… Angus had said we shouldn't push so far north, but I never thought…' A bitter laugh tore from his throat and he shook his head.

'Your friend, his son, they were killed?'

'Yes,' he whispered. 'His son, Peter, had just turned eighteen… There had always been disputes over borders, and routes, and furs, but I never thought it would go so far. What was done to them… I should've… I watched that boy grow up…'

Liam turned away from Rebecca's now all too penetrating gaze. He leaned back in the chair, stretching his legs out before him, and shifted his own gaze to the sickeningly bucolic pastoral scene above the mantelpiece. He'd never spoken of Angus and Peter to anyone. And now, telling her, it felt as if yet another burden he carried had been passed to her.

He wished he could tell her how it had felt, to find them, what had been left of them.

To find nothing but bones, and pieces of a carved necklace to identify the man who had offered him friendship, and a respite from the pain of his past. To know the boy he'd watched become a man—helped, he liked to think—only by the smaller bones. To be unable to bury them, for the ground was immovable in the harsh depths of winter, no matter how hard he'd scratched and torn at it. To see first-hand what devastation the greed and lust of man could wreak. To know he would have been no better, what he might have done had he found those responsible for Angus's and Peter's deaths.

He wished he could tell her how he hated himself for having failed to protect them.

Just as he had Hal.

He wished he could tell her that whatever small piece of him had still been capable of hope had died that day. That all that was left in him now was a frozen cold so much more bitter than that of the Arctic, and a dark soul, unredeemable. He wished he could tell her what else he saw in his nightmares—who else. His other torment, the other scene that haunted him endlessly. But he did not. Could not. Already too many boundaries had been crossed.

Enough, fool.

'It is no wonder that such things should haunt you, my lord,' Rebecca said finally. 'I am very sorry for your loss and your suffering. But their death was not your fault.'

Liam turned and glared at her, and she shrank back under his gaze.

'I only meant… You should carry their memory with you, but not…not the memory of them as you found them. Just as the monster is not that which it seems, so the ghosts that haunt us are more our own guilt and regret than true apparitions.'

Liam remained there, gaping at her, speechless, unable to voice any of his rising anger or bitterness. He had bared a part of his soul to her, a part of his grief, and she…she dared to…

To speak the truth.

Her stark and acutely perceptive evaluation was hurtful, and disconcerting. Altogether more unpleasant than pity or heartless sympathy might have been.

'Yet again, I have gone too far. Forgive me, my lord,' she said, rising again before he could stop her. 'It has grown late.'

'Mrs Hardwicke,' he called after her as she neared the door.

'Yes, my lord?'

'Why did you stay that night?'

'Because you asked.'

A curtsey, a rustle of skirts, and yet again she disappeared, his ghost of flesh and blood, leaving a thousand questions swirling in her wake.

Chapter Eight

Nearly three weeks since he had returned. It might have been a year—it wouldn't have changed anything. Liam knew he would have to face it. Face *her*. Sooner rather than later had been his plan, but that plan had been so much easier to make in the warm, safe confines of a London pub.

Countless times since his return he had tried, every time coming closer than the last. He had used the excuse of following Mrs Hardwicke's progress as incentive, somewhat successfully. Up the stairs. Down the corridor. Now, he stood before the door. It was there—*she* was there. Just out of reach, beyond the safe, solid barrier of centuries-old oak. He could feel her there. Feel her everywhere in this forsaken house.

Hal...

The door he had seen so many times in his dreams seemed unreal now. Different. In his nightmares it had been a great impassable barrier, full of ancient magic and dread. It had stood between him and his sister, taunted him as it kept him from her. Yet now, standing before it, Liam saw it in all its acute simplicity.

Only a door.

And beyond it, only a room.

Why could he not then bring himself to enter? He had faced the rest of the house, returned here and survived even though he'd been certain it would be the end of him. The nightmares had lessened. He slept somewhat peacefully for the first time in years. There had been no incidents since...well, since he had nearly killed Mrs Hardwicke.

Liam shuddered at the thought. But he'd faced that and come out the other side, alive.

Revived. Restored.

Facing the demons, exorcising them, had helped. This was it, the final demon.

The final ghost. Dammit, man, open the door!

He had faced barren, desolate, unforgiving wilds. Faced men whose hearts were black and who knew nothing but violence. He had faced death a hundred times over. Why not this? Why did his hand tremble as he lifted it towards the handle? Why did his heart beat so quickly and his breathing become so shallow he doubted he could draw breath?

Hal is not in there.

There were no such things as ghosts, only those of his own making. His own wraiths of guilt and shame. Mrs Hardwicke had spoken but the truth. It had helped, fuelled his determination to return here. But if there were no ghosts, then why could he feel Hal's presence? Feel her in every whisper of wind as it howled around the lonely tower? Feel her in every stone, every creak of wood?

Liam made to flee again, but stopped himself. He needed to be free. To see, to know. To ask forgiveness. To face his past so he could finally draw the poison of it from his veins.

This is why you returned.

Turning back would only prolong the torture. The

sooner he faced it, the sooner he could leave and never return.

With a deep, steadying breath, Liam drew the key from his pocket and slid it into the lock. A twist of the wrist, a click. His hand was steady and sure now as it swung open the door. Determined, he rushed in, and took the stairs two at a time. He didn't pause at the first door—he would go back there, but first he needed to go to her room. He needed to face the worst first. He needed to—

What in the name of...?

There was no darkness. No cobwebs. Not a speck of dust. Only...

Light. Order. Cleanliness.

Liam was stunned, his eyes taking everything in, an indescribable anger rising within him. His instructions could not have been clearer.

How could she have dared come here? How could she have robbed him of his purpose thus? Where had she even got a key? Nothing was to be touched. It was to be left as Hal had. His father had closed this room, and Liam had sworn to keep it thus.

Untouched.

Until he was ready.

But nothing remained. It had all been carelessly swept away by his new insolent, impudent, disrespectful house-keeper.

Liam howled, in pain, in anger, in regret. His eyes desperately sought a trace, any trace, of what he'd come to find. All they found was a tiny vase filled with dog violets on the mantel, beneath Hal's favourite creation she insisted be hung there, the painting which now mocked him. He remembered the day she had painted it, her fingers and cheeks covered in the full spectrum of colours. He should have known that day, should have seen it.

But all I saw was innocent romanticism...

He grabbed the vase and sent it flying across the room. How could she? Did the woman have no brain, no heart at all? What had she sought to do here? He stared at the mess of crystal and petals on the floor. Such a cruel jest to lay flowers beneath...

Liam screamed again. But this time it was a name.

'Mrs Hardwicke,' Liam bellowed at the top of his lungs. 'Mrs Hardwicke!'

Not even the multitude of thick stone walls, and three floors which separated them, could prevent Rebecca from hearing him. Indeed, the whole house seemed to reverberate, and Rebecca winced as her quill went scraping across the neat and tidy numbers she had just been entering into the ledger.

With a sigh, she set it back in its inkstand, and rose. Just as she did, Gregory burst in, flushed and frightened.

'I heard, Gregory,' she said calmly, smoothing her skirts. 'The East Tower?'

'Aye, m-ma'am,' he stammered.

'I am on my way. You and the others return to your duties.'

Shooing him away, for which he seemed rather grateful, Rebecca grabbed her courage, and her skirts, and began the long ascent to the East Tower.

Well, he was bound to take issue at some point... It really was only a matter of time...

Not that she had been afraid of what might happen when he discovered what she'd been doing in the place no one dared speak of. And if this was what sent him over the edge and got her dismissed, well, then, so be it.

'There you are,' Liam spat furiously as she entered the room.

Rebecca eyed the mess of crystal and flowers on the floor, and made to tidy them. 'Do not dare touch that.'

'I am here, my lord,' she said confidently, ignoring him as she collected the shards into her handkerchief, and laid the flowers back on the mantelpiece. 'Though next time might I suggest the bell?'

'You insolent, insubordinate, pig-headed, nosy, stubborn woman,' he raged, prowling around the room. 'It wasn't enough for you to disobey my orders with the rest of the house—oh, no—you simply had to push, didn't you! For there is no doubt you are to blame for this! Well? Have you nothing to say for yourself, then?' he demanded, ceasing his pacing.

'Have I missed a question again, my lord,' Rebecca said defiantly, standing proud and immovable. 'Forgive me if I have.'

'Why, woman, why?' he pleaded, striding over to tower over her. 'Why could you not leave this place be?'

'Because I could not countenance it, my lord,' she shouted, staring up at him. 'This room was a mausoleum. A sorrowful, hollow reminder of something terrible. I understand, believe me, I do,' she continued vehemently, 'the need to preserve memory. To honour the dead. But your sister, she deserved beauty, and light, and attention. And, yes, flowers. I have disturbed nothing but the dust and dirt. The rest is as it was, I swear.'

'Do not presume to speak of what you do not know,' he hissed, his hazel eyes flashing dangerously. 'You have no idea...'

'No,' Rebecca admitted softly. 'I have no idea what happened to her. Or you.'

Liam winced, and she sighed, shaking her head remorsefully.

'I apologise for upsetting you, my lord, it was not my intent. But I cannot—will not—apologise for doing what

I believed to be right. I will leave, if that is your wish. For if I stay, I shall continue to bring her flowers every day.'

'You have been sent to torment me, I think, Mrs Hardwicke,' he whispered, the anguish in his voice and heart tearing through her breast. 'More effectively than any demon from Hell itself.'

Rebecca's breath caught, and her eyes filled with tears. His words had cut her to the quick, and she felt sick.

What have I done?

'I shall leave,' she said meekly. 'I would never wish to cause you pain.'

'I forbid you to leave, Mrs Hardwicke,' he stated, his body tensing as though preparing to leap after her should she attempt it.

Rebecca's heart skipped and she realised she had momentarily forgotten to breathe. Liam was still staring at her, anguish, rage and challenge in his eyes. She searched them, hoping to find the meaning to his words, but she could not. Why would he not allow her to leave? Could it be he wished to make her pay, suffer for the pain she had unwillingly inflicted upon him?

How could he compare her to such terrible things one moment, then bemoan her offer to leave him in peace? He had obviously wanted her gone from the first, and indeed she'd given him every chance, every excuse to dismiss her.

And yet here he was, forbidding her to leave.

'I have duties to attend to,' she added when he glared at her warningly. 'My lord—'

'Just, go. Please.'

He sighed, finally turning from her, and Rebecca bobbed a curtsey and fled, feeling as though she might indeed be ill. He'd had the air of a defeated man in that final moment, and the thought that she might have broken him...

It made her heart twist and writhe. She was not a cruel

person. She had always strived to be good, and honest, and to spread love and care and joy, for she knew all too well what the absence of such things could do. And yet here was a man, already suffering, already on the edge with grief and God only knew what else, and she had pushed. Too far.

What were you thinking, Rebecca? Believing spirits had called you and instructed you...

Since arriving, she had tried to bring some light, and life, back into this house, and she'd thought she had. But then, he had returned, and nothing had seemed right anymore. Nearly every time they met it was a confrontation. Why could he not see?

Why are you so intent on making him see? On doing what you think right?

It was his house, after all. Not hers. Why could she not leave well enough alone? And why could she not leave *him* alone? Why, even now, did she feel the urge to run back? To fix him, or save him, or...

Even if he needed saving it would not be up to you to do so.

The night she'd found him in the library, she had admitted to herself that she liked and admired him. But now that seemed too easy an explanation, which did not even begin to define the pull she felt. The understanding, the connection.

As though...

As though he were a kindred spirit.

Leave well enough alone, Rebecca, she told herself as she passed the kitchens and gave everyone huddled there a glare, warning them to return to their work, and cease whispering about what had just occurred.

Cease trying to fix everything, and more importantly, cease trying to understand the master. Serve and obey.

Chapter Nine

Serve and obey. That is what Rebecca did to the best of her abilities in the days following her confrontation with Liam in the tower. She was careful to keep her distance again, keeping to the downstairs whenever she wasn't continuing her work restoring more rooms, which she did as discreetly, and as far from any place Liam might stumble upon her, as she could.

The only sign of her presence in the house was the flowers she continued to bring to Hal's room. She knew Liam had returned there since his first visit, but she found neither broken glass nor scattered flowers.

The day after their dispute she had stood there, flowers in hand, before the picture above the mantelpiece, for nearly an hour.

Am I wrong to do this? she had asked the forlorn Danish Princess, who seemed to peer out of the painting into her very soul. *Am I wrong to continue thus when I know the pain it has brought him?*

Ophelia had remained silent on her flowery riverbank, and Rebecca had not been able to find it within herself to relent.

It cannot be wrong to bring life into such a cold, dark place.

And so she had left the vase, and prayed that Liam might one day understand.

The others had kept their distance as well, attending to their duties as always, but careful to respect her need for solitude. They all sensed something important had passed between her and the Earl. Rebecca knew they all speculated as to what, but none dared ask. Not that they couldn't surmise well enough; they all knew very well the significance of the East Tower.

Mr Brown had taken to watching her closely, as though fearful she might take it upon herself to make more of a mess. Often Rebecca caught him staring at her, wearing an unsettling expression of confused wariness. He and the others had warned her against such actions, and she had not heeded them. She had neither served, nor obeyed, and now she and Liam both had to pay the price for her stubbornness.

Though she might have preferred to ignore the staff altogether, take her meals alone in her office and meet them only when absolutely necessary, she knew she needed more than ever to show stalwartness.

But as the days passed, and the wet, blustery winds and gales of October gave way to the frozen harshness of November, so the tension in the household seemed to grow, until finally Rebecca could not endure one more second within the confines of Thornhallow. Having neglected Mrs Ffoulkes, she decided a trip to the old woman's cottage would be just the thing. A cup of tea and a polite natter would do them both immense good, she posited.

She set off just after breakfast, with a basket of parkin and some supplies Mrs Murray had agreed to part with. Though Cook always fussed when Rebecca made the request, she always seemed to have a little stash set aside for that very purpose.

Yes, a long, solitary walk was just what Rebecca needed. Since she had arrived at Thornhallow, and particularly since the master had returned, it had felt harder and harder to keep her bearings.

In fifteen years of service, she thought as she set off through the park, deciding to take the longer path through the northern wood, not once had she felt so lost as to how to do her duty. Yes, there had been trying times. Failures, setbacks, disappointments. She was not perfect; no one was. But not once had she ever doubted *what* she was supposed to do. Never once had she felt so...confused. As though she'd forgotten who she was.

She stopped at the edge of the wood, and took a deep breath. The icy air stung her lungs but felt like a tonic. Marching onwards, careful to avoid the numerous puddles of mud and slush as she enjoyed the beauty of her surroundings, Rebecca wondered precisely what it was about Thornhallow that was making her doubt so.

An easy position. Simple. Quiet. That's what this was meant to be.

Only, everything about her life here was proving to be anything but.

In every other house she had served, she had obeyed dutifully—though, yes, she'd been wilful, and contrary at times. But then she had given her opinions with grace and diplomacy, not marched around doing whatever she pleased. Perhaps something in her was rebelling against the hierarchy, the order of things. Perhaps, in the freedom she'd been given by the master's absence, she had found...

What? Too much freedom?

As if there was such a thing.

In this world there is...

Rebecca slowed her pace when she realised that instead of enjoying her walk, she had taken to tramping like an ogre, crushing leaves and crunching twigs, scaring every living creature for miles. She knew what the truth was. She had let herself get attached to the master. She'd become invested in his life, and in his house. In the moments when she had seen *him*, unguarded and true, she had let herself be interested. Where she should have run, or held fast behind the solid, invisible and impenetrable wall of propriety, she had instead opened herself to more. To knowing him.

That was what lay at the centre of her confusion and unease.

Luckily, that was remedied easily enough. The distance she had maintained over the past few days would be maintained indefinitely. She would be a paragon of dutifulness and propriety. She would not engage. Easily done when she knew the master himself would most likely prefer never to see her again.

'You have been sent to torment me,' he'd said.

But I shall not torment you ever again, for you shall forget I even exist.

'Mrs Hardwicke!'

Or not, Rebecca thought with a sigh, as she turned to find the man in question striding towards her, raising his walking stick in the air as if waving to her.

He looked every bit the country gentleman today, in buckskin breeches, hessian boots, a forest-green waistcoat topped with a billowing greatcoat, and an old Eccentric hat.

'Good morning, my lord,' she said with a forced smile.

Solitude. Distance from you. That's all I wanted.

'Was there something you needed?'

'What? No. Well, yes.' He shrugged, his eyes scanning the ground as though the answer would be found there. 'You are on your way to Mrs Ffoulkes, yes?'

'Yes, my lord. Is that a problem?'

Is visiting the woman an offence now, too?

'No. No, I… May I walk with you? I'm overdue a visit as well.'

He finally met her gaze then, and Rebecca saw only an earnest hopefulness she couldn't have resisted in a thousand years. Against her better judgement, she nodded and began walking again. Liam fell in step with her, and so they continued on in silence, until Rebecca could remain so no longer.

If there was ever a chance to make amends, it was now.

'About the East Tower, my lord… I—'

'Mrs Hardwicke—'

'I should apologise, my lord—'

'Mrs Hardwicke, I am the one who must apologise,' he said gruffly, as though every word cost him. 'I…'

'You owe me no apology, my lord. I was insolent, and disobedient, and—'

'Yes, you were. But you were not wrong,' he sighed. 'I said some truly terrible things, Mrs Hardwicke, for which I had no right. Once again, I behaved a complete tyrant, and I do hope you will forgive me.'

'There is n-nothing to forgive, my lord,' she stuttered, stunned by his words. 'You had every right to be upset, and indeed, every right to throw me out of Thornhallow. Again.'

'Yes, quite,' Liam said with a wry smile. 'You asked me once—or stated rather, as seems to be your manner—that I had returned to Thornhallow to set things right. You were correct. You see, this place, this house…' He trailed off for a moment, searching for words. 'Well, there is truth to the tales I'm certain you've heard. I left to escape what happened here. And I returned…to face it. I believed that in order to do so, the ghosts I sought to preserve here had to remain intact. That things should be left, as they were.

So that I might see…understand… Well, the fact of the matter, Mrs Hardwicke, is that I was wrong.'

Liam drew a deep breath, and Rebecca chanced a glance over at him. A different man yet again stood beside her. A lost, tired, remorseful man, whose light now seemed to flicker in the low, golden autumn rays that pierced through the trees.

'Dog violets were my sister's favourite. She used to come out to the woods, fair weather or foul, to collect them, usually dragging me along.' He smiled a wan smile, then shrugged and returned to himself. 'All that to say, I am sorry. And thank you. For showing me that which I refused to see.'

They stopped, and Liam extended his hand to help her over a fallen tree. Rebecca hesitated for a moment, then took it graciously, trying to ignore the comforting warmth that seemed to emanate from his touch as she hopped over the trunk. Trying to ignore the twinkling of those hazel eyes that pierced through to her very soul.

'Thank you, my lord,' she said softly once they had re-sumed their walk.

'If there is another example of your disobedience wait-ing to be discovered, Mrs Hardwicke, I beg you tell me now. For I wish us to be friends. If that would be accept-able to you, that is.'

No. Say no, Rebecca. You cannot be friends with the master. Not this master. Say no. Remind him of your place, and his. You promised you'd keep your distance, you fool-ish lass. Now, say no.

'I would like that very much, my lord.'

Drat.

'And I believe you have witnessed the depths of my dis-obedience. Should I have any further desire to demonstrate my impudence, I shall be sure to quash it immediately.'

'Do refrain from doing any such thing,' he ordered with

a chuckle. 'You would be quashing your very spirit, Mrs Hardwicke. Infuriating though your contrariness might be, I dare say you would be less yourself without it. And I like you just as you are.'

'Then perhaps I shall simply give you fair warning,' Rebecca said, with a calm assuredness she most certainly did not feel. 'So that you might better prepare for battle.'

'A fair compromise indeed.'

A broad, cheeky smile spread across his face, and Rebecca could not help but return it.

Rebecca, you are surely the most dim-witted, weak-willed ninny in existence.

'May I ask,' Liam said thoughtfully after a moment, 'where did you get the key?'

'I don't know,' she admitted. 'I found it on my desk one morning. The morning— Well, it matters not. I thought of asking the others, but…'

'Whoever left it did so for a reason.'

Yes, I suppose they did.

Rebecca shrugged, unable to voice the words, and Liam nodded. They continued their walk in a companionable silence until they reached Mrs Ffoulkes's. Raising her hand to knock, Rebecca stopped, looked over at Liam thoughtfully, then reached into the basket and handed him the parcel of parkin.

'She has been quite eager to see you,' she said, in response to his enquiring look. 'Might help excuse your delay in visiting.'

Without waiting for an answer, she turned back to the door and knocked.

'Don't you think this parkin'll get you into my good graces, young man,' Mrs Ffoulkes said, eyeing him over her cup of tea once they'd all settled into her cottage some time later.

Liam had been right in thinking the old woman wouldn't have changed, and neither had the little cottage—still warm, cosy and filled to the brim with herbs, knick-knacks and books which Liam wondered whether she could still read.

'I know very well that cook of yours made them on this one's orders,' she said, pursing her lips and gesturing to Rebecca, who sat quietly, smiling into her teacup. 'It'll take much more to make me forgive your absence.'

'I am sorry for my neglect, Mrs Ffoulkes,' Liam said. Apparently today was the day for apologies. As someone unused to making them, it felt rather unsettling. 'Though I am relieved, and happy to see you've been keeping well.'

'Well enough,' the old woman said, shedding some of the sternness. 'And Mrs Hardwicke has taken good care of me.'

Liam glanced over at his housekeeper. She smiled at Mrs Ffoulkes with such genuine warmth and care, he wondered what it might feel like to have someone—*her*, really—smile at him in that way.

He took a breath and returned his attention to the old woman, where it belonged.

'You've taken good care of me, Mrs Ffoulkes,' Rebecca said. 'I've enjoyed our talks.'

'As have I,' she replied, placing her hand on the younger woman's tenderly. 'As have I. And you, Master Reid, where have you been, then, all these years?'

Liam hesitated for a moment, taking a sip of tea whilst he decided what to say. Rebecca eyed him, clearly also curious to know what he might decide to divulge.

'I was in the Americas, the Columbia District,' he said

finally, and a tiny smile of approval appeared on his house-keeper's face. It made him feel... *No.* 'Worked in trade.'

'An ocean was not far enough, was it, to escape Thorn-hallow?'

Liam was temporarily silenced by the woman's acute clarity.

'No need to tell me so, I know. Your father was a hard man—anyone who says otherwise is lying, make no mistake. And what happened here—'

'Mrs Ffoulkes,' Liam interjected, glancing at Rebecca in alarm.

She couldn't know. He...couldn't hear the words.

'All I mean,' Mrs Ffoulkes said pointedly, after a moment, 'is that I understand.'

Liam nodded, grateful.

'And trade, ha! That would've sent him into a right fit.'

The woman laughed, and he found a smile appearing on his own lips at the thought.

'Well, you always were more like your mother, you and Miss Reid. Thank God for that, too. She'd have been proud of you.'

'I barely remember her,' Liam said quietly, surprising them all.

'Good woman she were...kind heart. Were she that told the Earl to let me stay.'

She smiled, and all at once his father's generous gesture made sense.

''Tis easier, to remember the worst. But no matter how it hurts, you must remember the good. Take it from someone who tried not to.'

The room fell silent for a moment. Only it was a thick, warm silence. Not one of regret, of loss, but of shared remembrance.

'What was he like?' Rebecca asked after a moment, studying her tea. 'Your husband?'

'The most handsome man,' Mrs Ffoulkes replied, with a cheeky smile and a glint in her eye. 'Right rascal, but a good man. Hardworking and gentle.'

She glanced meaningfully at Liam, who might have reddened at the overt comparison, had that been something he did.

'I remember the first time I saw him, at the summer fair in Liveston. He was there with some friends, all dressed up to sell his father's livestock. He were a farmer,' she said conspiratorially, and Rebecca smiled. 'I was there with my friend Cecilia, and she went over to talk to a friend of his, and all I saw was him. His smile…warmed my heart. He came over and asked me to the dance that night. Gave me daisies when I went, and every day after that.'

'He sounds like a charmer.' Rebecca grinned.

'Aye, he was—though not as much as the one Cecilia was after,' Mrs Ffoulkes said pensively. 'He was a slick one. Nearly married him, she did, but there was some trouble with another lass. Lucky escape, I think. She ended up with the vicar.'

Mrs Ffoulkes stopped, and turned to face Rebecca squarely. She studied the housekeeper carefully for a long, uncomfortable moment.

'That's who you remind me of,' she said triumphantly. 'Couldn't think of it till now, but, yes, you look rather like him.'

Liam glanced at Rebecca and frowned. She was frozen, and what looked like fear had darkened her eyes.

'Merrickson, yes, that was the name. Grain farmers, they were. Any relation?'

'No,' she breathed, unconvincingly.

'Mrs Hardwicke, are you quite all right?' Liam asked, concerned. The woman had paled, and he might have sworn her hand trembled ever so slightly as she set down her cup. 'Are you unwell?'

'What's the matter, child?'

'N-nothing,' Rebecca stuttered, rising. 'I've just re-called that I have some urgent matters to deal with back at the house.'

'I'll walk you,' Liam offered, rising as well.

'No, please, no need to trouble yourself,' she said hast-ily, throwing on her coat and already making for the door. 'Lovely to see you, Mrs Ffoulkes. Thank you for the tea.'

With that, Rebecca disappeared, leaving both Liam and Mrs Ffoulkes staring at the door, confused as to what had happened.

Liam remained at Mrs Ffoulkes's for a while after Re-becca had gone, speaking with the old woman of nothing and of everything. Of the land, of her life, of his own, and most importantly, of what he had missed. Which had been so much. Too much. Not that he hadn't already realised that. Only, today it felt different.

As Mrs Ffoulkes gave him her own recounting of the area's history for the past ten years, Liam had felt more a spectator than ever, and less guilty than ever. For though things had been difficult, life had gone on.

As he walked back through the woods, then across the park towards the house, Liam realised that the weight he'd carried for years seemed slowly to be lifting. And all be-cause of one stubborn woman. The ghost of a smile appeared on his lips, then quickly turned into a frown as he recalled what had happened in the cottage. The way she'd paled...

Fear.

What is it you fear, Mrs Hardwicke? I would—

'Master Reid,' called Tim's voice. 'Master Reid, may I have a word?'

Liam turned, plastering on a polite smile despite feeling as though he'd already been put through the mill this morning.

He noticed that Tim was running. Liam couldn't remember having ever seen him run before; this must be spectacular news indeed.

'What is it, Tim? A problem with the horses?'

'No master, nothin' at all,' the groom said between breaths. 'I need… That is, there is something I must tell you, my lord.'

Liam eyed the groom carefully. Tim was intent on examining the ground, and toeing some mud. He looked sheepish, and unsure, and entirely unlike himself.

I cannot take more terrible news…

'Then you'd better tell me, Tim,' Liam said, steeling himself. 'And quick, for I now fear the worst.'

The groom took a deep breath, then met Liam's gaze and straightened himself as though he were meeting his executioner. 'I gave Mrs Hardwicke the key, my lord.'

'You gave Mrs Hardwicke the key,' Liam repeated after a moment, dumbfounded, his heart returning to its normal rhythm. 'And what key might that be?'

'The key to…to Lady Hal's rooms. You must not be cross with her, 'twas I that let her in there.'

Liam blinked, the confession throwing him completely. 'How did you even get it?' he asked.

Neither the first, nor the most important question, but then Tim might have told him a thousand terrible things, and he wouldn't be reeling as he was now. He couldn't think straight.

'I took it, when the Earl died,' Tim said, his courage returning slowly. 'I thought to keep it safe, keep her safe until you came back. But…'

'I never came back,' Liam said softly.

'I know it weren't my place, but I loved her, Master Reid. Don't think I could've loved her more had she been mine. And she were good to me.'

It was Liam's turn to nod, and bite away the tears misting in his eyes.

'I wanted to protect her, you see. And then, Mrs Hardwicke came, and I thought she was just like the rest of them. But then…I seen what she did to Thornhallow, master. And I thought, well, I knew, she'd take care of her. And Lady Hal, she wouldn't have liked the way things were.'

'She always hated the darkness,' Liam finished.

His eyes wandered to the glistening pool in the middle of the park, and he remembered sitting at its edge with Hal one eve, when she was barely old enough to form words.

'I used to tell her when she got scared to look out there. At the moonlight on the water. So she'd never be without light,' he breathed, speaking more to himself than the man before him.

'I am not sorry for what I did, master,' Tim said after a long moment. 'I just thought you should know.'

'Thank you, Tim,' Liam said simply, returning to meet the groom's gaze.

His gratitude was not only for the truth, but for everything the man had done to keep his sister safe. Tim nodded, knowing so even without Liam having to say.

'I am neither angry at you, nor at Mrs Hardwicke. In fact, I've just come from speaking with her. I am the one who should be sorry. For having abandoned you all. For being so blind. I will make things right. I swear.'

'Aye, my lord. We know you will.'

Tim bowed his head and turned back towards the stables. Liam stood there, unable to move for a long time as he processed all the day, all the past few days, had forced him to confront. He'd left Thornhallow that morning with the sole purpose of finding Mrs Hardwicke. Finding her, and finally making the apology he had realised she was due not hours after their confrontation in the East Tower.

For once his rage and regret had faded, it had been as though a veil had been lifted. Her words had rung incessantly in his ears until he'd been forced to admit that he had, in fact, been a blind, stubborn idiot, and that she was right about the house, and him, and Hal's room.

There were no answers there. No redemption. Only grief. Something everyone else seemed to have seen plainly. But for him, coming to terms with that had been the hardest part, and it had taken all his courage and strength to do so. Then to seek her out and say as much. To then be confronted with Mrs Ffoulkes's words, and Tim's…

Though the weight might feel as if it were lifting, Liam felt more confused and lost than ever. It was not in his nature to be so, and the worst part was that a voice somewhere deep inside told him that however troubling, unsettling and inconceivable it might be, Mrs Hardwicke might just be able to help him. Through whatever this was.

He had not lied when he'd said he wished for them to be friends. Improper though *that* might be. His housekeeper's company seemed to calm and restore him. She soothed his soul, and not even his pride could prevent him from comprehending just how exceptional such a gift was. Selfish, perhaps, but then, he was not so foolish as to throw away what fate had sought to bring him.

Are you happy now, Hal? he thought, taking a moment to admire his accursed home before returning inside. *I have made peace with her.*

Liam could see her then, standing at her window wearing a smug smile of satisfaction.

Chapter Ten

'So this is where you come when you are not haunting my library.'

Rebecca jumped a little at the sound of his voice, which, admittedly, did reverberate more than expected in the empty conservatory. He smiled reassuringly, approaching slowly so as not to scare her, though she looked more frightening to him in that moment. She had the look of a wraith, only the outline of her visible against the glass and the twilight.

'I might've guessed.'

'My lord,' Rebecca said. 'I didn't hear you come in.'

'But, please, do not even think about running away,' he said, coming to stand beside her, directing his gaze out into the night in an attempt to make her more at ease. 'I always loved this place, though when I was a boy it had more the air of a mysterious tropical jungle than now.'

'It shall see better days, I'm sure. At least Mrs Murray has kept some life here.'

'Ah, yes, the winter garden,' Liam said, gazing to the far corner, which had been appropriated by his cook. 'Most irregular, but then, who am I to say anything... I'm surprised you didn't go with the others.'

'I admit I preferred a quiet night, my lord. And I can see the bonfires well enough from here,' she said, pointing towards the village below.

'Ah, yes, right you are.'

'And you, my lord? Not one for Guy Fawkes's?'

'I'm afraid not, Mrs Hardwicke,' Liam said with a hollow chuckle. 'I liked it well enough when I was a boy, but now…I do not think I would be as welcome, lord of this land as I am. Though I do enjoy fireworks. Do you think they shall have any this year?'

'Indeed.' Rebecca smiled, drawing his attention back to her.

She seemed so different in this light, in this moment. Relaxed, open, even. And yet there was still always a wariness in her eyes. Not of him, but of something more.

Would you let me ease your burden as you have eased mine? he longed to ask.

'I have it on good authority from Gregory that this shall in fact be the best display in many years,' she continued. 'Though he might've been saying that to convince me to go.'

'Yes, most likely.'

Liam stared out towards the village. The bonfires looked like nothing more than torches from here, though he could almost feel their heat, and hear the chants and songs of those dancing around them. An image appeared in his mind's eye then, one, rather beguiling, of the restrained Mrs Hardwicke dancing around bonfires, hair unfurled, spirit free.

'They are meant to ward off evil spirits, and bring luck,' she offered after a moment. 'At least, that is what the Chinese believe, I think.'

'You are very knowledgeable, Mrs Hardwicke,' Liam noted, studying her profile.

If he'd thought her ethereal before, that first night in the library, now... In the moonlight, the sharp lines of her features accentuated by the shadows of the night, she seemed almost an asrai, translucent creature of the night who might fade into a pool of rainbows should the sun touch her.

'Wherever did you learn such things?'

'Are housekeepers meant to be dull in your opinion, then, my lord?'

'I meant no insult. Ah, I deserved that, I suppose.' He grinned, spotting her own smile. 'So, tell me, where did you learn such things?'

'Everywhere, really.' Rebecca shrugged. 'I have always enjoyed learning about the world, and... Well, I did not have a privileged upbringing, but by the grace of the Lord, I was given a second chance. Oh, look,' she exclaimed, pointing towards the skies, her eyes briefly alight with childish excitement. 'Your fireworks, my lord.'

'A most worthy display,' Liam admitted after a moment. 'And I dare say it is most pleasant to watch them from the comfort of one's own home. So...you taught yourself, then?'

'Everything I could,' she said, and Liam saw that darkness pass over her eyes again. 'Taught myself to read, and my sums, even embroidery, languages, sketching... All so that I might improve my station. I also worked for some good employers. Mrs Chealton, for instance, she was a lovely woman. Taught me the pianoforte so that she might hear music every night... She would lend me books, too, and then we would converse for hours about them... She first had me read *Frankenstein* when it was published.'

'Ah, I see... And your family? What do they think of you now, I wonder?'

Liam instantly knew he'd asked the wrong question, recalling that she had no family, and cursed himself inwardly as she turned away, wringing her hands. He made to place his own hand over hers, but stopped himself in time, and instead raked his fingers through his hair.

'I am sorry.'

'There is nothing to be sorry for, my lord,' she said with a strained smile. 'I like to think they would've been proud.'

'I'm sure they would,' Liam said gently. A thought occurred to him. 'What Mrs Ffoulkes said, that is, you speak like a southerner, but…'

'I am from here. Something else I taught myself,' she sighed. 'Born not thirty miles away.'

'Something which you have been careful to keep secret. It's why you didn't go to the village tonight. You never go, do you?'

Rebecca looked over to him, as though calculating odds. Liam's eyes narrowed, questioning, and she nodded sadly.

'You don't have to tell me,' he whispered, sensing she was ready to tell him her tale.

'And if I wish to?' she asked tentatively.

'Do you?'

'Yes… I do.'

Liam nodded, and waited, her demonstration of trust touching him deeply.

She took a breath, preparing herself to speak of whatever haunted her. He wondered for a moment how wise this was, to encourage such revelations, but he also wished to know. Wished to be there for her, as she had for him. Wished to know her better, no matter the danger.

'I was born a farmer's daughter,' she began, crossing her arms as though shielding herself. 'A rather improper young girl. Running amok around the countryside, fishing, climbing trees, generally causing mischief… My father said it was because I had no mother. She died giving birth to me. When he passed, my uncle took me in. He

was the only family I had, and he was... Well, suffice it
to say I only got worse, spending more time outside than
in. This once, I got stuck up a tree. My dress tangled in
the branches and I couldn't free myself. I never believed
in fairy stories, not until that day... The son of a neigh-
bouring lord passed by, and heard my cries. Rode up on a
white horse, if you can believe it. Really did have the air
of a prince.' Rebecca raised an eyebrow thoughtfully. 'He
got me down, took me home. I was so scared—my uncle
would be furious—but my prince offered to speak to him,
calm him... How could I have imagined?'

'Your uncle, he was a brute?'

'Oh, yes,' Rebecca said flatly. 'Drunkard, gambler. Hor-
rible licentious swine. Wasted away everything my father
had built. But he was nothing compared to my saviour.
When he took me home, I rushed to clean myself up, before my uncle could see and tan my hide. I was quick,
though—I wanted to see my prince again—and that's
when I heard them. Discussing my price, and the details
of my collection.'

'Your uncle sold you?' Liam asked, aghast.

Of course he'd heard of such things happening, but the
knowledge did nothing to assuage his anger at the idea of
it happening to her.

'He needed the money, and had little love for me...'
Rebecca shrugged, as though the pain were not as fresh
as it had been, which it undoubtedly was. 'They agreed
that my prince should return in the morning to collect me,
once he'd made arrangements for my *keeping*. I knew I
had but one chance—knew well what would become of
me should I stay. That night, I ran. Walked for days until
I made it to the city. I was lucky again, found a place as
a scullery maid...'

Taking a deep breath, Rebecca scanned the flashes of

colour in the sky, unseeing, lost in her memories. Liam clenched his fists, a strong desire to wring some necks rising.

'I thank whatever powers above daily for the chances that were given to me. So many things might've been different if I had not been so fortunate, and so many are not. What if he had taken me in the woods? What if I hadn't heard them, or if I'd been found? What if I had succumbed to the trials of living on the streets?'

'How old were you, when…?' Liam asked after a long moment of silence, the simmering rage in his breast somehow contained. 'When this happened?'

'Fourteen, my lord,' she said, finally meeting his gaze again.

'Dear God… Animal,' Liam blurted out before he could stop himself. 'And you continue to change places, to run, but…'

'Why should I? It's all right,' Rebecca said with a faint smile as she heard him curse himself, very audibly this time. 'Why still run, when I was nothing more than a peasant a lord once tried to buy? For one thing, I had to remain hidden until my majority, lest my uncle drag me back.'

Liam saw the flicker of fear in her eyes and steeled himself, waiting for the rest.

'Two years after I left, I was working as a housemaid in Norwich. I liked it, even thought I might stay there forever. I had friends.' She smiled sadly. 'I was returning from an errand, and there was my prince, striding right up to the front door. I stayed hidden, for hours, until I managed to get a message to one of the girls I worked with. She brought me my things, and told me his arrival was no accident. He'd come for me, armed with some tale of being my lost brother. I fled as far and as fast as I could. That is when I became Rebecca Hardwicke.'

Rebecca drew in a deep breath, and stared unseeingly at the glass before her.

'I was careful, I covered my tracks, I kept moving, years passed... Over time, I became complacent. I took a position in London, even though I knew that was where my prince usually lived. It had been twelve years...' Rebecca laughed mirthlessly and shook her head. 'I quite literally ran into him on the street. There was, this look, in his eyes. A promise. I had not been forgotten, and I would never be free. He would make me pay. I was lucky again that day,' she said, clearing her throat. 'I lost him in the crowd, and disappeared again. It will never end.'

'And you've never had a desire to settle down, been tempted? Somewhere quiet?'

'I suppose I could find some remote village, but would that not be another cage? I have a life, better than I ever dreamt of. Independence, and freedom many women can only imagine.'

'If you met someone...'

'I could never ask someone to give up their life for me. And I have never met anyone I cared enough for to be tempted. Well,' she sighed. 'Now you know. The truth.'

Liam nodded despondently and looked out onto the gardens, now a brightly glittering rainbow of colours in the fading lights of the fireworks finale.

He wished the man who had forced her into this life was before him, so he could show him the true meaning of suffering. He wished he could hold her hand, or hold *her*, swear that he would keep her safe, protect her. But he couldn't. It wouldn't be right, and she wouldn't accept it. But even so, he promised to himself. That so long as she was here, in his life, he *would* keep her safe.

She was his employee. He owed it to her as much as he owed it to the others.

Yes, that was all it was. And he liked her, no denying that. So he did not want to lose her.

Like he'd lost Angus, and Peter, and Hal.

Like he'd lost everyone he had ever cared about.

'Perhaps,' he said finally, 'one day you might find some-one willing to share a life, any life, with you.'

'Perhaps.'

'I thank you for trusting me with your tale, Mrs Hard—' Liam stopped himself. 'Might you share with me your true name? I shall not use it, unless in private, I promise.'

'Merrickson.' She smiled. 'Rebecca Merrickson.'

'Mrs Ffoulkes,' Liam said, fully understanding now. 'The man she spoke of...'

'One of my mother's cousins, I suspect. Some scandalous marriage as I recall.'

'She won't say anything, to anyone.'

'I know... It's just...'

'I understand,' he said gently, and Rebecca smiled gratefully. 'Well, it's a pleasure to meet you, Miss Merrickson,' Liam said with a bow of his head.

The chiming of the clock reverberated loudly through the hall, and all the way through the conservatory, bringing them back to themselves.

'I should return downstairs. The others will be back soon,' Rebecca said, pushing the past back to where it belonged. 'Good evening, my lord.'

'Good evening, Miss Merrickson.'

A tiny curtsey, a rush of skirts through the plants, and she was gone.

Liam remained there, watching the landscape fade away into colourless night, for a long while. Even the bonfires seemed to have dimmed now. He should have asked her, he thought belatedly, who the man was. The one who had tried to buy her virtue, her life. Though he sensed she would not have told him. She had already trusted him with so much. Too much, he knew she must feel, for had he not felt the same?

Instinctively, he knew her tale had not been shared before, and it filled him with pride that she should with him. Filled him with longing, to know it all, to know her fully, and for her to know him.

How tempting it would be to share the rest of his sorry tale with his elusive little housekeeper. She had seen many of his secrets already, and not shied away. For someone who had seen and experienced the wickedness and depravity of men, she had not been afraid of him, nor his demons. She had not been afraid of this house, of its secrets and its ghosts, as so many had before. She could see past the surface, see the truth beneath.

And yet he could see the danger there again. Of fostering, of allowing a closeness beyond the bonds of master and servant. Of fostering a bond with *her*. But he had not had a friend—a true friend—in so very long, was it not worth the risks? Surely it would hurt no one, a discreet, honourable friendship between them, at least for as long as he remained here. Her presence had made life at Thornhallow bearable, even in those moments when he'd felt she made it worse. Why should he question the sense of it all? There was no one here but themselves to judge.

Liam pondered it all relentlessly, and it wasn't until the conservatory was gloriously bathed in moonlight that he finally made his way to the library, decidedly too preoccupied and unfocused to deal with anything more.

A book, he decided, and a dram of whisky, would set him right again.

Chapter Eleven

'Ah, Mrs Hardwicke,' Liam sighed, glancing up from his papers, welcoming the distraction though he was still not entirely certain he could trust himself around her, despite their weeks spent apart. 'Come, please, sit,' he added, with a wave of his hand.

'Thank you, my lord.' Rebecca smiled, taking a seat before him.

The woman had the indecency to look the opposite of what he felt. Sprightly, inspired, entirely herself. Full of life, unplagued by the darkness he knew she carried. Unplagued by longings like his, reassuring and yet heartbreaking.

Our distance has not affected you; how I envy you that, too.

'I have come to discuss the arrangements for Christmas—if you have time, that is.'

'Heavens, I'd quite forgotten it,' he admitted despondently, rubbing the space between his brows with an ink-stained finger.

That explains the jolly mood...

'We can discuss this at another time, my lord, if—'

'Nonsense, I am quite in need of a distraction just now.'

He smiled faintly, gesturing to the mass of papers and ledgers strewn across the oak before him. 'And it is only what, a sennight away?'

'Indeed,' Rebecca said, and he felt her studying him closely.

When he caught her gaze, however, she hurriedly opened her notebook, and stared down at it.

'Well, Mrs Murray wished me to check that you would be happy with a cold dinner on Christmas Eve? And she wondered what you might prefer for Christmas Day? Venison? A goose, a turkey, or…? Unless you are dining away with friends, perhaps? Should we expect anyone?'

'No, I mean… That is, I shall be at Thornhallow,' Liam said, only realising it now.

His eyes turned towards the fire, and he remained lost in thought for a moment, before taking a deep breath and returning his attention to Rebecca.

'A cold dinner will be fine. As for the day itself, well, I admit I don't know… I'm unlikely to eat a turkey all by myself, nor a goose for that matter… Perhaps,' he started, studying Rebecca in turn, gauging what her reaction might be. 'Well, what are the staff planning? Will they all be here?'

'Yes, we shall all be here,' Rebecca said, surprised at his interest. 'It shall be a goose for us, I think.'

'Unless anyone has a preference for those infernal beasts, make it a turkey.'

'My lord—'

'Make it a turkey,' Liam said firmly, raising his hand. 'And have a plate of whatever is being had downstairs brought up, if you would be so kind, Miss Merrickson. It is nonsense to cook an entirely separate meal for me alone, and the staff deserve something special. I am quite sure they've eaten enough geese to last a lifetime.'

'Very well, my lord,' Rebecca conceded with a conciliatory smile. 'A turkey it shall be.'

'Anything else?'

'Well, yes… About decorations…'

'Must we?'

'I was only thinking perhaps a little greenery, and—'

'Do your worst, then, Miss Merrickson,' Liam chuckled, his mood improving. 'I see no point in attempting to dissuade you, for you shall simply go forth and do precisely as you please. And don't pretend otherwise,' he added, as Rebecca opened her mouth to retort. 'We shall spend an hour negotiating terms and then one morning I shall descend and find you have turned the place into a paragon of festivity.'

'Thank you, my lord,' she said, turning her eyes back to her notebook, desperately attempting to hide a smile, but unable, however, to conceal a slight and very becoming blush. 'Lastly, well, for St Stephen's Day, that is, I was wondering…'

'Ah, yes, of course, gifts,' Liam said with a sigh, leaning back in his chair.

He had forgotten that tradition as well. *Drat.* But, in truth, if anyone deserved gifts, it was his loyal little household. They had served him well, and the least he could do was make an effort.

'Thank you, Miss Merrickson, I will sort that myself.'

'Oh, yes, of…of course,' she stuttered, her eyes wide. 'You are certain, that is, you need not trouble yourself, I can assist—'

'Miss Merrickson, I am quite capable, I assure you,' he countered with a sly grin. 'And, no, before you ask, it shall not simply be envelopes, do not concern yourself.'

'Yes, my lord.' She nodded, closing her notebook.

'You have finished with me, then?'

'Yes, my lord. Unless there is anything you need, I shall leave you to your work.'

'That will be all, thank you.'

Rebecca rose and curtsied.

'Actually, could you have some coffee brought up? I feel as though I shall need it if I'm to continue wading through this mess...'

'Of course, my lord.' She nodded before disappearing.

Liam sighed heavily and looked up at the ceiling.

Christmas.

He'd forgotten the mere idea of it. It had never been anything other than a dismal, stuffy affair after his mother had...become ill. His father had always insisted they celebrate at Thornhallow, though why he ever used the term 'celebrate', Liam wondered. It had been far from anything remotely resembling a celebration.

Shaking his head, Liam remembered the faces of the staff as they'd lined up in the hall, awaiting the grace of their lord. Grim, tight-lipped, heads bowed in fear. That was what his father had inspired. *Fear.* In everyone he met.

Liam had always vowed he would never be like him. With a man like that as a father, it was no wonder...

Hal...

She'd been the only warmth during the season. She would always wait to give him his gifts until after St Stephen's, when their father would disappear back to the city until after the New Year. They would have their own private Christmas, and exchange homemade presents. His had always been dire in comparison to his sister's. She'd been a masterful painter and a delicate knitter, while he'd barely been able to fashion something recognisable from chunks of wood, however hard Tim tried to teach him.

Perhaps he would give Tim a proper new carving knife. *Yes, he would like that, I think...*

He could make little horses for his great-nieces and nephews, as he once had for Liam.

And Mr Brown? What shall we get you...

Liam went through the list of his employees, toying with ideas of what to get them. Lizzie arrived and set out his coffee, then disappeared again without a word. Liam barely noticed, so involved was he in his reverie of Christmas planning.

He felt...excited. For the first time in far too long, he felt excited by the prospect of Yuletide. It did not matter that he would be alone; all that mattered was that he might spread some joy, bring some pleasure to those who had faithfully watched over Thornhallow, and over him.

And what about you, Miss Rebecca Merrickson... What shall we get you, then...

Liam grinned, the idea already perfectly formed in his mind.

You will enjoy them, he thought, pouring himself some coffee. *Yes, and I think that after all I shall enjoy this Christmas...*

Chapter Twelve

'Come in,' Liam barked, grateful for the interruption, but frustrated by the Sisyphean nature of his work. 'Yes, Thomas, what is it?' he asked in a less aggressive tone when he glimpsed his butler's apologetic expression. 'Come, man, if it is important enough for you to interrupt, I suspect you should not be wasting time.'

'It's Mrs Hardwicke, my lord,' the butler said, cautiously approaching the desk.

'Whatever has she done now? Rearranged my chambers? Instituted mandatory singing of carols whilst cleaning? Out with it.' He grinned, realising that he wouldn't mind any of those things at all.

'I am concerned, my lord,' he said, in such a genuine tone Liam felt his stomach somersault. 'She hasn't returned yet, and…'

Liam followed Thomas's gaze and turned to the window. Outside, nothing was visible save for the swirling white waves of the snowstorm they had been promised for days.

'Returned? Do you mean to say that Mrs Hardwicke has gone out into this tempest?'

'Mrs Hardwicke expressed some concern for Mrs

Ffoulkes... I did tell her she would be seen to, but Mrs Hardwicke was most insistent—'

'That dratted woman, what on earth was she thinking?' Liam exclaimed, jumping to his feet and making for the door, Thomas on his heels. 'How long has she been gone?'

'Three hours, my lord. She left this morning, before the storm arrived, and promised she would return before it descended...'

'Yes, well, she was most evidently wrong.' Liam strode out of the study, and threw open the coat cupboard in the hall. 'Knowing our stubborn housekeeper, she won't have stayed put at Mrs Ffoulkes's, oh, no, she'll have attempted to make it back.'

With a groan of frustration, Liam grabbed his greatcoat, fur coat, scarf and beaver hat, and made his way down the servants' stairs.

'Ensure there is a hot bath waiting by the kitchen hearth. Towels, blankets and the warmest of Mrs Hardwicke's nightclothes you can find.'

Wrapping himself up as he made his way through the servants' quarters, Liam ignored the worried looks of the staff, and focused instead on silently cursing Rebecca with every breath. Anger helped to keep his own concern in check, and his mind focused on the task at hand, rather than on the sick feeling in the pit of his stomach.

'Here, my lord, some hot potatoes for your pockets,' Mrs Murray said, handing them to Liam as she burst out of the kitchens and fell in step with him. 'Do bring her back, my lord, and mind yourself.'

Liam slipped the potatoes into his pockets and slid into a pair of the pattens that lay by the door, before wrenching on his thick, fur-lined leather gloves. The Columbian winters had seen to it, at least, that he was attired to face what awaited.

'Do not let anyone else leave the house, Thomas,' he instructed. 'No matter what.'

'Yes, my lord.'

With a nod, Liam pulled his scarf over his face, threw up his hood, and without any further ado opened the door and stepped out into the blast of wind and snow that greeted him.

He watched as Thomas leaned against the door with all his weight to close it again, and braced himself before turning back to face the storm.

When I find you, my little Miss Merrickson, the storm shall be the least of your concerns...

The scarf wrapped around his face had frozen, clumped with ice and snow. His feet were soaked and numb, as was the rest of him. Still, he marched on through the growing drifts, clutching his coats tightly, his eyes scanning the white, blurry wasteland before him as best they could.

The wind howled and whistled around him, warning him to turn back while the heavens unleashed their fury on the world, but Liam marched on, the crunch of his steps a whisper compared to the bluster around him. He had to find her. He would freeze to death himself before he left her to the elements. She was lucky he knew this land well enough to make his way in this hell storm. Lucky that the moon still had some light to offer, and that the snow reflected what little it did.

Foolish, careless, reckless woman!

For the hundredth time since he'd set out, he wondered what precisely the woman had been thinking. Did she not know how quickly storms descended here? And now here *he* was, forced to trudge out after her since she seemed terminally incapable of staying put and doing as she was told. Incapable of doing the sensible thing. He should let her freeze to death out in his own park. That would serve her right. Perhaps then she might understand, might listen.

Even as he thought it, he cursed himself loudly, his warm breath spreading through the scarf and warming his nose for a brief moment.

No. Please, God, let me find her. Let me save her, as I could not save the others...

If she died...he would not be able to bear it. Not another soul on his conscience. And most certainly not *hers*. She might be the most infuriating, contrary, wilfully disobedient wretch of a woman he had ever encountered, and yet... If she left him, if she was taken from him, Liam knew his life would never be the same.

He felt his heart twist in agony at the thought and shouted to the heavens. No. He would find her. He had to. All would be well.

'Miss Merrickson!' he screamed out into the whirling void, stopping his progress only to listen for something, anything, that might help him. 'Rebecca!'

There... A faint...something.

Liam forged onwards, eastwards, in the direction of what he hoped with every fibre of his being was her voice.

'Rebecca, thank God!' he cried, finally spotting her kneeling silhouette against the blanket of swirling snowflakes. 'What were you thinking?' he vented, kneeling before her.

'I...I...'

With that, Rebecca's eyes fluttered closed, and she slumped forward against him.

'Oh no you don't,' Liam growled, sliding one arm around her, whilst the other dug out her legs from the snow and lifted them. 'No dying on me now. Not until I've given you a piece of my mind, woman.'

Liam heaved himself to his feet with a grunt, Rebecca

in his arms, held tightly against him. She was frozen to the bone. No warmth emanated from her.

Incorrigible, insufferable, stubborn...

Liam quickened his pace again, his own body screaming out against the effort and the cold. His anger and frustration fuelled him onwards, and he treated the unconscious body in his arms to a colourful slew of expletives he would never have dared use whilst she was awake. It masked the desperation, and the overwhelming relief he'd felt when he'd finally spotted her in the snow.

For she was close, so very close to death. He could feel it. He had seen good men taken the same way in the mountains too many times before. She looked so pale, so ghost-like... And her breathing was slowing, the rise and fall of her chest against his telling him so.

'No. You will not die!' he cried, pulling her in closer. 'Not like this. Not ever.'

And, as if the heavens had heard his pleas, Liam spotted the faint orange glow of a lantern in the distance before them.

'There, see, almost home now.'

Warmth. A wave of thick, stifling heat. It pulled Rebecca back through the frozen fog of her mind, back to the present.

Thornhallow. Home. Alive.

She was alive. She still couldn't move, her entire body unwilling to respond to the feeble demands of her mind, but it didn't matter. In truth, she didn't want to move.

'Is the bath ready?' she heard Liam shout.

He found me.

Yes, she remembered that—only just. A tall figure appearing in the storm like an ancient demon of legend. She'd heard his voice calling on the wind, and with the last of her

strength, she had called back. And he'd found her. She was
in his arms now, safe against his chest. She could smell
wet wool, fur and leather, and was that his heartbeat in
her ears or her own?

She was vaguely aware of others around them, but her
eyes refused to open.

'Yes, my lord,' Thomas said, following closely behind
as they made their way through to the kitchens. 'Everything is prepared, as you asked.'

'Oh, my lord!' Mrs Murray screamed from down the
corridor, spotting them. 'The poor mite's frozen to death!'

Not yet frozen... But nearly.

Now there was a thick haze of fog in her mind, a heavy
dullness inviting her to sleep. To rest her cold, weary
limbs, to rest her mind. She resisted, concentrating instead on how weightless she felt, how delightfully safe she
was in her master's arms.

For even in that moment, Rebecca knew the dangers
of giving in.

'Indeed, Mrs Murray, quite near to it, I fear,' Liam
shouted back, though he needed not, at the rate he was
approaching the flapping cook. He spotted Lizzie and the
others behind her, watching on in horror. 'But do not fret.
We will see Mrs Hardwicke to rights soon enough.'

Pushing past them and into the kitchens, Liam laid Rebecca down on a cleared table, and began peeling off his
own layers of protection, most of it with his teeth as his
fingers refused to cooperate.

'Help, please,' he said to Gregory as the boy rose from
pouring the last bucket of boiling water into the copper
tub set before the hearth. 'Pattens. Boots.'

'Aye, my lord,' Gregory said, swiftly complying.

'We should take care of her, my lord,' Lizzie said tentatively from the doorway.

Liam stopped, and was about to tell them all where they could go with their suggestions, that *he* would see this done, propriety or not, when Thomas stepped forth.

'My lord, Mrs Murray and Lizzie will see to her,' he said, in a tone that not even the King himself would have dared disobey. 'We shall get you warmed as well, in my rooms.'

'Fine,' Liam growled. 'But time is of the essence. Gregory—vinegar, water and cloths in her bedroom, and make sure that there are plenty of blankets and a bed-warmer as well.'

'Yes, my lord,' Gregory said, scurrying out.

'You fetch me as soon as she is ready to be put to bed,' Liam told the women, glancing over at Rebecca one last time.

'Yes, my lord,' they reassured him in unison, steering him out through the door.

'Mrs Hardwicke,' Lizzie called, a few moments after she'd heard Liam leave.

A groan was the only response Rebecca could manage. She tried to open her eyes, but felt a rush of tears when she did. Where was she now?

No longer in his arms, it's cold and hard here.

'Can you hear me? Mrs Hardwicke!'

'Lizzie,' she croaked, managing to open her eyes finally.

The kitchens, she saw through the blur. *Why are we in the kitchens?*

'I...'

'We need to chafe you, Mrs Hardwicke,' Mrs Murray said gently. 'I need you to sit for me—can you do that? We'll help you.'

Rebecca nodded feebly, and the next moment she felt everything scream out in pain as the women pulled her up to a sitting position on the edge of the table. All the blood rushed to her head, and there was pounding unlike anything she had ever experienced before. She whimpered, swaying, and Lizzie's hands came to rest on her shoulders for a moment. Drawing a deep breath, eyes closed again, Rebecca managed to hold steady.

Fingers began swiftly and meticulously trailing along her body, taking away every last frozen, soaked thing. Pattens, boots, stockings, coat, hat, gloves, skirts, chemise. Somewhere in the back of her mind a protest formed, but the release from the garments felt so extraordinary, nothing escaped her lips. Even as she realised what they would see, she could not stop them.

The warm, moist air felt like a blanket against her glacial, numb skin, and Rebecca found it easier to breathe. She managed to open her eyes again, just as Mrs Murray's hands dropped to her waist and, with impressive strength, slid her forward.

She felt the hard tiles beneath her feet as the world once again blurred and dizziness swept over her. But the women steadied her again, before returning to their task. The last of the sodden garments fell to the floor, and then their hands were against her skin again.

It was a trial to stand as they began chafing her, so vigorously it seemed her skin was now on fire.

'What were you thinking?' Mrs Murray admonished. 'We told you the master would see to Mrs Ffoulkes, and now see what you've done. Scared us all right to death.'

Mrs Murray's voice broke, and Rebecca felt a lump of emotion in her own throat. Someone cared about her. More than *someone*, everyone here. It had been a long time since people had truly cared for her, cared what happened to her.

No matter what she did, she could not help the tears that rolled down her cheeks. Neither of the women said anything, nor acknowledged that they had witnessed her weakness. They simply rubbed every frozen inch of flesh, from her shoulders down to her toes. She managed to prise open her eyes slightly, and she saw them, like warm sprites of summer, glowing in the light of the hearth. She was relieved to note that their own eyes were thankfully full of serious purpose as they swept across her body with the interest and dedication of doctors.

They do not judge me...

Before that thought could develop, or any others could take its place, they stopped their work, set their arms under her own, holding tight about her waist, and guided her to the bath, helping her in.

'Now, just stay in there for a while,' Mrs Murray instructed, before disappearing.

Rebecca did as she was told, letting the warmth of the water and the fire lull her into near senselessness.

She let it soothe away her sorrow, let it soothe away her hurt, until Mrs Murray and Lizzie returned to dry and clothe her. Even then, she was barely present, her mind somewhere far away, in a land where she'd found home and could finally rest. The darkness and the heavy slumber called her again then, and she found she could resist it no longer.

The last thing she felt was a pair of strong arms lifting her up as a whisper in her ear told her it was time for bed.

Liam laid his troublesome housekeeper gently down in her bed, and tucked her in with as much care and tenderness as his mother had when he was a child. She was still pale, though a faint wash of colour had returned to her cheeks.

Had he managed to find her in time? He'd done his best, but she was not out of danger yet. If she developed a fever, if...

Sighing, Liam dropped into the chair by her side.

Waiting. That was all there was to do now. Wait. And so he would wait. She, at least, would not die on his watch.

No, Rebecca. You, I vow I shall not lose.

During the middle of the night, Rebecca took a turn for the worse. The fever Liam feared came upon her, the chill having set into her lungs despite his best efforts.

He was awoken by the sound of chattering teeth and whimpers as she tossed and turned, winding the blankets around herself. Immediately Liam set about trying to break the fever, alternating between soothing her with cloths soaked in cool water and vinegar, and chafing her legs—at which point he discovered some very peculiar inking on her skin, which he determined he would ask about when she was herself again.

For she shall be. I swear it.

Not until mid-morning did the fever break. Rebecca finally fell back into a restful, or at least not fitful, slumber, and Liam did the same, half lying on the bed, half in his chair, the cloths still clutched in his hand.

Thomas woke him some hours later, insisting that if he would not sleep in his own chambers, he might at least refresh himself and have a proper meal.

Lizzie took over watching Rebecca whilst Liam relented and did just that.

And so it was for the next four days.

Outside, the storm raged on. Inside, Liam kept to Rebecca's bedside, leaving only to refresh himself. The staff took turns watching over her when he did, and Mrs Murray brought him trays of food along with broth and tea for

Rebecca. No one said a single word about his presence by her side, nor his devotion to her care. They all understood that the master would not be swayed from his task—and, indeed, they all felt keenly for the new housekeeper they had once seemed so intent to despise.

Christmas came and went, uncelebrated and nearly forgotten but for private prayers, which all seemed to feature one Mrs Hardwicke.

Rebecca had only very few moments of consciousness, and none of lucidity. Though the first fever had broken, the infection in her chest worsened, and other bouts of fever came and went. Her body shut down, fighting the sickness, and perhaps it was best, for if not, she might have fought Liam's devoted nursing.

Not that fighting him would have helped. Liam cared for her with everything he had. Something deep inside drove him on, and he was relentless in his tending. He had sworn he would not lose her, therefore he would not. And so he soothed her, fed her, gave her water, even brushed and braided her hair after the women bathed her.

By the time the doctor could be sent for, and arrived on the fifth day, there was nothing left for him to do.

'What do you mean, there is nothing to be done?' Liam exclaimed, half-delirious with the lack of sleep and worry. 'By God, man—'

'My lord,' the doctor said in his most soothing tone. 'There is nothing more for me to do as Mrs Hardwicke is well on her way to recovering. She is awake now, and there is good colour in her cheeks. I think a few more days in bed, and she shall be as right as rain.'

'Oh,' Liam said dazedly, swaying slightly as exhaustion, physical and mental, crashed upon him suddenly. A thousand emotions and thoughts were running through him, making him dizzy. But he could neither voice, nor understand any of them.

Thank God.

'Thank you, Dr Sims.'

'Of course, my lord. Now, I suggest you get some rest yourself.'

'Yes, I think you're right.' Liam nodded. 'Thomas shall see to your fee.'

They shook hands, and the doctor disappeared upstairs.

Liam sighed, and leaned back against the wall.

Rebecca will be fine. She is safe now.

She was awake. He wanted to go to her, to see for himself, perhaps even see her smile, herself again.

You really are tired...

A woman in his life had been in danger. And he'd wanted with his entire being to save her, where he had failed to save others. But admitting there was anything else to that need would only bring trouble. He had to resume his position as master, before it was too late. It seemed callous. And it hurt him—physically pained him—to leave the servants' quarters then, and return to his own. Filled him with regret to pass on Rebecca's care to Thomas and Lizzie, to leave her in the hands of others.

Nonetheless, he did just that.

For he knew that if he did not, he would soon be the one in danger.

Chapter Thirteen

Liam's resolution to keep away from Rebecca's bedside lasted the rest of that day. The following morning, after pacing his study for an hour, staring aimlessly at his work for another, and wandering the house for two, he finally relented, grabbed a selection of books from the library and made his way downstairs.

Chin high, he ignored the disapproving stares of his staff, as well as Mrs Murray's rather pointed use of the cleaver on a joint of beef as he passed, and went straight for Rebecca's quarters. He let himself into her office, but hesitated before the door to her bedroom.

Deciding he would only eventually return at some point later in the day, having wasted countless more hours pretending to work, he knocked on the door.

'Come in,' came her voice, fainter than usual, but a welcome sound. 'Oh, my lord.'

Liam felt his heart soar for the tiniest moment when he saw her there, propped up against the headboard, a smile on her face, and a healthy glow in her cheeks. Though he could tell she was weakened, she seemed well on the path to recovery.

'Good morning, Miss Merrickson,' he said once he'd

closed the door again. 'Welcome back to the land of the living.'

'I… Th-thank you, my lord,' she stammered, and Liam might have sworn she blushed slightly. Perhaps to hide just that, she set about rearranging her dressing gown and blankets. 'To what do I owe such a visit?'

'I thought you might be in need of some *divertissement*,' he said after a moment, with the faint impression of a smile. The realisation that she remembered nothing of what he'd done was both a relief and also, deep down, something of a disappointment. 'I brought a selection of books for you.'

'Thank you, that is very kind. However, I fear as much as I wish to, my mind is still not at its best. I'm not sure I will make any sense of whatever you've brought me.'

'I have for you today some Austen, as well as *The Antiquary*—and, more for your amusement than anything else, *Nightmare Abbey*,' Liam said, staring at the books' spines. He caught a smile and the beginnings of a laugh out of the corner of his eye and grinned. 'Perhaps later. I shall leave them here for you.'

Liam was acutely aware of her eyes following him as he went to place the books on her bedside table, though he tried his best not to think about them.

Or her.

Or how he wanted nothing more than to stay in this room.

'Thank you, my lord,' she said softly.

It was then that Liam made the mistake of looking at her again. Sure enough, she was staring up at him, those dark brown eyes of hers soft and inviting. Despite the toll the illness had taken, she glowed, as though she had been reborn from the trial and returned to him, renewed.

Returned to me. What a preposterous notion.

'Well, I should leave you, then, Miss Merrickson,' he said abruptly, turning back towards the door.

Halfway there, he stopped again and sighed. Why was he making this such an ordeal? Were they not friends? Could he not offer her comfort and company as she had?

'Unless, that is, well, if you cannot read... That is, shall I read to you for a while?'

Turning back, Liam found Rebecca wearing an unreadable expression, halfway between consternation and curiosity.

She cocked her head, studying him for a long moment, before a smile broke. 'You are not busy, then? Or perhaps you are using me as an excuse to get away?'

'And if I am?'

'I do enjoy Walter Scott...'

'*The Antiquary* it is, then,' Liam said, unable to stop grinning as he sat himself in the chair beside her again, and opened her selected book.

They sat there all day together.

Trays of food were brought in and out, Rebecca drifted off to sleep now and then, and Liam occasionally took to reading whilst walking about.

But nothing truly interrupted them as they lost themselves to the words, letting themselves drift together into another world, for a little while, at least.

Night fell, the candles burned to nearly nothing, and Rebecca fell fast asleep to the sound of Liam's voice.

He watched her for a moment, watched the rise and fall of her breast, the peace in her face, and the way the shadows danced around her with the flicker of the dying candlelight. He felt the pull he had that first time—a pull which seemed even stronger now.

He told himself he should not return again. And yet,

even as he blew out the candles and made his way from her rooms, he knew that tomorrow he would return. And the day after. Until she was fully herself again. For he could not resist the temptation, the lure of her company.

For a short while he could bend the rules. So he would, and damn the consequences.

Liam did return the following day, and the day after. He continued to read to Rebecca, as though they'd agreed that this was how she would pass the time recovering, with him.

The others might have had something to say, if Liam hadn't given them a look to warn that he would broach no comment on the matter.

It was all kinds of improper. Everything about their living situation, about Thornhallow in general, was improper and should be frowned upon. But Liam was well past caring. Any reason he might still have had, disappeared with Rebecca's illness.

But the respite would not—*could* not—last forever; that much was clear.

They both knew, as he finished *Northanger Abbey*, that their time was at its end.

'May I ask,' Liam said, his lip curling faintly upwards as he leaned back in the chair, the final volume safely stowed in his pocket. 'Well, that is, you see, when I was… When you were…' Liam's eyes roamed across her body as he searched for the words to describe what he referred to in a gentlemanly manner. 'I may have glimpsed some of your…'

'Tattoos, my lord,' Rebecca said firmly. 'I have no shame in calling them thus.'

There was no judgement in his eyes, she noted then.

Only curiosity and, most frightening of all, warm complicity.

She could not resist, and somewhere deep down, she wanted him to know. As much as she longed to know him, she also wanted him to know and understand *her*. Fully. To understand everything she was, for then she could be very certain indeed that he would never be tempted by the familiarity which had grown between them again.

For men like him, innocence was everything when payment was not involved.

'Yes, quite. And why, I wonder, Miss Merrickson, do you have them?'

'When they are sinful, and naught but for sailors and scum? It's all right,' she reassured him when he winced. 'They are memories, things I did not wish to forget. Some ladies have diaries; I am quite incapable of keeping one, so...'

'So you have those instead? Quite an alternative... Did they hurt?' he asked suddenly.

'A little. One gets used to it, I suppose.'

'Interesting... And...'

'You may ask,' she said softly when he stopped himself. 'I will not be offended.'

'Well, were you never concerned that...well, that is, that a man, a suitor, perhaps...'

Rebecca chuckled again, enjoying his discomfort.

Liam's cheeks reddened. 'I know you've said that, well, that you hadn't considered it, but... Oh, forgive me, I really do go too far.'

'You know so many of my secrets already, what is one more?'

Liam bowed his head slightly.

'Even before I was forced to run, I never imagined...

marriage, settling down with a good and proper husband, as part of my future.'

She couldn't quite remember what she *had* imagined, only that there was adventure.

Shaking her head, Rebecca continued. 'But when I left home, my future was cemented. And I had made no vow of celibacy.'

Rebecca watched his expression darken as he grasped her meaning.

There it is...the realisation...

'The truth is, the first time I took a man to bed...I did it so that if my prince ever found me, I would not be... You understand. I wanted to reclaim my own body. So it was with the tattoos, I suppose. And, as it happens, I enjoyed myself. Over the years I found solace, and pleasure, in the arms of men—discreetly. None were offended by my tattoos, nor my lack of virtue. But then, I asked for nothing more than an evening or two. I only... I wanted to feel less alone,' she admitted quietly, before she could prevent her tongue running away with her.

She felt as though if anyone could ever understand, it might be him.

'I could make no friends, never get close to anyone, be part of a family again, save in that way. For one small moment in time, I had a measure of closeness.'

'And your heart was safe,' Liam said flatly.

She looked up, ready to see admonishment in his eyes, but instead she found understanding yet again.

He sighed, flashing the briefest and most wan smile she'd ever seen, and nodded. 'You know even before it begins how it will end. You owe nothing, you are owed nothing. You can pass through life as though not even a part of it.'

'Yes.'

It should have hurt her, those words, that vicious and cold truth laid bare, a truth she'd known somewhere in the depths of her heart but always refused to recognise. Only, it didn't. It made her feel…

Less alone. But then, here, with him, with the others, you never feel alone anymore.

'Why do you call him your prince? The man…'

'I don't know.' Rebecca frowned. 'I suppose… It takes some of the fear away. Takes his power away. For if he is only a prince in a fairy story…'

'What harm could he do you?'

Rebecca nodded.

'You truly are a spectacularly unconventional woman, Miss Merrickson,' Liam said.

'And it is getting spectacularly late, my lord,' she replied huskily after a moment.

His eyes seemed only to hold admiration as they remained affixed to her own.

And light, a magnetic light…

Which threatened to thoroughly undo her should he gaze at her like that any longer.

'I have talked quite enough of myself, and I think perhaps you wish to retire.'

'Indeed. You are not yet fully recovered,' he conceded, rising, a sad smile lingering at the corners of his lips. 'I have interrogated you enough for one evening. I shall let you rest.'

'I think perhaps, my lord, you should not trouble yourself so much. I am feeling much better, and I think it shall not be long before I'm back on my feet again.'

'Indeed.' Liam nodded, as acutely aware as she was of the danger more time together might bring. 'Goodnight, Miss Merrickson.'

'Goodnight, my lord.'

Liam bowed and left, though his scent—indeed his very presence—lingered in her room, just as the man lingered in her mind, despite all her attempts to rid herself of him.

For, try as she might, she could not. She had hoped at least to lessen his opinion of her, to force him to leave her be, in peace. That was why she'd told him all the sordid details of her life, wasn't it? To discourage his attentions? Why should she even have to? There was nothing *to* his attentions. He was being attentive, caring, because she was his responsibility. A good master takes care of his servants. True, he had been more *involved* than most—than any, really—but then... He knew of such things because of his life in those wilds. And the house was isolated, so who else could tend to her?

Literally anyone...

No. The others had their duties, so he was simply being considerate to everyone by tending to her himself. By reading to her for hours, and soothing her fever with cool cloths, and... By looking at her with those eyes...

Instead of pushing him away, it felt as if he'd drawn closer. Not only had he not found her truths repellent, but he seemed to understand her.

No.

He had saved her life. And she was grateful. And he was undeniably an attractive man. So, these tender feelings were normal. They had been forced together too closely, and she owed him her life.

It would all be right again when everything returned to normal.

Chapter Fourteen

'You have recovered, then?' Liam asked as Rebecca laid down a tray of coffee on his desk.

Apart from the New Year, when they had all gathered in the hall to hear the chiming of midnight, and raise a glass of sweet wine, she hadn't been allowed from her rooms. Even then, she'd had Gregory, Sam or Tim at her arm every second of those blessed twenty minutes of freedom.

Today, despite everyone's protestations and cooing, she had insisted she was more than fit enough to return to work. If she was honest with herself, she also wanted to prove that regardless of whatever fancy had come over her during her illness, she could still face Liam without feeling anything...*untoward.*

'And have wasted no time returning to work.'

'Yes,' Rebecca said, rather more breathlessly than she could have hoped for.

But something in his offhand tone and his proximity as she set down the tray...

Drat the man.

'I also wish to ask,' she began tentatively. Apparently she was *not* fully herself yet. 'Well, that is, as the staff missed the chance to celebrate Christmas properly, because of me, I thought perhaps, as Twelfth Night is in two days, you might allow us to have a belated sort of Christmas. Mrs Murray still has all the food in the icehouse and the larder—'

'Fine.'

'Thank you, my lord.' She smiled, intent on not taking his gruffness to heart. Not that he saw the smile regardless, staring down at his papers as he was. 'And I…I've not had the opportunity to thank you properly, my lord. Not only for, well, for coming for me, but also…'

Lord, why is this so difficult? Rebecca sighed, focusing on a nick in the polish on the edge of the desk. She would need to see to that.

'But also for caring for me as you did. I may have seemed unaware, but I was not.'

'Indeed, you make too much of it, Miss Merrickson,' he said dismissively.

'I know of no other, my lord, who would've spent such time, nor gone to such lengths tending to their housekeeper,' Rebecca retorted, finally finding the courage to raise her eyes.

He was no longer looking at his work, and she sorely wished he were.

'Yes, well,' Liam said after a moment, clearing his throat as though to hide what looked to Rebecca like a wince. 'Perhaps, Miss Merrickson, such ministrations might not have been necessary had you not acted so recklessly.'

'I…I am sorry for any trouble—'

'Trouble,' he spat, rising precipitately from his chair, and pacing at the window like a caged animal. 'Miss Merrickson, what the Devil were you thinking, running out in a snowstorm like that?'

'I… That is, Mrs F-Ffoulkes,' Rebecca stammered,

completely taken aback by his sudden agitation. 'She needed to be looked after, and I thought I would make it—'

'Did you think I would not look after Mrs Ffoulkes?' he barked, rounding back, with a wild look in his eyes that set her even more on edge.

'Indeed, my lord, but I—'

'Did you think at all, Miss Merrickson?' he continued, as though she'd not said a word, making for her abruptly.

Rebecca took a step back, but he continued his advance.

'Did you think at all of what consequences your actions might have on others? Of what might've happened to you?' Liam asked fiercely, prowling towards her until she was backed against a bookshelf, and he'd yet again cornered her. 'Did you think at all of the concern others might have for you? Did you think at all, I wonder, Miss Merrickson, of what would've become of me had you been taken from this world?'

Rebecca blinked, her heart pounding, blood rushing in her ears so loudly that her mind struggled to hear the words, to make sense of them.

Frowning, she stared into those tempestuous eyes, trying to find the meaning of his words, of his entire manner at this particular moment. But what she found there seemed to be genuine hurt. Had she imagined the slight crack in his voice at that final question? Was she imagining his laboured breathing now? The pleading in his eyes that reminded her far too much of a wounded animal begging for mercy?

She opened her mouth to speak, but found her voice yet again absent, and instead swallowed loudly.

His eyes searched hers, asking a thousand unspoken questions.

'No, Miss Merrickson,' he breathed, with a sadness that pulled at her heart. It seemed as though his search for answers had yielded none. 'I think, in fact, you thought of nothing before you so carelessly risked your life.'

Only then did Rebecca fully realise how incredibly close he was. She hadn't so much heard the words as felt his breath against her cheek, soft as a caress, and yet cold enough to freeze her blood.

So close.

Close enough that she could see every detail, from the tiny flecks of grey in the stubble of his beard, to the flicker of his lashes.

So close.

His warmth and his scent were enveloping her, trapping them both in some strange sort of bubble, removed from the rest of the world.

As though...

Almost as though he meant to kiss her.

Nonsense. Impossible.

And yet...there was something else in his eyes now.

Heat.

The shimmering gold flecks had melted, become pools of glistening, molten liquid. Rebecca felt her breath catch as she watched his eyes roam across her face down to her lips. Watched the question form behind his eyes in the almost imperceptible twitch of his eyebrow.

And if he did? Rebecca would not stop him. She would welcome it. Though every bone in her body told her it would be wrong, and bring only agony, she would welcome it a thousand times over.

But it never came.

Only coldness as Liam turned away, almost flying back to the window, hands firmly clasped behind his back, once again the master.

'Good day, Miss Merrickson,' he said dispassionately.

'Good day, my lord,' she breathed, her voice cracking with the feeling of utter loss that swept over her.

Rebecca bolted from the study, stumbled down the corridor, and out into the garden through the conservatory. She breathed in deep, welcoming the daggers of cold, frosty air into her lungs. She welcomed the nip at her nose and ears, and the shiver which ran through her, unclouding her mind.

No matter how whatever had just happened came to pass, what mattered was that it must never happen again. That way lay only destruction. Broken lives and broken hearts—neither of which Rebecca could afford. Temporary insanity, weakness of the flesh, exceptional circumstances—whatever it might have been, there was no use trying to make sense of it.

Whatever closeness she had allowed thus far, must cease. Things would return to the way they were meant to be. Master. Servant. Invisibility. Speak only when spoken to. Nothing had happened, therefore returning to normality would not be a problem.

Wouldn't it?

For she had promised herself just that before, and failed miserably.

Liam stared out the window, seeing none of the wintry landscape. All he saw was Rebecca, the image of her as she'd been in those fateful seconds before he'd turned away. It had taken every ounce of willpower he had to do so, to turn away from those eyes gazing up into his own, filled with the same heat which had risen from the very depths of his soul.

So close he'd been to crossing that final line, to giving in to his now undeniable need to touch, to kiss, to possess. She would not have stopped him. He'd seen surrender in those fathomless inviting eyes, and it had nearly been his undoing. *Their* undoing.

How had he let things go so far? Desire, lust, need... These were not things he'd never felt before in his life. These were not feelings he was unable to conquer—though admittedly he was used to conquering them by surrendering. But when that had not been possible? He had walked away. Closed his mind to the possibility. Distracted himself.

Was the problem simply that he could not walk away? That he could not be rid of her? He should have dismissed her when he'd had the chance. But even then...

Even now. He *could* walk away. She was his servant, she belonged below stairs, out of his realm, out of his reach—and yet every time she retreated there, he found ways to seek her out. He enjoyed her company. She brought him comfort, and was a witty, intelligent conversationalist. So he'd indulged in what he'd thought to be a harmless relationship.

Friends...

Only, he'd been lying to himself. It had never been harmless, or meaningless, or trivial. Nothing about the damned woman was.

Contradictions.

That was what he'd seen from the first, what had attracted him. There was danger in indulging himself, in getting to know her better. He'd known *that* very well from the start. Why else had he been so intent on pushing her away? But he'd seen too much, and she...had seen too much. Of him. Pieces he'd never shown to another soul, he had shown her, and she'd not turned away.

The woman had wormed herself into his very being; he knew that now. He'd known it the night he'd gone after her. He'd known then that her loss would leave in him another void impossible to fill. Break him in ways that could never be repaired. But just because he'd grown attached, it did not mean he should give in to his baser instincts.

He could have her body; he knew that now, too. Or, he could have *her*. He could not have both. That thought had been the only thing to pull him back from the edge, to force him to wrench himself from the nearness of her, her intoxicating scent, the welcoming heat of her body. The thought that surrendering to his animality would mean jeopardising everything else. She would not risk dishonour, or discovery, or shame. Their relationship as master and servant would be broken. She would leave him.

And so, even as his body had screamed out in pain, as though he had torn flesh from flesh, he had stepped away. He would not lose her. He had sworn that in the snow. So he would keep his distance. They would return to the way things had been—or at least should have been.

Master. Servant. Two separate worlds.

Thus resolved, Liam returned to his work, which was more than sufficient to keep him occupied, distracted and far from temptation. He had returned to set things to rights, not to worsen the situation and that of those who depended on him. He'd returned to free himself and so he would. Of everything.

Including her.

Chapter Fifteen

'I will take up His Lordship's tray,' Rebecca said, before anyone else could claim the task.

Nothing else fuelled her but the need to ensure he was well. Despite whatever else had happened between them in that study—*again*—he'd held true to his word and given the staff half the day today, Twelfth Night, as well as Epiphany, ordering them to *'pretend it is Christmas'*. She felt keenly the fact that he would spend the time alone, whilst below stairs such merriment would be had.

'I'll only be a moment, so everyone can get settled.'

'All right, then,' Mrs Murray said, sliding the tray over. 'Mind you, be sharpish—won't have dinner getting cold. Thank the master for us.'

Rebecca nodded, and was unceremoniously shooed from the kitchens.

As she made her way upstairs, surrounded by the taunting smells of turkey, pies, roast vegetables, cinnamon and spice, she could hear a flurry of activity behind her. Delighted shouts and laughs as everyone readied themselves for dinner.

Picturing them all, dressed in their Sunday best as they were—even Sam had asked Gregory to assist with the tying of his fresh white cravat—scurrying about like excited children, Rebecca smiled to herself. She hadn't been able to *stop* smiling recently.

Earlier, as she'd donned the elegant wine-coloured silk confection one of her previous employers had gifted her, worn and out of fashion though it may be, as she'd woven the gold ribbon—the only adornment she possessed—into her braids and fashioned them into a crown, she'd caught herself smiling into the mirror like a fool.

Making her way to the library, where Liam had asked for his meal to be brought, Rebecca found her smile fading, and concern for him growing. He, too, had missed out on Christmas, and when they'd spoken of the arrangements, what seemed a lifetime ago now, he'd seemed almost... excited. But since her illness, something had changed; *he* had changed. And though he would've spent Christmas on his own in any case, for him to be alone tonight... It somehow felt *wrong*.

Grabbing a sprig of holly from one of the arrangements, she set it on the otherwise sad-looking tray, and knocked on the library door.

'Come in,' Liam called. 'Ah, Miss Merrickson.'

'I come bearing your dinner, my lord,' she said, setting it down on the small table by the chair he was currently slouched in, nursing a whisky. She tried not to notice how very dashing he looked in his fine evening dress, nor how very sad it was that he'd donned it. 'Is there anything else I can do for you?'

'No, that's all I need, thank you,' he said, his eyes sweeping over her from head to toe, making her feel as though the silk was utterly transparent.

Appreciation and a wistful sort of longing mingled in his eyes, as though he'd never known her till now, nor ever would again.

'The colour suits you,' he said finally, turning his attention back to the flames, which seemed to always possess the answers to his unasked questions. 'I'm sure everyone is waiting for you. Enjoy the celebration, Miss Merrickson. A belated Happy Christmas to you all.'

'Thank you, my lord. Happy Christmas to you,' she said, wishing yet again that she had it in her power to make this day a happy one for him, in some small way at least.

But you cannot.

'Someone will collect the tray later. There shouldn't be any wassailers. I've been advised there haven't been these past years.'

'No, there wouldn't be,' Liam said as she made for the door with a curtsey. 'And I will see to the tray. You should all enjoy yourselves.'

'As you wish, my lord.'

With one last glance at the melancholy figure of the Earl of Thornhallow, Rebecca made her way back downstairs to the others.

This is how it must be. This is how the world is. Nothing to be done. Though if I had one wish for today, Lord, it would be that there be no sadness in this house. If only for a little while...

If Rebecca had thought Mrs Murray an exceptional cook before, she was astounded to find that the woman had quite outdone herself with the feast she'd prepared tonight. Every single detail had been seen to with care, and every dish was more delectable than the last, worthy of a king's table. By the time they arrived at dessert, everyone was already moaning, having eaten far too much.

Whilst they indulged in pudding, gin and pies—with Tim being made King when he found the pea in the Twelfth Cake, whilst Betsy became his queen—they all exchanged the small trifles they had got for each other weeks ago.

Rebecca received some paper flowers, a new knitted scarf, some ribbons, and a little tin thistle brooch from Mr Brown. Then, they moved on to the games—charades, Up Jenkins and Throwing the Smile—whilst they all continued to pick at the food and drink which seemed enough to feed an army.

Before long Tim took out his fiddle, and they alternately sang carols and folk songs, increasingly bawdy as they went. It was during one such vivacious rendition of a local tune that Tim stopped abruptly, his eyes widening like saucers.

Gregory, Sam and Thomas were next, their eyes travelling to the same spot, widening when they saw whatever was there.

'What the blazes is wrong with you lot, then?' Mrs Murray tutted, turning to witness whatever it was that had rendered them silent. 'Oh, my...' The rest of her words were swallowed by the shock.

Rebecca and the others on her side of the table turned, and she realised what had brought them all to silence.

It seems my little prayer has been answered...

Liam stood at the door to the servants' hall, wringing his hands. Not even his immaculate evening dress could counter the boyishly hesitant, unsure and pleading air about him.

The men suddenly came to and scrambled to their feet, and Rebecca might have sworn Liam blushed slightly as he waved them back to their seats.

'Please, everyone, I didn't mean to interrupt your festivities, nor indeed to disturb you all,' he said. 'Quite the contrary, I only... That is...'

His words trailed off and he bowed his head, as though cursing himself.

Rebecca turned back to the others, silently pleading.

They all looked between themselves, hesitant, and wary.

It was not unheard of for masters to fraternise occasionally with their staff—particularly at village fetes and the like—but here, now…for the Earl to wish for their company…

And yet, even though it meant awkwardness, and a touch of censure, none of them could refuse. For it was, after all, Christmas—*somewhat*—and they all held him in their hearts.

Thomas turned to Rebecca and nodded solemnly. She smiled and turned back to Liam, who had taken to raking his hair as he searched for words, unaware of the silent conversation between his employees.

'You are more than welcome, my lord,' she said softly. He looked up at her then, with such gratitude she felt her heart melt. 'Gregory, a chair for His Lordship.'

'And a drink mayhap, my lord,' Gregory said, jumping to do as he was bid. 'We've a nice sloe gin—'tis Hardy that makes it.'

'If it is Hardy's then I must try it,' Liam said graciously, taking his seat. 'Though I imagine I should be wary. I remember the last time I tried his concoctions I woke in the middle of the moors.'

Everyone laughed in unison, relaxing as they all returned to their places.

Rebecca chanced a glance at him across the table, and was rewarded with a gracious smile and a nod of thanks. The sincerity in his eyes, mingling with the extraordinary light she'd come to know too well, sent her stomach fluttering, and she quickly turned her attention back to Lizzie, who was currently trying to engage her in talk about the Hardys.

As they all settled back into their conversations, passing around the bottle of gin, helping themselves to pies and sweetmeats, Liam watched them, letting the warmth and joy of their company wash over him. He watched as they laughed and teased, talked and played, and for the first time, felt as though he was surrounded by family. He watched the woman across from him, engaged with everyone around her, tying them all together in a perfect harmony he knew had not been there before.

Liam realised then the extent to which she had managed to bring life back into the house. The extent to which she'd brought life back to him.

And though he did not realise it quite yet, in truth, it was at that very moment, when she burst out laughing at something Tim said, eyes afire in the candlelight, her auburn hair a flaming crown, that Liam fell completely in love with the housekeeper of Thornhallow Hall.

'May I?' Liam asked some time later, waving to the chair beside Rebecca.

Everyone had broken into little parties of conversation as they enjoyed the musical entertainment. Rebecca had been left alone—not that she minded.

'I do not wish to intrude.'

'Of course, my lord.' She smiled, careful to turn her attention quickly back to Tim.

Liam sat with a weary sigh, extending his legs out before him. His eyes may also have been on Tim and Gregory, as they finished their joyful ditty, but his attention was solely on her. She felt it, as though everything in his being was reaching out to hers. A strange energy had come between them, linked them, and refused to be broken, despite her best efforts.

'Are you enjoying yourself, then, my lord?' she whispered, intent on refusing the lure of gazing into his eyes, or giving in to whatever folly these feelings were in any way. 'Downstairs celebrations are more lively than those upstairs, I think.'

'From my experience, yes, that is certainly true,' he whispered conspiratorially. 'But it has been many years indeed since I've lived the life of an upstairs gentleman. This feels much more…comfortable. Familiar. So, yes, I am enjoying myself. And you, Mrs Hardwicke?'

'Yes, my lord,' she breathed sadly, that name foreign and cutting now.

Fifteen years she'd borne it; it had been hers, and yet now she despised it. Despised him saying it. She longed to be called Miss Merrickson. She longed to be called Rebecca again, to hear him—

God, what is wrong with me? she chided herself abruptly, trying to focus on the music.

The music. That's it.

The food, the drink, the atmosphere… It was intoxicating. Clouding her judgement and her mind. He was being kind, and friendly, and she…was once again making mountains out of nothing and letting her feelings run away with her. It meant nothing that he was here, now, with them.

Rebecca drew a deep breath, and focused again on Tim's fiddling. Only then, she realised the tune had changed, and that Gregory had returned to his seat. Lizzie stood beside Tim now, breathtaking and haunting as she sang the 'Coventry Carol'.

Rebecca felt the harsh sting of tears at the back of her eyes, but found she could not move to wipe them away. She could not wrench herself from the scene before her, the melody permeating every fibre of her being, resonating chords within her she had long forgotten existed. The purity, the beauty, filled her heart to the brim and stole her breath. And then, when she thought it might be impossible to feel anything more, she felt the faintest of touches against the little finger of her right hand.

Him.

Liam.

His own little finger almost imperceptibly there, against hers, their hands linked by the slightest of touches. Had anyone looked over, they wouldn't have seen it, seen the connection, and yet to Rebecca it felt as though his entire body had wrapped itself with hers, as though they'd joined together in some pagan, magical, forgotten way.

She knew she should move, tear herself away, and yet she couldn't. She didn't understand it, and she did not want to. She only wanted to feel it, to feel *him*. To believe for the smallest of moments that he was hers, and she his, in a world beyond this one. For that moment they lived together, beyond time, beyond convention, beyond rules, somewhere only the other existed. Where their heartbeats kept in time with the music as one.

Sorrow, and a profound feeling of loss mixed with the elation she'd felt moments before, for she knew well that the magic could not, and would not last. That soon it would be stolen, and then she would spend years trying to understand it, without hope of ever doing so.

Lizzie finished the carol and was met by an enthusiastic round of applause. All at once the connection shattered; the moment faded into something of a distant memory.

Had it really happened at all?

Rebecca decided that it hadn't. Coming back sharply to the room, she rose and excused herself.

When she returned minutes later, mostly herself again, she was glad to discover that Tim had returned to more spirited, lively tunes. Before long the table and chairs were pushed to the corners of the hall and everyone was on their feet dancing.

Rebecca avoided Liam; and he her. Though that prevented neither of them from enjoying the rest of the night as much as any of the others.

It was close to midnight when the drinks stopped flowing, the music died, and everyone began wandering off to bed, feet sore and hearts full. They left Mrs Murray sleeping in her chair by the fire. No one really had it in them to rouse her, and besides, it would be neither the first nor the last time she slept there.

Soon all that was left in the servants' hall were the remnants of the evening's festivities, and a snoring cook.

Half an hour later, Rebecca was certain she was the only one in Thornhallow still awake. She had volunteered to close the house for the night, acutely aware that sleep would not be easy to come by. Some quiet time alone, and the ritual of locking up, might help her find some normality and peace of mind again.

It wasn't only that which had passed with Liam—that which she remained intent on convincing herself hadn't happened at all—it was all the rest that was troubling her. The whole day, indeed everything about her life at Thornhallow. Over the years, she'd lived in many homes, met many different people, shared many celebrations, but somehow it all felt so different here.

Unique. Rare.

She hadn't spent such a wonderful time, felt loved and cherished, and part of a family, in, well…twenty years. Nearly her entire life. Her father had tried so hard to give her that, and he *had*, but when he'd been taken… Well, everything had changed. Over the years she had purposefully and instinctively kept her distance from those she served and worked with. Even from those she took to bed.

Liam had been right about that. She'd passed through

life alone in a sea full of people. Always knowing she would leave, that she need only rely on herself, had helped keep her safe in more ways than one.

Rebecca sighed heavily as she checked the door and window latches in the dining room, and closed the curtains on the moonlit frozen landscape. She'd done well convincing herself that the life she lived, that she'd built, was enough. Coming here… She'd realised just how wrong she had been. Thornhallow felt like home.

Familiar. Safe.

And everyone here, despite difficult beginnings, had become like family. Perhaps it was the circumstances, the lack of constraints of a normal household, which made it easier to grow close. Whatever it was, they'd all managed to insinuate themselves into her heart, and Rebecca dreaded even more now the day that would take her from Thornhallow.

But you know full well the day will come, Rebecca… He will never stop hunting you.

Pulling the curtains in Liam's study closed with more vehemence than she meant to, she knew that no matter how she wished it otherwise, she would have to resign herself to the fact that she would leave Thornhallow. No matter how delightful, how wonderful today had been, in the coming weeks she would need to take care to regain some distance from, well, everything.

Yes. You know the rules Rebecca. Chin up, she thought, pushing open the door to the library with purpose and confidence.

'Devil, Miss Merrickson, are you trying to frighten me to death?' Liam exclaimed from the other side of the room, jumping nearly as high as Rebecca. 'Whatever did that door do to you?'

'Apologies, my lord,' Rebecca said, trying to calm herself. 'I thought everyone in bed.'

'So you decided to come lurking in the library again?'

'No, that is, I wasn't tired, so I told Mr Brown I would see to closing the house.'

A tense, thick silence took over the room as they awkwardly stood there, staring at each other. Liam seemed as awake and yet as tired as she felt, and though it hadn't even been an hour since she'd last seen him, seeing him now, standing there in his rolled shirtsleeves and waistcoat, lit only by the fire, Rebecca felt her heart skip a beat.

He must have noted her gaze; the next moment he was unrolling his sleeves and slipping his jacket on.

'I should retire,' he said, downing the rest of his drink. 'It is late. Please, don't let me prevent you from finishing your rounds.'

'Thank you, my lord,' Rebecca said with a nod, moving to do just that.

She checked the latches, closed the curtains and glanced quickly at the fire, before finding herself retreating from the library in unison with him.

'Goodnight, then, my lord,' she said, as lightly as she could manage.

'Goodnight, Miss Merrickson.'

With a smile, Rebecca turned away and made for the drawing room. She heard his footsteps across the tiles, and then on the stairs, and they seemed the saddest sound she'd ever heard.

Shaking her head, she cursed herself yet again for her foolishness.

'Wait,' Liam said sharply.

Rebecca turned, shooting him an enquiring look.

He stood halfway up the staircase, with the strangest expression on his face. Rebecca cocked her head, and he nodded to something above her. Glancing up, she spotted the branch of mistletoe above the door.

An ambivalent mix of feelings washed over her as she realised what he meant to do. She could laugh it off, move away, break the moment, and she could do so easily enough, for he was still on the stairs, waiting for her to make the final decision. She could do it—refuse, walk away, force them to continue as they had these past weeks, save them from themselves. She could do all that, if only she could will her body to do so.

Instead, she stood there, rooted to the spot, her feet unwilling to comply with her rational mind. Her eyes found him again, and as soon as they did he nodded, almost imperceptibly, and descended the stairs. Slowly, he made his way to her, and in those precious seconds Rebecca decided that she was not being foolish at all. That she would allow herself this one tiny, brief moment in time, to imagine, and to dream. She would offer her cheek and revel in his closeness, in the lightest of touches, and then they could return to reality. To life as it should be.

Yes. It is Twelfth Night, after all.

Rebecca smiled, concentrating on controlling her shallow breathing and rapid heartbeat. This was nothing. Tradition. It would be a swift, chaste kiss on the cheek, not some monumental event. How many other friends across time had met thus and survived, unchanged and unharmed? The world had not come off its axis before for such kisses—why should it today?

She quietly ignored the impact the slightest of touches of his hand had on her not hours ago.

Liam stood before her now, the makings of a smile at the corners of his lips, and his golden eyes twinkling in the fading firelight of the candles around them. Rebecca turned her face slightly, offering her cheek, only to feel not his lips upon it, but the back of his knuckles as he gently brushed against her skin, asking her to turn back to him.

What could she do but obey? How could she resist so sweet an entreaty, so delicate a command?

But she should have, she knew, as soon as their eyes met again. There was resignation and determination behind the warmth and excitement. Rebecca's heart nearly broke with the realisation that she had just allowed them to jump over a precipice, and with a sigh, she rose to meet him.

All at once their lips had joined, his hand had found its way to the back of her head, and her own clung to his lapels. It could have ended there; *she* could have ended it there. His kiss was slow, and sweet, and gentle, not tentative, but *kind*. Chaste enough that she could have pulled away. But she might sooner have ripped her heart from her chest. She could not part from such sweetness, such delicacy—she could only savour it, enjoy it for as long as it might last.

She should have stopped it. Before, almost in unison, they opened themselves further to each other. Before the kiss deepened with their exploration of each other's mouths. Before their tongues entwined and raw heat and pleasure coursed through her body. Before her soul was warmed by his touch. Before she was lost again with him in their place beyond time, beyond reality, where only they existed. Before they molded together, their mouths moving in such divine unison it was impossible to say where one ended and the other began. Before his arms were around her, and hers around him, and their chests pressed together, wound up in each other's heat, their bodies sharing both breath and heartbeat.

Rebecca had experienced many different kisses in her life, but none like this. None so deep, so raw, so full of passion and tenderness it threatened to tear her heart in two should it stop, should she be taken from this other being who had become part of her. None that threatened to sweep her feet from beneath her, threatened to make her forget who she was. None which promised so much more should they forget themselves.

For behind the lingering, slow exploration, behind the savouring, the testing, the teasing, the offering, lay an even hotter passion which, should they unleash it, would consume them both.

It was only dread of that, fear of what might happen should she let go completely, that pulled Rebecca back from the edge. With a breath, and a slight push against his chest, she broke the kiss. Taking a step back, she dared not even look at him, preferring instead the hall tiles.

Still, she could taste him, could feel him around her as though she were still enveloped in his embrace.

'I think perhaps, my lord,' she whispered sadly, 'you should not have done that.'

'Yes, Miss Merrickson,' he groaned. 'I think on this occasion, you are right.'

'Goodnight, my lord.'

'Goodnight, Miss Merrickson.'

Rebecca's eyes did not leave the floor until she'd heard his footsteps traverse the hall and climb the stairs.

Not until she had heard the distant echo of Liam's door closing did she raise her head, tears pricking at the back of her eyes, feeling utterly bereft and lost. Pushing away everything that had just happened, Rebecca finished seeing to her duties.

An hour later, however, safely ensconced in her bed, she finally allowed herself to cry the tears which had threatened to fall since she and Liam had parted.

For everything was always better once one had cried.

Chapter Sixteen

Thomas's rather loud and abrupt opening of the curtains, along with the outpouring of stark, bright winter morning light, woke Liam with a start. He blinked, the sun's rays piercing through the foggy mist of his still half-asleep mind.

He'd barely slept. Most of the night he'd spent tossing and turning, the events of the previous evening repeating themselves in an endless loop. Not until the sun had begun its ascent had he finally managed to drift off into a dreamless, restless sleep.

He wondered grimly if someone else in this house had spent such a wretched night.

'Good morning, my lord,' the old butler said, somewhat too cheerfully for Liam's taste. 'I trust you slept well?'

'Quite,' Liam lied, knowing that after yesterday's festivities nothing less would be expected. 'Thank you, Thomas. You enjoyed yourself?'

'Yes, my lord. And if I may say so,' Mr Brown said, lighting the newly laid fire, 'it was a delightful surprise to have you join us.'

'Thank you, Thomas.'

'Will you be having breakfast downstairs?' he asked, resuming his normal self. 'Or shall I have it sent up?'

'I will come down, I think, Thomas, but, please, no hurry. And I shall dress myself this morning. As I recall, I instructed you all to take the day...'

'Yes, my lord, as you wish.'

'Go.' Liam waved at him, sitting up in his bed, not quite ready to leave it entirely. 'I order you to find something to amuse yourself, Thomas.'

'Very well, my lord.'

'If you could, however, ask everyone to find me at some point this afternoon in my study? I have something for you all. A belated St Stephen's gift, as it were.'

'I shall tell them, my lord,' he said with a bow, heading for the door. 'A kind and sure to be much appreciated gesture, I'm sure.'

With that, he left Liam to his quiet, lazy solitude.

Liam wondered for a moment what indeed the old retainer would find to occupy his time. He'd come to the realisation, when trying to decide on everyone's gifts, that he did not in fact know much about Thomas. About who he was, beneath the mask of dutiful butler. A sad thought, considering he'd known the man his entire life.

Though he'd been brought up to be the master, prepared with every lesson, every moment, to be a proper lord, he'd never truly been able to reconcile himself to the notion. When he'd left for the New World and discovered a society without such expectations, when he had found a society where any man could rise, given he had the will...it had opened his eyes and he'd felt, for the first time, that he'd found a society in which he could live, and believe in. Where his blood did not thrust upon him a way of life he neither desired nor could defend. Where work and industriousness defined the man—not his title, nor his family.

Though his idyllic view of that society had been shattered as well, the precept of it remained nonetheless ingrained within his beliefs.

When he'd joined the staff for their celebrations last night, it had been in that spirit. The spirit of equality. When he'd shared their food and drink, danced with them, he'd felt at home. *That* felt right. It had convinced him that the course of action he'd set himself upon was the right one— that he would never be his father's son. Not that he'd ever wished to be. In fact, that was the very last thing he would ever wish for.

The sun's rays caught upon the crystal of the vase on the mantelpiece, sending rainbows of colour dancing across the wall before him.

Flowers...everywhere... Miss Merrickson and her obsession with flowers...

He smiled to himself. That simple gesture reminded him so much of his mother, and of Hal. They, too, had been intent on filling the house with colour and sweet fragrances. They, too, had sought not to cultivate hordes of exotic species, forcing blooms out of season, but to seek out those blossoms which nature provided at any given time. Uneven, wild and imperfect they may have been, but there had been inexplicable beauty in the simplicity and disorder of the arrangements they'd made. As there was in this one.

Liam's mind turned inevitably back to the events of the previous night. He wished he could feel as he should. Ashamed. A right cad. But he could not.

That kiss...

It had awoken something within him. *She* had awoken something within him. Despite his lack of sleep, he felt so *alive*. Last night his restlessness had not been due to worry, or fear, only excitement and...

Happiness. Elation.

When he thought back on the touch of her, the feel of her

beneath him, her scent swirling around him, her warmth seeping through him to the darkest, coldest corners of his being…it filled him with wonder. And pleasure. And joy.

There had been such purity, such unguarded gentleness in that kiss. She had opened herself to him, and he to her, in a way he'd never known before. He had found comfort and pleasure with women he'd encountered over the years. But with Rebecca… Everything had melted away as he'd folded himself into her, offering, receiving. And then…

She must have felt it, too; he knew it. He'd seen it in her eyes when she'd pulled away. The possibility beneath the simplicity. The passion, which, left unchecked, would consume them until nothing at all was left of who they were before. Had she not found the strength to move away, there was no doubt of what might have happened. What could have happened.

What could *still* happen.

What he desperately wanted to happen, had since the first moment.

'Was there anything else, my lord?' Rebecca asked that evening as she set down the master's coffee tray.

Though he'd been true to his word, and asked nothing of the staff all day, he had asked Lizzie to have some coffee brought up when she'd seen to him. Rebecca remained the only one who hadn't gone to him as requested, so she'd reluctantly volunteered herself to bring up the coffee.

'And Mr Brown bade me ask if you wished him to attend to you this evening?'

'Tell Thomas he is not to attend to me, he is to enjoy the rest of his day, as instructed. As for you, yes, there is something else,' Liam said with a wicked glint in his eyes as he reached into the top drawer of his desk. 'I have not forgotten you, though you've been intent on disobeying again, and have not come to collect your gift, as instructed.'

'I, that is, I was…'

Pretending to read. Gnawing at my fingernails. Reliving that damned kiss incessantly.

'Enjoying my day, as instructed.'

'Indeed,' he said, offering up a neatly wrapped box.

Rebecca gaped at him hesitantly, eyeing the box as though it might bite her. She'd hoped he might be sensible and decide that it was best, after the previous night's events, to forgo the tradition. It was with that hope that she'd steered clear of his study, despite his instructions.

Liam gestured for her to take it, looking increasingly embarrassed as the silence thickened between them.

'You need not have gone to the trouble,' she said, flustered, finally taking the box. 'But thank you, my lord.'

'My pleasure, I assure you, Miss Merrickson. And no trouble at all.'

The dangerous heat returned to his eyes and Rebecca swallowed, unable to break her gaze away from his.

A log shifted in the fireplace, saving her by bringing her sharply back to the room.

'Goodnight, my lord,' she said with a curtsey, fleeing as quickly as possible without it appearing a flight at all.

'Goodnight, Miss Merrickson.'

Proper daft you are, thinking everything would go back to the way it should, she thought, nearly tripping over herself in an effort to put as much ground between them as possible.

All day she'd tried to convince herself that things *could* go back to the way they should be. That what had happened meant nothing, changed nothing. And then, at the first gesture of thoughtfulness, the first moment alone with him, all those hopeful thoughts had fled, leaving only a rapid heartbeat, flushed cheeks and a stomach full of butterflies.

Slipping into her office, Rebecca threw the box onto her desk reproachfully. Why couldn't he have forgotten her, or at least pretended to? Made everything easier for her?

Because it's easy for him. Last night meant nothing, and he's trying to prove it.

Yes, that was it. She should be grateful. She was overreacting.

Right ninny.

This was nothing. A token no different from anything the others had received. For Thomas it had been his own grooming set. Tim had got a new carving knife. Mrs Murray an apron with her name embroidered on it. Lizzie had been given a delicate ivory hair comb, and Gregory a book on roses. Sam had received a new cap, and Betsy some fur-lined mittens. All thoughtful gifts, simple tokens of appreciation.

That is what this is. Just a tiny, insignificant token, she thought, opening the box, determined to prove her own point.

She froze, however, as she spotted the contents: a small, worn little book. *Tamerlane and Other Poems, by a Bostonian.*

She extracted it reverently, gliding her fingers over the worn edges, opening it to the title page. The words *Liam Reid* were inscribed in the top right corner, in faded ink.

His.

This was his, and he'd gifted it to her. Personal, thoughtful.

And still it means nothing, you overly excitable nincompoop.

Rebecca slid down into her chair, and laid the book open. It did not take very long for her to become utterly engrossed in the poems. They were unlike anything she'd ever read before. Haunting, disquieting, enchanting. Whoever this Bostonian was, she decided she liked him very much.

Just as she was beginning to forget herself, Thornhallow and most importantly Liam, she fell upon a dog-eared page. Frowning, she scanned the page. Halfway down, a verse had been underlined. Recently. There could be no mistake; the ink was too fresh, too vivid. It was the only mark she'd found on any of the pages, save for Liam's name.

Her heart racing again, her mouth dry, Rebecca ran her fingers over the underlined words.

And I turned away to thee,
Proud Evening Star,
In thy glory afar,
And dearer thy beam shall be;
For joy to my heart
Is the proud part
Thou bearest in Heaven at night,
And more I admire
Thy distant fire,
Than that colder, lowly light.

A meaningless token. That was what she had tried to convince herself this was. Liam had accused her of being *his* torment. Was he not hers, behaving thus?

Rebecca wished she didn't understand the meaning of this. She wished she didn't understand the declaration, that he'd left her to wallow and suffer alone. But this...

Was it an invitation? Permission? A request to make the final leap, take the final step? He'd been as bold and demanding as she knew he could last night. Anything further—anything more—would be her choice, and hers alone.

Snapping the little book shut, Rebecca slid it back into the box and cast it away into the bottom drawer of her desk. The choice *was* hers. And she was making it. There would be nothing more. Already her heart was in shreds.

After a kiss. Nothing but a simple kiss.

What would become of her if she succumbed to anything more?

No. Work.

She would work until her mind was numb and her fingers bruised and bloody. No matter what he had to say about that. At least then she would feel something other than this. The rest would pass. In time. Soon enough. She would see to it.

That was her choice.

Chapter Seventeen

It had been a half-hour at least that she'd been standing here, at the foot of the main stairs, her candle flickering as tiny gusts of the blustery wind swept through the hall. She'd waited until she'd heard the familiar sound of Mr Brown's door closing—waited long enough to be certain she wouldn't be seen nor heard—before creeping out of her rooms, giving not one thought to what she intended.

She'd come thus far almost entranced, her feet carrying her with solemn purpose. And then, at the bottom of the stairs, her mind had taken control and she'd balked before the rest of the journey. All at once the questions, the doubts, had assailed her. They would not be silenced, and swirled, endlessly, in her mind.

What if she was imagining things? Finding meaning where there was none? What if Liam had underlined the words to note that they were his favourite. To *share*, not to express any hidden thoughts or feelings.

If she was wrong about this, it would be…

Humiliating. Disgraceful.

More than enough to warrant dismissal. The presumption. The sheer *wantonness*…

And if she wasn't wrong?

There was an attraction—no denying that. Even if she had wished to chalk it up to her overactive imagination, she wouldn't have been able to. She had seen the heat in his eyes, felt the current when they'd dared get too close. Felt the pull, the magnetism, the desire. And the kiss they'd shared—there had been a connection no one could deny.

Was it not the danger of what might happen that had given her the strength to pull away? The fear of the depths she'd succumb to, of the heartbreak and sorrow which lay therein, which had forced her to break away? And now she was actively seeking it out, seeking *him* out, willing and eager to explore those tempting depths? What sort of consummate fool was she?

The wanton, fallen, brazen kind...

If she did march up those stairs and offer herself, what would he think then? In the cold light of the morning, what would remain of him as master and she as housekeeper? If she bridged the fragile chasm between them, separating their worlds, what would she be condemning herself to? Would he ever be able to look at her the same way, once she'd shared his bed? Or would whatever was left of his respect be gone?

It wasn't as if he thought her an innocent. He'd seen the tattoos, and she'd been quite thorough in her revelations, telling him all about the men she had welcomed into her bed. Was this sort of behaviour all he expected? Did he dare invite her *because* he thought her a woman such offers could be made to?

Yet he had seemed to understand her choices, her search for comfort. Perhaps that was all he sought, too. Which was reassuring. Wasn't it?

Reckon you won't answer any of those questions just standing here, getting right nithered in your nightclothes...

Two choices. Accept the consequences of offering herself up to the master, or go back to bed and wonder forever what might have been.

With a deep breath, she took hold of the banister and made her way up the stairs. If there was one thing life had taught her, it was that there was no time for regrets. If Liam did not want her, so be it. She would live with the shame. But she would not live with the regret of having let what she knew to be something special pass her by.

Her resolve got her to Liam's door, though once she stood before it she found herself yet again paralysed. But turning back, returning to her own rooms, seemed even more impossible than going through with this. And so, her hand as steady and sure as her heart was not, Rebecca made to knock on his door.

Just as she did, it swung open. She and Liam stood there, staring at each other in shock for a long moment. There was no doubt he'd been intent on going to her, and Rebecca's heart sank. It would have been so much easier had he not wanted her. Rejection she would have recovered from. But his own desire, she would not.

Liam backed away slowly, and Rebecca stepped into the room before she could convince herself to flee as far from him and Thornhallow as she could. He closed the door gently, leaning so close she was certain he could hear her heartbeat, pounding away against her ribs as it was. She could certainly hear it.

She could hear his shirt rustling as he moved, the gentle patter of his bare feet against the rug, the crackle of the fire in the hearth. Every sense had heightened when she'd stepped inside. The faintest of touches as Liam took the candle from her, and set it down by the door, sent an electric current through her entire body.

Rebecca took a steadying breath before she dared look

at him. 'I ask nothing of you,' she breathed as he stood before her. 'Not now, not ever.'

'And I ask only that you not leave me.'

Rebecca nodded, sealing the perilous pact, and Liam, his eyes alight with molten heat as he swept her into his arms, kissed her with a hunger and a passion she'd never known.

All his restraint evaporated, and he claimed her with that kiss, his hands tethering her as close to him as he could, as if he could meld their bodies together with that simple contact. And perhaps he could, for Rebecca felt as though she was tumbling into him, with him, to the place beyond the world where only their souls existed, entwined, connected.

Rebecca felt her dressing gown drop from her shoulders, and felt herself sweep away Liam's. They were moving, moving away from the door towards his bed, neither willing to break the kiss that heated their blood and tied them together. Rebecca felt the same hunger she sensed in Liam rise within her. Desperate, unyielding and destructive desire which could never be satisfied. Not in a thousand years.

Liam broke away with a gasp, long enough only to send her nightdress flying into a crumpled mess across the room along with his shirt. Rebecca's breath caught in her throat when she glimpsed him in the firelight, a sculpted paragon of male beauty, a god or an angel of light. Even his skin seemed to glow with the same magnetic pulse that shone in his eyes, drawing her to him with everything he was.

Her hands had a life of their own as they swept across his chest and abdomen, her fingers greedily mapping every inch of him as he took her mouth again. Their initial hunger sated, now they savoured each other, feasting slowly on what the other gave. Gently, fiercely, tenderly. Each touch was a breath, giving life in a way air could never.

Rebecca's heart soared and felt as though it had leapt from her own chest into his. She pulled herself closer, so that she could feel his chest against hers, feel his breast against hers.

A low growl sounded in Liam's throat and then his hands were on her hips, pulling the rest of her against him. She felt his desire pressing against her inner thigh, and her body decided it wanted more of him. All of him. Her hands found their way to his neck, then to his face, her fingers trailing along the lines of his jaw, his brow, his cheek, until they were running through his hair and she was entwined around him.

He lifted her, wrapping her legs around his hips, and carried her the last few steps to the bed. He laid them down together gently, his weight upon her, and the feel of him within her arms reassuring. A promise of all that he gave. He broke away and gazed down at her with such adoration and appreciation Rebecca's heart skipped a beat. His thumb brushed her cheek before his fingers found their way to her long auburn tresses and fanned them out around her head like a crown.

His eyes swept across her face, simultaneously mapping and feasting, as Rebecca's did. She wanted to commit every detail of him to eternal memory.

You will be the end of me, William Reid, she thought as he silently asked the question she could not in a million years say no to. She had already said yes, a thousand times since she'd first seen him.

So she slid her hands down, unlaced his breeches, and within seconds they and his drawers had joined the other garments on the floor.

And then he was trailing kisses everywhere. From the

corners of her lips, along the line of her jaw, down her neck, to her shoulders and clavicle. Reverently, he explored every inch of skin bared to him, searching, listening to the shifts in her breathing, to the tiny moans escaping from her throat, finding those places which responded most to his touch.

Rebecca's hands took over, guiding him, searching for his own secret places.

His mouth found her nipples and she arched back, the rush of scorching, glowing energy through her veins a jolt of life. He kissed and suckled gently, trailing a path of kisses across her chest as he moved from one to the next. His hands roamed across her belly and her hips, brushing as lightly as feathers, igniting every inch of skin beneath until they found their ultimate purpose.

Rebecca knew where he would touch her next and she guided his mouth back to hers, needing to quench her sudden thirst. Needing to fall into him again as his fingers slid along secret silken folds, as calescent as the core which awaited him there, slick and eager and welcoming. She gasped as he slowly explored her, and she felt him smile against her lips, his tongue trailing across her bottom lip. She bucked and arched, still drinking from him as he deepened his exploration, teasing, retreating, faster, slower, driving her to the edge she thought she knew.

'Come with me,' she told him, wrapping her legs around him again, begging him to take her fully, to complete their journey.

'Rebecca,' Liam whispered hesitantly. 'What if—?'

'I know how to ensure there are no consequences.'

He studied her for a long moment, and she knew how much trust she asked of her. She willed her promise to shine in her eyes, the promise that she would keep them safe.

'Come with me,' she repeated softly.

And so he did, unable to resist her entreaty, sliding himself into her with one sure thrust.

Rebecca cried out, and he brushed his hand soothingly against her forehead, asking if he'd hurt her. She opened her eyes and smiled, her eyes so dark with passion there was no doubt it had been sheer pleasure and not pain which had driven the cry from her lips.

So he kissed her again, and again, punctuating each movement inside her until once again she neared the edge. Then, cradling her, he rolled them over. Few men she had ever encountered preferred this way, yet somehow Rebecca was not surprised he would trust her, ask her to share the control, the drive.

She trailed kisses across *his* skin now…along his neck, which he bared to her, a wolf trusting her with his life. Across his shoulders, down his arms, down his chest. She, too, covered his nipples with her mouth, tasting, sampling, sending waves of pleasure coursing through him. He moaned and growled as she paid homage to every inch of incandescent skin.

She straightened herself upon him then, and his hands came to rest upon her hips, steadying her, guiding her as much as she did him. The dark hunger was in his eyes again—she could see it there, beneath the hooded lids, edging her ever onwards, matching her own. And behind it, the same resignation, an acceptance of what they had given in to.

It was wrong, improper, unacceptable, forbidden by the laws of God and man alike. Though together as one, as they were, neither could think this was anything but what *should* be. What *had* to be.

Liam rose, encircling her with his arms, begging her to stay close. Comfort, need, desire, all mingled when he kissed her again. Their eyes would not close, locked into each other's, steadying, securing the invisible thread between them as they rocked and rose and moved with silent complicity.

Nothing Rebecca had ever experienced before with any man came remotely close to what she felt then, as they climbed ever higher together. Her heart beating in time with his, a calm surrender of everything that she was, had been and would ever be. She had been born for this, to love him and only him. She had been made for him, and he for her.

Overwhelming fear and regret rose to swirl inside her breast along with the sweet pleasure and love she felt.

Love. Impossible, heart-wrenching, desperate love. God help me...

And then they were rolling upwards towards the peak of their pleasure together, their cries mingling in the dusky haze of firelight and darkness. A kiss, to seal it. The promise of an eternal bond and connection that would be tried and tested, but never broken. His mouth declaring all his words could not, and her own screaming the words she could never say out loud.

I love you. I am yours. Always have been. Always will be.

Still she stayed cradled in his arms, her body refusing to part from his lest this all be naught but a dream. They remained entwined thus for a long time, until slowly they came to lie beside each other, their gazes still locked.

My love. My light.

'*Stay,*' he'd said, when she'd crawled from the tangle of his body, and from the soft blankets and sheets which had witnessed their coupling again a short while before. '*Please,*' he had whispered, his hand outstretched when she'd finally found the strength to do what she must. Leave him. *'Stay with me...'*

And so she had.

Lying in his arms as she was now was dangerous, even more so than what they'd done before. Everything else she could dismiss as madness. Unbridled passion. She could convince herself it had been inevitably primal, nothing more, even though every inch of her body, heart and soul screamed out in denial. But this, this infinite tenderness in the safety of his own private world, this was far more threatening to her peace of mind, and heart, and soul.

Still, she lay there, her head rising and falling with every one of his breaths, her fingers trailing the lines of his body. She should not speak. She should not ask. She should not share anything more with him. And yet she could not stop herself.

'Will you tell me, my lord—?'

'Liam,' he whispered. 'Please.'

'Liam,' Rebecca repeated softly, trying not to enjoy the sound and taste of it. 'Will you tell me what really happened here?'

She heard his heartbeat quicken and thought, as the silence thickened, that he would refuse. Ask her to leave.

'I'm sorry, I shouldn't ask.'

'No,' he said with a heavy sigh, stroking her hair gently. 'I have thought many times I should tell you. How I would like you to know. Now, perhaps, it is too late to shy away from bearing secrets.'

Rebecca's hand came to rest on his belly, steadying him for the painful tale. The secret to his soul, to who he'd become.

'My sister, Halcyon, Hal, she was... God, how I loved her. She was the most beautiful, the kindest creature to ever walk the earth. Not even our father could break her generous spirit. She was younger than me by ten years, and I think he resented her, blamed her for our mother's descent into madness and death. It was easier than to admit it was he who caused her demise.'

'Mrs Ffoulkes… She said he was a hard man.'

'An understatement of infinite proportions,' Liam said bitterly. 'He was cruel, and cold. I didn't know my grandfather, so I do not know if I may lay blame at his door for what my father was. Oh, my father never raised a hand to any of us,' Liam told her, spotting the question in her eyes. 'He didn't need to. His words, his cutting reproach, his disgust and disapproval—they were enough. He hated for anyone in this house to feel pleasure. To feel…anything but fear. Hal, her horses, that tower… Despite all the resentment he felt towards her, somehow he allowed her those things. Perhaps because no matter what he said or did, it did not seem to change her. Hal was…so full of life nothing could touch her. I would have fetched her the moon had she asked. But then…'

Liam stopped, the words caught in his throat. The memories of that time resurfaced with a vengeance, the pain visibly as raw as ever. He took Rebecca's hand, entwining their fingers, anchoring himself to her.

'I went away. Only for a couple months, to get some respite from *him*. I spent it drinking and gallivanting about town with the few friends I had, but I came back for the New Year, and…everything had changed. Hal, she was broken. Withering away… I didn't understand, I tried to help her, but she wouldn't talk to me. I woke up one morning, and I swear, I heard her calling on the wind.'

Liam's breath was shallow now, and hot tears slid from his eyes.

'I found her in the river. Caught between a branch, and the ice… I…I knew. What she'd done. I lifted her out, carried her home. I always wondered if I could've done more… If she had confided in me…'

'You did what you could, Liam,' Rebecca breathed. 'I'm sure she knew you loved her.'

'Then why did she not trust me to help her?' he pleaded, voicing the question he had clearly spent so many years asking himself.

'I don't know. No one can. But I do know that she would've wanted you to remember her as she was before. That she would have wanted you to carry her memory with you, not fear it.' Rebecca kissed his chest, knowing it was easier said than done, but hoping the words brought him some comfort. 'That's why you kept her rooms untouched. You thought…'

'That I might understand,' he breathed, the confession tearing at her heart. It all made sense now.

'That I might find clues, an answer to why she'd done it. There was nothing.'

'There was everything she created.'

Liam kissed her knuckles tenderly and nodded.

'Why—?' Rebecca asked after a moment.

'Why do they say I murdered her?' he finished with a wry smile. 'Because I said as much. When I laid her down before my father, at the bottom of the stairs, God… I was so angry, so distraught. I felt I *had* killed her, with my negligence. I said things… Some of the servants heard, and, well… I refused to deny it publicly, as otherwise, soon enough the town would've known how she really died, and…'

'She would've been denied a proper burial.'

'Yes… The magistrate… He declared it an accident.'

'And your father?'

'A year after Hal died, he had an attack of the heart. I was admittedly surprised to learn he did possess one,'

Liam spat bitterly. 'He fell down the stairs, and his head was injured. The servants who found him were convinced it was murder, either myself or Hal's ghost, whom they swore roamed the corridors. I was long gone—I'd left the day we buried Hal—but once people have convinced themselves of something...'

'I understand.'

'You always knew, didn't you?' he asked, looking down at the figure in his arms. 'That there was more sorrow than malevolence in this house. That I was not the monster so many make me out to be.'

'I have known monsters,' she said, her eyes rising to meet his. 'And I knew from the first that you were no such thing.'

'I never...spoke of her, before. I never...shed tears for her,' Liam admitted. 'Not until...'

Rebecca smiled, and squeezed his hand.

'Never spoke of any of them. Still,' he whispered. 'There is a void in me, one I fear will never be filled.'

'In time, when you are ready. The loss will never leave you, but you will live with a full heart again.'

'In time,' he said pensively, his eyes roaming her face. 'Perhaps.'

Perhaps we will both live with a full heart again.

For a brief moment Rebecca's mind conjured an image of them here together, at Thornhallow, quiet peace in their hearts, and laughter in the air on a bright summer's day. It was a strangely vivid daydream, so vivid it seemed a vision of the future.

An impossible future.

And just like that, reality once again swept over her.

Liam saw the longing and the regret come into her eyes, matching his own. He bent down and kissed her, with gratitude and affection, to make her forget, to allow them both to forget the world they lived in.

And then he took her again, lost himself in her embrace so deeply it felt as though her essence was seeping into him, healing him, her entire being a balm for his broken soul. He found himself within her then, himself who he'd thought lost forever.

Not that he would admit it to himself once they lay together later, sated yet again, Rebecca peacefully asleep in his arms. It was a trick of the mind, of the body. Bliss, pleasure, played tricks on one's rationality. Yes, he had found a pleasure with Rebecca that he had never before with any woman. Yes, he had revealed parts of himself to her that he'd thought he never could. Yes, he enjoyed her company, her mind, her friendship.

But that was all it was.

Two lost souls, finding solace together in this dark winter night.

Their attraction had been undeniable, *inevitable*, given their living situation. He would not make this out to be anything more than it was. He could not.

For here, in this room, in the dead of night, time might stop, the world might fade away, but it would not be so in the cold light of day.

Chapter Eighteen

The week that followed was surreal, a lost moment in time. Not just because of the nights she spent with Liam, when they lost themselves in each other. Nights, when not only their bodies met, but also their minds. When they spoke for hours of books, philosophy, politics…even sometimes the estate. She amused him with tales of her old masters, and he her with his boyhood pranks. In the firelight, in those short hours they spent together, they became friends, lovers and equals.

Though it did not escape her notice that neither seemed ready to fling open wide the doors to their souls again. To discuss things which *truly* mattered.

The house itself was quiet. A strange sort of normality resumed after Epiphany, a return to chores and work, albeit a slow return. Everyone was in high spirits, brought together by the celebrations. It was as if they'd come to accept that they were family, and that, for a time any social conventions which separated and dictated their lives, could be cast aside. Though they all knew, soon this extraordinary time would come to an end.

Rebecca was perhaps the most acutely aware of the impending return to life as it should be. Every night, as she left Liam's room, she said a silent prayer, thanking whatever powers above for another day, another moment at Thornhallow.

That first night, standing in the cold darkness of the corridor, Rebecca had nearly been overwhelmed by a sudden awareness of what she'd just done. The dread, the fear of what might come next, had crept up on her as the sun had crept towards the horizon and she'd listened intently for any trace of the others.

But then, it had all seemed...*inevitable*. So perfectly *right*.

The realisation she'd come to in Liam's embrace—that she had fallen in love with him—tormented her. Though it hadn't prevented her from returning to him, however aware she was of dooming herself to more suffering.

By allowing herself to give in to temptation, she'd condemned herself to heartbreak, and a pale imitation of a life. There was no question that she'd never loved a man as she did Liam—no question she would never love again after they parted, which they inevitably would. Nothing could ever come close to what she felt; there was a calm certainty in her heart about that. Even though she wished she could believe otherwise, convince herself that it was only the pang of first love every girl must experience.

But she was not a girl. She was a woman who knew her heart and soul too well.

And tonight, as she lay prone on the pile of blankets and pillows they had made before the hearth, Liam beside her, staring into the flames, her soul told her something else.

This is your last night.

Liam took a lock of her hair, and let it flow through his fingers like water. Torn from her melancholy reverie, she turned and offered him a smile. She would miss him. Miss *this*. Not simply the comfort, the pleasure, even the laughter they shared. But this *connection*. It seemed so natural to lie here with him, naked. There was no shame, no discomfort, no fear.

No, when he looked at her as he did now, lazily and yet reverently, his head propped up on his hand as he lay on his side, twirling her hair, she felt nothing but... *Peace*.

'What is this for?' Liam asked softly, his fingers trailing over the roman numerals inked on her shoulder. '1822?'

'The year I became a housekeeper. I'd worked so hard to make something of myself. And finally I had. I wanted to mark the occasion.'

'Quite right,' he agreed seriously. 'So young...an extraordinary achievement.'

Slowly, Liam bent over and kissed the numbers, his breath seeping into her bones, marking her in a far more eternal way than any other caress. She shivered slightly as his fingers moved to skim over her ribs to the head of wheat inked there.

'And this?'

'For my father,' she whispered, not missing the flash of sadness in his eyes. 'He used to pluck one, and roll it between his hands, to see if it was ready. He would let me do it, too, not that I knew how to tell the difference. But it smelled of him.'

'You loved him very much.'

'Yes.'

Envy shone along with regret in his eyes as his lips covered every inch of the wheat. She understood. Her father had been everything to her, all she'd known, all that had been *home* for her. And his...

Had not.

'What about this one?' he asked with a small smile, drawing the lines of the robin between her shoulder blades.

'The first man I...*knew* was called Robin. A sweet fellow, a footman in the second house I served. He was gentle, and never made me feel...*less*, for having been with him.'

'Hmm.'

Rebecca laughed when she was granted a dark look from Liam, and the robin extra attention from his lips. Moving down her body, he found the rose on her hip, and raised a brow.

'My mother,' Rebecca said, surprised by the depth of emotion that filled her heart then. 'She had a rose bush by the kitchen window. I think it was her most prized possession. It's all I had of hers. Papa...he parted with all else but her ring. It was to be for my wedding. My uncle took it and sold it.'

Liam's jaw clenched as he stroked the rose, and the display of anger on her behalf was heart-warming.

'The roses here were my mother's.'

'Was she like Hal?'

Liam nodded. 'I remember...her light. The warmth of her touch. Like the sun on a spring day. And I remember it dimming. Day by day, until she was gone. I was twelve when my father sent her to a sanatorium. He announced her death over breakfast two months later, as if it was the latest winner at the races.'

Tears pricked Rebecca's eyes as Liam reverently kissed the rose, then lay down beside her, his mind clearly very far away.

'How did you get this?' she asked, trailing her fingers across the scar on his brow. If this was well and truly her last night with him, she wanted as much of him as he would give. To keep, to hold, to treasure.

Always.

The last thing Liam wanted to do was answer.

Beyond his confession of what had happened to Hal, they hadn't indulged in any of this soul-bearing business, and he had been grateful for that. It was enough—too much, really—to share the nights with her, to be with her, without opening doors which had been long closed and would do better remaining so.

Wrong.

At every turn she had prised pieces of his soul from him, and he'd felt better for it.

So why not now?

Rather than answer his own question, he answered hers. 'I got that the night I decided to sail across the sea,' he sighed.

He felt her penetrative gaze studying him, waiting, giving him the space as always, to back down or give more. *Give her everything.*

'After I left Thornhallow, I just kept...trying to get further away. I crossed to Amsterdam, made my way to Frankfurt, Rome, Lyon... Drinking, gambling away what money I made. I fought in prize fights. Worked in a vineyard near Bordeaux for a while, served as a night guard for a brothel in Milan. I wanted to forget. All of it. Myself. I did...things I am not proud of.'

He turned to face her, willing her to understand that though he might not be the monster others purported, neither was he some tragic hero.

'I have marks on my soul.'

'As do we all,' she said.

Liam nodded, the weight he had been ignoring—that of her potential repudiation of his life and his actions—lifting from his heart.

'I ended up blind drunk, beaten, in a gutter in Brest. Still unable to forget. The crew of a ship bound for Boston passed by, Angus among them. And he stopped. I asked him once, why, and he told me he'd recognised the look in my eyes. He'd had it when he lost his wife. He convinced me to take a place onboard, working for my passage, and luckily the captain agreed that, despite my state that day, I would be useful.'

'Did you find any peace in Columbia?'

'Yes, I suppose, for a while,' he said, slightly taken aback at the question, as though it were somehow more personal than what he'd just revealed. 'I found a measure of freedom, and in that, some peace. Life was harsh, and hard. But knowing your survival depended on yourself and those with you... Being so close to nature... It felt primal. *Natural.* But when I found Angus, and Peter, dead...'

Liam shook his head, hoping to chase away the images he could never erase from his mind.

'What little peace I'd found, it shattered.' The realisation he had never voiced, never acknowledged, became real in that moment. 'I wanted my life as it was then to be my life always. I tried so hard to convince myself it was right, that it was everything I wanted... I refused to see the violence, the greed, the death and the suffering there. It was to be my utopia, where I became myself, with no expectations. When I found their bodies, it was as if a veil was lifted. I saw the world as it was, truly, and I saw myself as I was. Not a new man, but the same man who had run all those years ago. Still heartbroken, still...incomplete.'

'Not even the other side of the world was enough?'

'I remember standing at the edge of a lake one night,' he breathed, the image as clear as ever in his mind. The words tumbled from him, as if, yet again, with her mere presence Rebecca coaxed them from him. 'Some months after arriving in Columbia. The water was black ice, surrounded by pines, and there were the tallest mountains you can imagine, capped with snow that seemed like beacons in the darkness. And the stars... There were more stars than sky. It felt like if you reached up, you could touch them. It was the most awesome sight I'd ever witnessed.

And yet…I couldn't help but think of Thornhallow. Of the way the sunrise turns the heather pink, and the twilight erases the boundary between Heaven and Earth.'

'Why did you leave it to rot, then? If you love this place so?'

'I don't love Thornhallow. I hate it. All I can feel is pain, my father's cruelty, and it is as suffocating as it was then. It's the land. It's in my blood. My soul.'

Rebecca nodded, and he knew she felt it, too.

'With time…new memories… If you found a measure of happiness here…perhaps, you would not feel it so.'

I don't feel it so…not anymore.

Not since she'd come here. Since she had infused her own light into the walls, as if chasing away his father's darkness, his own darkness, and the terrible memories of Hal and his mother. He wanted to tell her that, to tell her…so much more.

Instead he nodded, wound himself around her and kissed her, willing the unspoken words to somehow flow into her heart.

It is with you I have finally found peace. And myself.

Dawn was still hours away when Rebecca crept out of Liam's room, wishing as she had every day that she could stay there, basking in the warmth and tenderness of his arms forever. But that, too, was an impossible dream.

As she slid back into her rooms, her body and heart aching, demanding at least a few hours of rest before the coming day, Rebecca could not shake the feeling that everything was about to change. That the moment she'd dreaded—the moment when everything came abruptly to an end, when the world demanded things be righted— was fast approaching.

That was your last night. You know it in your heart.

Chapter Nineteen

'Ah, Mrs Hardwicke.'

Mr Brown's sharp voice startled her as she stepped out of her office some hours later. Rebecca nearly jumped out of her skin, but composed herself in a second, and smiled.

'If I may have a word?'

'Yes, of course. Good morning, Mr Brown,' Rebecca sighed.

The butler looked like he was on a serious mission, and she would have preferred to deal with whatever it was after breakfast—but, given his expression, that was not an option.

What terrible news awaits me now...?

'Should we adjourn to my office?'

'No need, Mrs Hardwicke. No need,' he said, surveying her in his usual unnerving manner. 'I have just come from His Lordship. It seems we are to have guests. The Marquess of Clairborne, an old school friend.'

'Oh, how delightful!' Rebecca exclaimed, with what she thought was convincing enthusiasm, considering her exhaustion. 'How many, and when do we expect them?'

'The Marquess and another gentleman are to arrive over-morrow, according to the note which came this morning.

I am sure His Lordship will wish to discuss arrangements with you, but I thought it best we make some preparations without delay.'

'Yes, an excellent idea, Mr Brown. We have so little time.'

'Particularly regarding service at mealtimes.'

'Yes, it would be best to not be seen wanting.' Rebecca smiled again, and Mr Brown cocked his head, as if he'd been expecting a different reaction to the news altogether. 'I will speak to His Lordship about trying to hire more staff in the village, but I doubt any will come. I think, if you and Gregory serve, Lizzie and I can bring everything up from the kitchens. That shouldn't be too unseemly...'

'Indeed, Mrs Hardwicke. Shall we discuss this further over breakfast? With the rest of the staff?'

'Yes, I would be grateful for their thoughts—and some coffee.'

With a nod, Mr Brown turned, and led the way to the servants' hall. Rebecca sensed he was still very much aware of her, still gauging her reactions. She understood then that he knew something had passed between her and Liam. How, or how much, mattered little.

The Marquess, an old school friend...

The old butler had, in his effortlessly subtle yet obvious manner, emphasised that information so that the significance of the visit was clear.

They've come to welcome him back.

The Marquess would be the first of many who belonged to Liam's old life, to his future. People who belonged to the same society Liam did, no matter how hard either of them tried to forget. Liam was not Liam. He was the Earl of Thornhallow. As such, he would take his place among them, do what was expected.

Whatever had been between them both, was over. The

time had indeed come for the world to be righted. And Mr Brown had sought to prepare her, to help her avoid any surprise or discomfiture when Liam told her the news.

She was immensely grateful, despite the wave of shame that washed over her at the realisation that he knew—or suspected, at the very least—the nature of her relationship with their lord. Though there had been no judgement in his manner, only a strange sort of concern. He had sought to, discreetly and kindly, prepare her for the inevitable future, remind her of her place, and the reality that came with it. He'd granted her time, to ensure she was nothing less than professional when facing the others. When facing Liam.

'Thank you,' she whispered, passing him as he held the door for her.

A nod, and it was as though nothing had passed between them. They both took their places at the table, and as Mrs Murray served them breakfast, discussed the news and arrangements to be made with the rest of the staff.

Rebecca was like an automaton, going through the motions as she had countless times before when advised of guests' imminent arrivals, concealing her emotions beneath a mask of professional collectedness. Later, she would take a moment to reconcile herself with the notion that whatever she and Liam had shared, whatever they'd become, was now officially at an end.

Chin up, you daft moppet. You will be a model of grace and dignity if it's the last thing you do.

It was her own folly that had brought her to this, her own choices which now cut through her like knives. No one would see how much it hurt. Not now, not ever. She had crossed so many boundaries, allowed herself to behave in a fashion so improper already... That was quite enough. No one would know. No one would see.

Least of all Liam.

Once the staff had finished their breakfast, and all their preparations had been set in motion, Rebecca retired to her office. She allowed herself a moment of wallowing, allowed herself to feel the pain which took her breath away, and threatened to stop her heart.

When the bell she'd been expecting rang out shrill and sobering, she wiped away the escaped tears, smoothed her hair and skirts, and made for the study.

Liam stood as he had countless times before at the windows in his study, hands clasped behind his back, the very picture of a lord surveying his domain. Yet again he stared unseeing at the white, glittering landscape before him. Yet again his thoughts were affixed somewhere else. On the door behind him. On who he waited for.

Rebecca.

Absent-mindedly, he fiddled with the cuff of his jacket, desperately attempting to find the right combination of words. Still, he was no further than he'd been when he'd learned of his friend's imminent arrival. When he'd realised he would have to tell Rebecca.

He wished he could regret all that had passed between them. Wished he could hate, curse himself—and her—for having succumbed to temptation. But he could not. The only person he could find it within himself to curse was Henry Spencer, Marquess of Clairborne. For he was the one breaching the world he and Rebecca had created. The *home* they had created. Spencer, and the world beyond these walls, were destroying this beautiful place they had made. This haven.

Deep down, Liam had known this day would come—but not so soon.

And not like this.

He hadn't had enough time with her. Though something

inside him whispered that he would never have enough time with her. Not in a thousand lifetimes.

Damn you, Spencer.

As much as he looked forward to seeing the best, and perhaps only, friend he'd had before leaving England, this visit was so much more than a simple reunion. It was the beginning of his reintroduction into the society he'd forsaken. The first steps into life as an earl. A life he wanted not one whit.

And likely Spencer's mother, the Dowager Marchioness, had also precipitated her son's escapade, determined as she was to see Liam joined to her daughter. Had he not been so disgusted by her obvious husband-hunting, he might have admired her for it. He'd been in the country for a little over three months, had avoided any social gathering or locale which might indicate he was in want of a wife, and yet here she was, sending her son as a harbinger of the future he wanted nothing to do with.

Had Spencer given him any more than two days' warning, he would have found a way to deny him. He would have made it clear this was the very last thing he wanted. But with not only Spencer, but another gentleman arriving overmorrow, he would be forced to welcome them.

He could only pray it would be a short visit, only hope they would be off on their merry way before Spencer could even think to do his mother's bidding, and set the stage for Liam's reintroduction to his sister as well as society. Even if he *had* been in search of a wife, he would certainly not have looked to the chits society bred for that purpose. He would want someone to match him. A partner. Someone with whom he could share everything, be everything he was.

Someone like Rebecca.

No. That way lay only anguish, disappointment, destruction for them both. Stories like theirs did not have happy endings. No matter how much he may wish it were possible.

If I were free... When I am free— Focus, man! She'll be here soon. What am I to say?

They were expecting guests. A friend of his. She would know what that meant, and...hate him. But she would hate him just as much if he presumed too much, and tried to explain. Tried to tell her that he wanted none of it, wanted only what they'd had, if only for a little longer. That he wanted more.

His plan...

She will hate you for that, too.

And presuming to say any of that would break their unspoken pact, the fragile balance. Presuming that she did not know her place—nor his—would be an insult. He knew her well enough now to understand that.

It did not stop the fact that he wanted to yell and scream his displeasure. To promise her that he wanted no part of this. To beg her to believe that he would never cause her pain—if indeed the news could hurt her as much as it had him. He liked to think it would, that what they had, meant as much to her as it did him.

And then he would tell her that all he wanted was time with her. It always came back to that.

'Come in,' he said, his heart sinking at the sound of the knock.

He heard her confident steps approaching, then stop by his desk, and he found he could not face her.

'We are expecting guests, Mrs Hardwicke.'

Rebecca. My—

'Yes, my lord. Mr Brown has already seen fit to advise me,' she said simply.

Liam turned, not bothering to hide his surprise.

'Two gentlemen arriving overmorrow.'

Liam nodded slowly, stunned by her coolness. He had expected any reaction but this—*wanted* any reaction but this.

'Excellent,' she continued. 'We've already begun preparations. I thought to give the gentlemen the Blue and Yellow Rooms in the West Wing. Mr Brown will be going to the village to see if he can convince some extra hands to come, though I suspect we will have to make do as we are. He will also be putting in Mrs Murray's orders, so if you could advise how long the guests will be staying?'

'I...I don't know. I hope to see to it that it isn't long,' Liam managed, after realising a question had been asked of him, his mind still reeling.

'We shall plan for a week, then, and proceed from there,' Rebecca said. 'The Marquess is presumably coming with a valet, so I do not believe we will be stretched too thinly. It isn't ideal, and I apologise, for I know it will look quite unseemly for us to be so few. Nonetheless, I hope this suits, my lord. Do advise if I've missed anything, or if there are any further arrangements to be made.'

'Nothing shakes you, does it, Rebecca?' Liam asked bitterly after a moment. He thought he saw her wince slightly, but a moment later she was as collected as before.

'How imperturbable you are.'

'Do you know what makes an excellent servant, my lord?' she asked.

'No. Do enlighten me.'

'An excellent servant anticipates their master's needs. Knows what to do, how to fulfil their desires even before they themselves are aware of them. I am an excellent servant, my lord.'

'Be that as it may. You don't have to...' Liam groaned, his frustration growing. 'None of this bothers you? You feel nothing?' he demanded finally, unable to rein in his own emotions any longer. 'Nothing at all?'

'Cast me as cold, and unfeeling, my lord, if that is your wish,' she bit back. 'But know that I am neither. What I am is acutely aware of my duty. To this house, to you and most importantly to myself.'

'And nothing will prevent you from doing it?'

'No, my lord. Now, if there is nothing else?'

'You have everything in hand, it seems, Mrs Hardwicke,' he said, turning back to the window, unable to bear the sight of her any longer, lest he give way to the urge to rush over and shake her from her damned composure. 'I shall not detain you from your *duty*.'

He listened to her retreating footsteps, heard them pause momentarily before the door was opened and shut again.

Liam knew he should be jubilant. Any other man would leap for joy at the realisation he would face no anger, no tears, no pleas. Any other man would laugh with relief at the prospect he would face no consequences from the unholy relationship. That he was *free*. But Liam felt only hurt. He was not free. He would never be free of her. Though she was apparently of him.

Things between them had always been more than simple. More than master and servant. He had returned to Thornhallow to break the hold the house had upon him, and instead he'd entangled himself in a far more perilous way.

I suppose I should thank you, Thomas...

Liam suspected the old butler had had more than just preparedness in mind when he'd warned Rebecca of their guests. That little act of underhandedness saved him from delivering the news himself. Saved him from making an utter and complete fool of himself, debasing himself beyond reparation in the face of his housekeeper. The damned old butler had subtly found a way to set everything back to its proper place.

I should be grateful, but I regret that you denied me a glimpse past her otherwise impenetrable armour...

A ride. That was what he needed to clear his mind. Fresh air—that would do the trick. The snow was nothing he and Orpheus couldn't handle.

Abandoning any hope of work for the day, Liam strode out of the study, grabbed his coat, scarf and hat before Gregory even realised he was there, and marched out to the stables.

Damn you, Spencer. Damn you, Rebecca. And damn this house.

Chapter Twenty

The grandfather clock in the hall had just rung ten when a carriage was heard on the drive. Mr Brown, who had been attentively awaiting the arrival, rang for the others immediately, and within seconds the hall was filled with the animated fluttering of the staff as they made for the door.

They were perfectly lined up outside, looking fresh and spotless, when Liam joined them. He swept a disaffected gaze of inspection over them all, before Mr Brown was graced with a nod of approval.

Rebecca, he dared not even look in the eye. Facing what he must, he could not bear to look at her, and be any more tortured than he already was. Enough had been said. There was nothing more to be done but greet his guests and move on.

Plastering as jovial and welcoming a smile as he could manage, he straightened, and stepped before them all to greet the carriage.

Within seconds, it pulled up, and the door swung open.

'Reid, you rascal!' the Marquess of Clairborne shouted in his usual warm, slightly mocking tone as he descended with a hop, hand extended, barely looking like someone who had been travelling.

He hadn't changed at all since Liam had last seen him. The same boyish looks, golden curls and clear blue eyes, the same cheeky smile. He was as impeccably dressed as ever, his dark pantaloons, vibrantly green waistcoat, crisp linen shirt, blue jacket and billowing greatcoat all perfectly tailored in the latest fashion and finest materials. There was not a crease to be found; even the Gordian knot of his cravat had withstood the travails of travel.

'It's been too long, old fellow,' he said, with that grin which had cost many a woman her wits and heart.

'Indeed it has,' Liam agreed, shaking Spencer's hand warmly. Truth be told, he *was* pleased to see him. 'Welcome to Thornhallow.'

'Should've waited for an invite, I know, old chap, but I feared one would never come. As we were spending the festive season not a hundred miles away, I couldn't resist surprising you. Besides, I really had to get out of Clairborne House.'

'How are your mother and Mary?' Liam asked.

'Yes, jolly well, they send their regards, of course,' he laughed. 'Had to beat them off with a stick, they wanted to join so. But I thought we should save the larger reunion for another time.'

Spencer winked and Liam thanked his stars the whole family hadn't come.

Beat them off with a stick, indeed.

It wouldn't surprise him if it were actually true in this instance.

'Ah, here is my good friend Mr Walton,' the Marquess continued, indicating the simply but elegantly dressed and rather pleasant-looking young man just descending from the carriage. 'Walton owns a shipping company—don't you, Freddie?'

'Guilty,' Freddie said, with a warm smile as he bowed. 'How do you do, my lord?'

'Reid, please,' he insisted, offering his hand.

The young man took it, surprise and appreciation in his eyes.

'Welcome.' Liam felt his smile fading, and forced himself to forge on. 'Shall we adjourn inside? There is coffee waiting for us in the drawing room. Then I imagine you will wish to refresh yourselves?'

Spencer concurred with a nod, and Liam led him inside, closely followed by Freddie.

The door closed, and Rebecca and Gregory divested the gentlemen of coats, hats and gloves, whilst outside Thomas, the grooms and the Marquess's valet saw to unpacking the carriage. Liam then guided his guests to the drawing room, where, by some magical feat only servants could manage, Lizzie awaited them with the promised refreshments.

They talked and sipped coffee, sampled little sandwiches and freshly baked scones, spoke of the journey and the weather and everyone's health for nigh on two hours, until finally, Liam convinced his guests they should rest and settle into their quarters.

He was glad when he was left alone in the drawing room.

It was mind-numbingly easy to resume his place in society—and it made him want to scream. Though it was pleasant enough to see Spencer again, he could not help but feel none of it was right. He no longer belonged. He no longer wished to.

Had he more courage, he might have run away before they arrived. Had he more courage, he might have done a great deal many things.

Soon, you will be able to be rid of them. Soon...

* * *

'I was asking, Reid,' Spencer said loudly, a glint of mischief in his eyes, tearing Liam sharply from the reverie he'd slipped into, staring at the flame of the candles before him on the dinner table.

He looked around to find his guests staring at him expectantly, and graced them with the polite smile he had been using all too often today.

'What are your plans, now that you've returned to England?'

'None that are quite cemented enough to be shared, I fear,' Liam said, returning his attention to his plate, intent on savouring Mrs Murray's beef roast. Intent on ignoring everything *but* the roast, really.

Today had felt interminable, as though time had been slowed to purposely lengthen his torture. To an outsider, the day would have seemed an altogether quiet and convivial affair, filled with tours of the house and gardens, a lively afternoon meal, a game of billiards and spirited conversation. To Liam, however, it all had served only as a reminder of the dull emptiness that filled such a life as he was meant to live.

A life without true purpose.

He'd found some solace in the time he'd spent with Spencer—who, for all his airs, was a shrewd, practical fellow—and Freddie—who proved himself to be an intelligent, enterprising young man, who had built his own company and fortune from nothing, and was a self-made man such as Liam liked. But for all the camaraderie he'd found, his spirits had only worsened. With every passing moment, so grew his restlessness and desire for his guests to take their leave, even as they had only just arrived.

To top it all, he'd received a letter that afternoon from

Leonards, stating in no uncertain terms that his dream, his plans, were impossible.

All he wanted was to return to the world as it had been before his guests' arrival. The world in which Thornhallow actually felt like home, complete with a family. Complete with Rebecca.

It was a terrifying thought, that his hatred of the place had been so diminished, yet it also felt inevitable. Rebecca's light had finally pushed back the darkness, and he... When she was gone the darkness returned.

At odd moments throughout the day, he'd found himself praying that she might come to him, or that he might find the courage to go to her. He longed to say *Damn it all*, and rush down to the servants' quarters and tell her everything, beg her forgiveness. But he did not. Rebecca had made it clear that any feelings either of them had were to be forgotten, pushed away into some dark, forgotten place.

She had remained unseen, out of reach, more a wraith haunting his house than Hal had ever been. Hidden in her own realm, she had ensured, with her usual flair, that the household ticked along like clockwork. She'd made her presence felt, to him at least, by her absence, and the hole it left within him. The world they had created existed only in a time which had passed, and could never be found again. Not for all his wishing.

Though now he found himself wishing that she'd remained unseen. Rebecca had been forced into his presence for dinner, if only to bring in the food with Lizzie, and her nearness taunted him more than her absence.

Focus. Spencer. Unwanted questions.

'It is only months since I've returned, and there is much for me to reacquaint myself with.'

'Surely, you have returned for a reason,' Spencer continued, his conviviality now verging on interrogation.

The tension grew, not only at the table, but also among
the servants. Thomas and Gregory straightened almost
imperceptibly. Though whether it was because someone
was questioning the master, or because they too desperately longed for the answer, was anyone's guess.

*I, too, long for answers. But I have none to give, even
to myself.*

'As you say, it is months since your return,' Spencer
said, lazily sipping his wine, though the sharp intent in
his eyes belied his relaxed manner. 'You must have for-
mulated some scheme, made preparations for your future,
and that of the Earldom.'

'Plans which, as they are in their fragile beginnings, I
cannot share, old friend. You will learn of them when the
time is right.'

'The counsel of friends can be most illuminating.'

Liam nodded tersely, still refusing to take his eyes off
his plate, though at the rate he was devouring the meal
upon it, tasting none of it, the distraction would be short-
lived.

It wasn't that he didn't want to confide in his friend,
didn't want to trust him with everything—only he couldn't.
There was no telling what either of them would say or do,
what would be left of their friendship if he revealed it all.

The table fell into silence again, the delicate tinkling
of cutlery and refilling of wine glasses the only sounds.

'Well, whatever your plans,' Spencer said finally, wiping the corners of his mouth delicately, 'society will be
enthralled when you finally decide to grace it with your
presence. Already the mamas and debutantes are working themselves into a frenzy to ensure they are thoroughly
prepared for the Disappeared Earl. Why, when we were in
town before Christmas, you were all that was on anyone's
lips—isn't that right, Freddie?'

'Indeed,' Freddie agreed warily, eyeing both friends, careful not to put himself in the midst of what he sensed was a conversation verging on less than amicable. 'I expect you will have a most entertaining Season.'

'That is an understatement, Freddie,' Spencer chuckled. 'Novelty is all that keeps those creatures entertained, and you, my dear Reid, are the most novel thing to happen since Napoleon escaped Elba.'

'Are you not one of those creatures, then?' Liam said coldly, his irritation growing. He had managed to avoid talk of the future, and his plans so far; he would not be taken in now. A flash of hurt shone in his friend's eyes, but he forged on. 'As for the Season, I have absolutely no reason to take part in that dreadful occasion. I have quite enough to satisfy me here at Thornhallow.'

The silence which followed was painfully tense but thankfully short, as Liam nodded to Thomas and then began the dance of clearing the table, and setting it for dessert.

'Yes, well, I do hate to notice, Reid, but comfortable though you may be,' Spencer drawled, swirling the vintage red Liam was now sad Thomas had unearthed from the cellars, 'there is a lack.'

'A lack,' Liam repeated, raising a brow.

'The servants, Reid. Indeed, the whole management of this house. I know you are accustomed to much more savage conditions than these,' he forged on.

Liam clenched the arms of his chair so tightly he might have torn them off. Better that than unleash the well of anger inside him at Spencer, who was still his friend, and a guest, even if he couldn't quite see his *friend* at the moment.

'But, truly, you need a proper hand here.'

'Mrs Hardwicke has everything well in hand,' Liam

managed to say evenly enough, through gritted teeth. 'She keeps things as I wish them to be.'

'I'm sure she does.' Spencer smiled. He paused, just long enough for everyone to think they might make it out of what was quickly becoming a dreadful evening, alive. 'But this house—as do all grand houses—requires a mistress to guide it.'

That was it.

The last of Liam's patience snapped.

He could endure an interrogation—indeed, he'd expected one. It wasn't precisely Spencer's fault that every plan Liam *had* made was now shattered into a million pieces. He could endure the vague insinuations about his lifestyle. What he couldn't, he found, was any insult on Rebecca, or his household, paired with an overt if subtle attempt at matchmaking.

He'd never thought his friend would succumb to the business as his mother had, but here they were.

And he'd had enough.

'As far as I'm concerned, Mrs Hardwicke is mistress of this house,' he said, the words tumbling from his mouth before he could stop them, pinning Spencer with a stare to shatter ice.

The entire room froze.

From Freddie, who had just reached for his glass, to Gregory, who was laying out terrines of jellied fruit on the sideboard.

Spencer matched Liam's stare for a moment, then his eyes flicked to the doorway at Liam's back, and a smirk grew on his lips. Only too late did Liam realise what precisely Spencer had fixed his attention upon.

No... What have I done?

'Well, then, Mrs Hardwicke,' Spencer said congenially, though there was as much ice in his tone as there was in

Liam's eyes. 'It seems you are to be complimented indeed for all your efforts.'

Liam's voice died in his throat as he turned just enough to see Rebecca standing in the doorway, frozen just like the rest of them, as she handed Thomas a coffee tray.

He felt her shame and her hurt radiating off her in waves, and it kept him silent even as he wished to salvage what he'd done. Her duty, her pride—he knew how important those things were to her. How much a part of her they were, and now… He had shamed her—before guests, before a peer, before her own staff—all but announcing to the world what they'd done.

Her eyes flitted to him, searching for something, for anything.

Forgive me, Rebecca.

Spencer opened his mouth to speak and Liam came to. 'Leave us,' he ordered them all.

No one needed to be asked twice. With eerie grace, calm and silence, the staff bowed and curtsied, dropped what they were doing, and slunk out.

'If you'll excuse me,' Freddie muttered, following in their wake with haste.

Liam tried his utmost to rein in his emotions as Spencer leaned back in his chair lazily. He was walking a dangerous line, risking either more dishonour for Rebecca, or his friendship—which, no matter how much he detested Spencer at that moment, he had no wish to lose.

'Such an exquisite find, Reid,' he drawled. 'A rare flower, indeed.'

'Mind yourself,' Liam warned.

'Though what flower, I wonder?' The Marquess smiled. 'If my sister were, for instance, that perfect English rose which we all know she is,' he said pointedly, 'what do you suppose Mrs Hardwicke might be?'

'Spencer...'

'A briar rose, perhaps,' he offered. 'Too simple. Lady's mantle? Very hardy... No. I know. A foxglove. Such a beautiful bloom. Delicate, perfect symmetry, enticing colours, inviting. Some even seek it for its healing properties. But beneath it all, it is poison.'

I should wring your throat, Spencer.

Instead, he grabbed his glass, nearly shattering it, and downed his wine.

'A flower not to be trifled with,' Liam sneered. 'A rose, other than beauty, thorns and a sweet scent, what does it offer in its short life?'

'Every flower has its uses. One must only know when to sample one or the other,' Spencer advised, with less hostility, and more sincerity in his eyes. 'Everything in its proper place. As with all things.'

Spoiling for a fight—for anything that might make him forget the despair currently residing in his chest—Liam rose and marched over to the sideboard, pouring himself more wine, and knocking it back before turning to Spencer, who was still lazily lounging in that damned chair as if nothing at all was wrong with the world.

'Enough with the pretty words,' Liam growled. 'What is this? If not for the friendship we once shared I would lay you out right now!'

'All because of a housekeeper?' Spencer asked tauntingly.

'She isn't just a housekeeper!' he shouted, tossing away the glass, which shattered against the wall into as many pieces as his own life, and took a step towards Spencer.

'Precisely,' Spencer snapped, all false humour and pretence gone, his eyes flashing dangerously as he rose, nearly toe to toe with Liam. 'We'd have to be blind not to see it. I'm only looking out for you.'

'What...?' Liam asked meekly, his mind reeling as his anger was replaced with shock.

'I am still your friend,' Spencer said earnestly.

His eyes were now devoid of anything but pleading, and Liam was lost.

'Always will be.'

'You're just looking out for yourself,' Liam spat, afraid of acknowledging what Spencer was saying.

He set about pacing the room, hoping it would help dispel the feelings of helplessness and despair from rising again. Anger—anger was safe.

'This is about you, and your mother, working towards marrying me to your sister.'

'Goddammit, Reid!' Spencer shouted. 'This isn't about me or my sister. Yes, I would be happy to see you two wed.' He sighed, raked his fingers through his hair, and Liam stopped. 'But this is about you. You're burying yourself here, taking your housekeeper to bed. And don't you dare deny it,' he warned. 'You are an earl! Nothing can come of whatever is between you. She knows her place, and her duty, but you refuse to see it.'

'I am acutely aware of my duties.'

Now I sound like Rebecca...

All at once, anguish took hold again. Liam managed to fall into the chair Freddie had vacated, defeated. He knew Spencer was right. His friend *was* trying to help him. Trying to open his eyes to the impossibility of the situation, just as Rebecca had. Liam *had* known, but refused to acknowledge it.

Spencer gently put a glass of whisky in his hand, and sat again.

'You must know,' he said softly. 'She can never be a countess. And I know you too well, despite all these years between us, to know that is what you want of her.'

No, I want—

Her.

He did. Not as his countess, perhaps, but only because he never wanted to be Earl. But he did want to share a life with her—he saw that now. Wanted her always by his side. Only, whatever way he looked at it, he couldn't ask that of her. Spencer was right, he couldn't make her his countess. The scandal would bring nothing more than hardship to her, even if they ran again, far away. As much as he might dream of them living quietly, exiled alone, even then it would be too much to bear.

And wouldn't there be shame for her, too, if he asked her to be his, if he by some miracle enacted his plans? Would there not be dishonour in that, too? Was that not why he hadn't breathed a word of his intentions? Because he knew she would see him differently? Not as the man come to set things to rights, but as the coward who didn't know his place. His duty.

There would be shame, too, in making her his mistress.

She already is.

No. What they had, it was more than an arrangement. More than him setting her up in some apartment, paying her way. Paying the way for any children their nights together might bring. What they had shared…it was more than that.

'I ask nothing of you,' she'd said that first night. She had simply given, everything of herself. And he…couldn't ask her to give up her dignity for him.

Closing his eyes, Liam tossed back the drink, and looked over to his friend.

'I am sorry, Reid,' Spencer said quietly.

'As am I.'

'Freddie and I will leave in the morning.'

'You don't—'

'Yes, we do.'

With a nod, Spencer rose and left Liam alone to his thoughts.

And as he sat in the chair that night, attempting to drown his frustration in fine wine and whisky, he could not shake a growing feeling of impending doom. Perhaps it was that he'd been caged into a role today, forced to become that which he despised. Perhaps it was his inability to further his plans. Perhaps it was what he'd done to Rebecca.

Whatever it was didn't fade with the copious amounts he drank.

Chapter Twenty-One

The clock in the servants' quarters had not long sounded nine when Rebecca heard the bell ring for Gregory. The guests were leaving, then. The Marquess's valet had advised them of that last night, and Rebecca knew it was her fault.

It might have been easier to blame Liam's outburst, but she couldn't. The hours of fretful sleeplessness had shown her that. This—this entire mess—was her fault. Her shame, her embarrassment, Liam's fracture with his friend—all of it—was because she'd not been strong enough to keep away from him.

All her life, she had prided herself on being a woman of honour, and dignity. It was all she'd ever had. Men and masters might control the lives of those beneath them, but they had no control over one's heart, and self-respect. But now... Her actions had not only compromised her own honour, but also Liam's.

Somehow, she knew Liam wouldn't stop fighting what everyone else saw—*knew*. The Marquess, Mr Walton, even Thomas. They all accepted that this was how things were. That this was the way of the world. By fighting it, saying what he had, Liam had dishonoured himself—but not beyond reparation.

Men did not suffer the consequences of affairs as women did. He still had a chance to be seen as the lord he was—by his friend, by his servants and by society. If she was no longer part of the equation.

It was now up to her to set things to rights. Time for her to leave Thornhallow forever. After all, not only did their stations divide them, but also her past. What had happened, it precipitated things, but her leaving had never been in question. So, she would take a few days to gather what was left of her wits, then find somewhere quiet to go until she found a new position.

Before you make any more trouble. For any of them.

No one below stairs had said anything; they'd given her a wide berth, and quite a few supportive glances and small smiles. But while their loyalty bolstered her courage, and her pride, it was all just one more slash against her already breaking heart. Very soon, she would leave them, the closest thing to family she'd ever known.

You always knew it would come. This is your life. Better sooner than later.

Conscious that the current line of her thoughts was neither productive nor pleasant in any way, Rebecca rose from her desk. She decided she would go up and help the others clear the breakfast room, now the house was quiet again, and hopefully Liam was nowhere to be seen. It was as good enough an excuse as any to escape herself, and find something to occupy her mind.

The others were already well on their way to having the room cleared, but when they saw her arrive they tempered their haste, and took more time between each ascent and descent, returning only to collect the piles she'd gathered, until eventually, Rebecca was left alone to wipe, and sweep, and polish, for which she was grateful.

The bell rang at the front door, and she heard Thomas's

footsteps travelling across the hall. She gave no real thought to their visitor, half suspecting it to be Mr Bradley.

That was until she heard Thomas's clear and commanding voice through the half-open door of the breakfast room.

'His Lordship the Viscount Rochesdale,' Thomas announced.

Oh, God, no...

Rebecca felt her stomach drop, her mouth go dry and her blood run cold. Had anyone seen her then, they would have seen her blanch, eyes darkening with terror. Clutching the edge of the table to keep upright, she knew she had to move, to run, but she couldn't. Her mind was numb; her feet wouldn't respond.

There were voices now, Liam's and her prince's. Francis Mellors, Viscount Rochesdale. She heard them, vaguely over the blood rushing in her ears, rendering her near deaf.

So he'd found her, then.

So quickly.

Was this her punishment? Her *reckoning*?

You knew you shouldn't have come here. Too close.

A shrill burst of laughter tore her from her thoughts and shook her into action. She moved as quietly as she could from the room and down the stairs. Only when she was safely ensconced in her office did she allow herself to stop. She leaned against the door and slid to the floor, her legs now failing to support her.

The initial shock had passed, and now the reality of her situation came crashing upon her. Her prince was here. Fifteen years of running, of successfully evading the demon who sought to claim her, and now, here he was. In the one place she'd been foolish enough to believe for a moment was safe.

She let out a hollow laugh that was quickly followed by a pitiful sob. But she would not cry. She would not break.

There was no time; she had to run. As always, without warning, without goodbyes. She would pack her bag, and disappear today. This instant. Leave Thornhallow behind. Leave Liam behind.

Already she'd suffered, knowing it was coming, that it had to be thus, and yet now, with the hour upon her…

God give me strength.

Steadying herself with a deep breath, closing her heart to the pain which threatened to overwhelm her, Rebecca pulled herself from the floor. Then, as though the hounds of hell were on her heels, she grabbed her travelling bag, and threw as many of her belongings as she could into it. There would be no taking the portmanteau, but she would make do. She had to.

Leaving her keys on the desk, Rebecca listened at the door for a moment to ensure no one was about. Only Mrs Murray could be heard, shouting her usual orders across the servants' quarters. Quietly, Rebecca slipped out of her office, down the corridor and out the tradesmen's entrance. Daring not even to take a final look, she scurried along the house, and across the park into the woods, before she could convince herself there might be another way.

Once in the shadow of the trees she allowed herself to breathe again, and prayed that she would make it far enough before anyone noticed she was missing.

Liam had stood beneath the portico and watched his guests—*friends*—depart, then remained there, staring at the empty drive for a long while after that for good measure, not even feeling the cold, his thoughts too entangled to allow him to feel or see anything beyond them.

Not even the copious amounts of liquor he'd downed last night had helped him find any rest. His own words, the look on Rebecca's face and the conversation with Spencer had whirled endlessly in his mind.

What a right mess of things he'd made. He'd come to untangle himself, to free himself, and instead… He had wrecked what little he had left, and now he felt more lost than ever before.

When he'd lost Hal, it had been simple. He'd had to run. To leave this place, his father, the person he was destined to become. When he'd left Columbia, it had been simple. Return, and cut ties forever.

Now… He didn't want to be Earl, but he would be. He could run, but the prospect tasted bitter. Even though Spencer had shown him he wanted absolutely nothing more to do with society. With that world, those people… To spend the rest of his life living as society prescribed, speaking and caring about nothing of importance, gliding through his days with feigned insouciance… There lay only madness.

Yet if he stayed… What choices then lay before him?

You have to tell her. You have to…say something.

Yes, Liam thought bleakly, wandering back into the hall distractedly. Through all his meanderings of the mind, only one thing was inescapably clear. He had to speak to Rebecca. Well, first, he had to apologise.

Beg forgiveness, more like.

Beg her forgiveness for shaming her, though he could not will himself to regret his words. Damning though they might have been, he realised the truth in them. Rebecca was mistress of Thornhallow. Mistress of him, and his heart.

He'd tried and failed so many times to distance himself, when he'd known from the first she would bewitch him. When he'd known the night he'd gone after her in the storm that to lose her would mean his own end, and not because of the guilt he would carry.

The past days, living here, in a world so separate from hers, so close and yet unreachable…it had been torture. And despite his reluctance last night, this morning had brought another certainty. He may not like the prospects he had to offer Rebecca, but he had to at least offer them. Hear her rejection of him, of his plans, in her own voice. He couldn't take the choice from her.

The bell at the door echoed loudly in the otherwise silent hall, tearing Liam from his thoughts. Thomas swept to the door in a blur, and Liam moaned, rubbing his hand over his face, unsure he wanted—or was able—to deal with whatever this was now.

Can a man not get one moment of peace?

Sadly, neither could he find the will to move. He cursed his own body's failure as Thomas stepped aside and admitted an unfamiliar, elegantly dressed fellow about his own age, who rather looked like a red squirrel.

Liam strode to the door as Thomas shut it, passing him the man's card.

'His Lordship the Viscount Rochesdale,' Thomas announced.

'Mellors is fine.' The Viscount smiled sweetly, which did anything but endear him to Liam. 'We are, after all, neighbours.'

'Reid,' Liam answered gruffly, extending his hand.

He vaguely remembered Rochesdale, somewhere on the other side of town, and who must have been the old viscount, one of his father's acquaintances.

'My apologies for arriving unannounced,' Mellors said with false contrition. 'I heard you were in residence and thought to introduce myself. Our fathers were friends once, and I hoped to lay the foundations of such a connection again.'

'Indeed.'

Liam warred with himself. He didn't want to invite Mellors in, foster *any* connections—but, as much as he despised having to be part of society again, he knew good relations with neighbours were always better for an estate.

Whether I am here or not.

He nodded to Thomas, who took the Viscount's coat, gloves and stick, clenching his jaw as he resolved to entertain this unexpected guest for a short while before going to find Rebecca.

'Have some coffee brought to my study.'

'Yes, my lord.'

'Very kind,' Mellors said with a bow of his head.

He looked a bit too much like the cat who'd got the cream for Liam's liking.

Definitely should've sent him packing.

'I do hope I am no imposition.'

'Not at all,' Liam said through gritted teeth, leading Mellors onwards.

Liar.

'An impressive house,' Mellors commented as they settled in his study, his eyes flitting everywhere, as if taking note of every speck of dust.

Of which, thanks to Rebecca, there are none.

Liam decided he didn't like this Mellors much—and not solely because between the tailored silks and wool, and bejewelled fingers, he looked every inch the representative of all Liam generally despised.

'Very…old-fashioned.'

Liam forced himself to return the sneer. 'It was built by the first Earl of Thornhallow,' he pointed out.

'Naturally,' Mellors conceded, a glint in his eye. 'You

should visit Rochesdale some time. Not as *historical*, but just as grand.'

I'd rather visit Gehenna.

'Yes, I must.'

Liam was about to say *Hang society*, and put an end to this strangely off-tone conversation, when Mr Brown appeared at the door, *sans* coffee. The look in the butler's eyes told him there was a reason for that.

'If you will excuse me,' Liam said, in what amounted to a gracious growl.

'Of course.'

'What is it, Thomas?' he whispered as he reached the butler, shooting Mellors a falsely placating smile. 'I swear, if you find an excuse to get me out of here, I will raise your salary to an obscene amount.'

'There is something you should know, my lord,' Thomas breathed. 'Though I am not sure whether you will be so thrilled once you hear it.'

'Out with it, man,' Liam said sharply, giving the butler his full attention. 'What is it?'

'It's Mrs Hardwicke. She's gone, my lord.'

'Gone,' Liam repeated, uncomprehending, dread growing in his stomach. 'What do you mean, *gone*?'

'I happened to see her heading towards the village via the west woods, my lord. She had a travelling bag, and when I went to her office…I found these.'

Liam looked down at Thomas's outstretched hand and saw Rebecca's set of keys.

A hundred emotions and questions vied for attention within him but he pushed them all away, focused on only one thought: *I need to stop her.*

He looked at Thomas, and in an extraordinary show of opinion, the butler nodded and stepped aside.

'I'm afraid a matter of urgency has arisen,' Liam said

to Mellors, who was on his feet in an instant. 'You will excuse me. We'll resume this another day.'

'Of course.' The Viscount bowed.

'Thomas will see you out,' he threw over his shoulder, already marching out of the room.

He marched straight to the stables, not even bothering to stop for his coat, borrowing instead the one Tim kept hanging in the tack room. Neither Tim nor Sam said anything as he strode past to get Orpheus, his expression warning against any interruption. He jumped bareback astride the stallion, the two grooms threw open the doors and Liam galloped out as though his life depended on it.

There was not a second to waste. He didn't know what had prompted Rebecca's hasty, and cowardly departure, for surely if this was about last night, she might have fled earlier, but he knew that he couldn't let her go. Not like this.

He deserved more, something, *anything*, he thought as he rode across the park, caring little for his own safety. She was utterly witless if she imagined things could end like this. To think he would *let* them. To believe he could bear for things to end between them, and that he could part from her.

Liam slowed Orpheus as they approached the woods. He might not care about his own safety, but the animal had done nothing to deserve any further carelessness. Rebecca could not be much further. At least, so he hoped. He had no desire to offer the village a public spectacle. He needed to find her quickly, and bring her back before she could harden her heart any further against him.

I will not lose you, Rebecca.

Finally, just as he was beginning to lose hope that he would find her before she reached the village, Liam spotted Rebecca on the path ahead. He saw her turn, stumbling on some roots as she did, and felt his stomach flip when he caught her expression before she recognised him.

Utter terror...?

Liam slid off Orpheus as she turned from him, her pace quickening as she continued to flee.

Oh no you don't, he thought, breaking into a run.

She must have heard him, for she, too, began to run, though luckily her bag and skirts impeded her.

'Rebecca, stop, please!' he shouted, easily catching her up. 'Not like this!'

'Go back to Thornhallow, my lord, I beg you!'

'Damn it, Rebecca!'

'Let me go!' she screamed, even as Liam grabbed hold of her arm and whirled her around to face him. Tears were streaming down her face, though she was trying valiantly to fight them. 'Let me go, Liam!'

'At last we have dispensed with the *my lord*s,' he growled, grabbing her other arm, too. 'You cannot fight me, so relent—please, Rebecca—and explain yourself! I at least deserve that!'

Her attempts at wrenching free ceased, and she slackened beneath his fingers, his touch alone keeping her upright.

'If this is about last night—'

'Liam...'

It was more a breath than a spoken word. His heart lurched as he searched her face, imploring her silently to look at him. She looked so defeated, so *tired*...

God help me. Please say I alone am not the cause of such pain...

'Now. Tell me. What are you doing?'

'Leaving,' she said meekly. 'I thought it obvious.'

'Why?' Liam asked, unable to conceal the pain in his voice.

There had to be something more to this—but what else *could* there be?

'It's time. You knew I would one day.'

'Not like this. Rebecca, please, I beg you, tell me. I know something's wrong—you won't even look me in the eye, damn you!'

She did look at him then, and his heart broke with the pain and fear he saw in her eyes.

There is something more.

'Why?'

'I can't,' she breathed, her voice faltering.

'I won't let you leave like this, not until you tell me the truth.'

I won't let you lie to me as Hal did and risk losing you.

'I will drag you back if I must.'

Rebecca shook her head despondently and he felt her lose what little strength she had left. He guided her gently to the ground, and she stayed there, on her knees, until finally a sob wrenched free of her breast.

This most certainly wasn't just about them.

This was worse, much, much worse.

'Oh, God,' Liam said, all at once understanding.

Only one other thing has changed...

'It's him, isn't it? Mellors?'

Rebecca nodded, and he pulled her close against his chest. He let her cry all her tears, her sobs cutting through him like daggers, until she had none left to cry.

'You should've said something, come to me... I would've...'

'I swore I would quit the house if my secrets endangered it,' she croaked.

'It is not up to you to quit this house. He will never set foot here again—'

'He knows!' she exclaimed, and the terror in her voice

shattered his soul. 'If I stay, he will stop at nothing. I must go. It is time.'

'It's time when I say it is.'

Rebecca wrenched herself from him and stared at him reproachfully. 'And when is that, *my lord*? When you are married? When more discover what has passed between us? When does it end—*how* does it end—if not now, like this? This story does not end well. We both know that. Now, let me go,' she pleaded.

And even as he knew he should, as he could not before, so he could not now.

'Please, Liam.'

'No,' he rasped, taking her face between his hands. 'I cannot. God help me, I cannot.'

He pulled her to him then, and kissed her with fierceness and passion, possessing, demanding and unyielding. He would not let her go; he would end her torment and set her free, as he could not free himself. He would not think of what might come to pass, of how things might end. For now, he knew he would die if he released her.

And so he took everything she had left to give.

Took everything which meant she could leave him.

'God help us both, Liam,' she cried as he finally broke the kiss.

'I will keep you safe,' he whispered to her after a moment, his hands still clutching hers. 'I swear it. We'll find a way. Now, please, come home.'

Unable to speak, Rebecca simply nodded, and let Liam lead her back to Thornhallow.

Chapter Twenty-Two

'Here,' Liam said gruffly, forcing a glass of whisky into Rebecca's hands before resuming his pacing, looking every bit a caged, snarling beast.

He'd been doing that since he'd dragged her back inside, sat her on the sofa and thrown a blanket on her shoulders, nearly half an hour ago. There was nothing to do but let him. Soon, he would come to the same conclusion she had years ago.

Rebecca was numb, terrified and yet resolved. There was no doubt in her mind that her prince would find a way to her. The only thing she could do now was ensure Liam wasn't caught in the middle. That he didn't suffer trying to protect her. And he would. For, just as before, Liam refused to stop fighting.

If it hadn't been so heartbreaking it might have warmed her. Chased away the cold numbness inside.

That's what the whisky is for.

'We'll go to the magistrate,' he declared finally to the flames, nodding his head as if trying to convince himself more than her.

'And say what?' she retorted flatly.

He turned, his eyes alight with indignant fire.

'Francis never touched me. Even if he had, I have no proof.'

'Ford is a good man,' he bit back. 'He'll help us find a way. He helped with Hal.'

'This isn't covering up a tragedy such as that, Liam!'

He winced and she sucked in a deep breath, forcing her voice to remain even. His hopefulness and conviction were salt in the wound. Once, she, too, had believed there was a way. But no longer.

'This is an accusation against a peer. Your neighbour. *No.* I will not stay hidden here, living in fear. I have to go.'

'Then we'll go together,' Liam said, striding over and taking her hands in his.

Rebecca stared at him, uncomprehending, a vicious sliver of hope nearly clouding her own judgement as she looked into those eyes that would forever be her downfall.

'Please,' she begged, her voice cracking and what little remained of her strength wavering. The numbness was fading with every one of his protests, with his every touch, and the pain of it all tore into her. 'Stop it. You cannot leave again. Not like this. Not for me.'

'It wouldn't be just for you,' he breathed, looking down at their hands.

'What?'

Sighing, Liam rose, and loath as he was to, he released Rebecca's hands and returned to the hearth. This wasn't how he'd imagined having this conversation, but then, Fate was a cruel mistress. So he would tell her why he'd truly come back. Somewhere in his heart he was grateful—the choice he'd been dreading was being made for him.

I will run, for her.

'I only came back to rid myself of the Earldom,' he said, turning to face her.

'Is that even possible?' She frowned, searching his eyes for the lie.

'No.'

Raking his fingers through his hair, he tried to find the words that would make her understand, that would make her stop looking at him that way.

As if she doesn't know me at all.

'This life was never for me. The people who live on the estates need—*deserve*—a strong hand to lead them. To care for the lands, and them. That is not me. It never was, and never will be. I came back to rid myself of it all, make the arrangements for the title to pass to my cousin. But Leonards could not find a way. So we'll leave.'

'You want to run again. After that scene out there,' Rebecca said, emotion tightening her voice and his heart with it, 'your offer is to run again?'

'I have means,' he pressed on, knowing it all sounded as weak as it felt. 'We will be safe. We'll be happy.'

'No, we won't, Liam!' she shouted, jumping to her feet, the blanket falling back like a cape.

She tossed her glass onto the table disgustedly, and his heart fell to his boots.

'I don't *want* to run anymore! I do so because I have no other choice! But you... You ran halfway across the world,' she said, her eyes pleading, anger melting into sorrow. 'Still you found no peace.'

No, no, no...

'If we were together—'

'Not like that. I can't.' She shrugged weakly, biting back tears.

He took a step towards her, but she pulled away.

'You're not the man I thought you were.'

Liam froze, halted in his tracks by the words his heart

had feared all along. He'd always known what she would think of him if he told her the truth, but hearing it now...

'You're a coward, Liam.'

'What are you, then?' he spat, the harshness in her eyes spurring on his own, anger mingling with guilt and despair in his breast.

'God only knows. What I do know are my limitations. When a battle cannot be won.'

'So you retreat?'

He hated himself for hurting her, but he couldn't seem to stop himself. This wasn't how this was supposed to go, any of this.

'Yes,' she seethed. 'Call it cowardice, or self-preservation— what you will. But you...you have a name, a title, means, as you say. You have *power*. To be, to build, whatever you wish.'

Liam turned away, back to his old companions the flames, but her words would not release him. *She* would not release him.

'You searched for ten years—or rather, I think, your entire life—for some ideal world. And you failed to find it. Instead of staying, and fighting to make that world yourself, you would run again. For how long, Liam? How far?'

'As long and far as it takes.'

'You will destroy yourself on that path,' she croaked.

He felt tears of his own burning his eyes.

Only from the flames. Not the searing truth.

'The man you feared you were when we first met, that is who you'll become. But I will not be there to see it.'

'We aren't finished,' he declared in his most lordly and commanding tone as he heard her begin to walk away. 'If you truly wish to leave, I will make arrangements and keep you safe. You are not to disappear, and I'll instruct the others that Mellors is not to be allowed within a mile of my land.'

'You should tell the others the truth, then,' she said flatly. 'They deserve as much.'

Liam nodded. There was a moment, the tiniest sliver of a second, when he knew he could make this right. When he could go after her, and fix everything he had just shattered into a million pieces. Only the man who could, would be the man Rebecca had thought he was.

And I can never be that man.

He heard her footsteps, the click of the door, and he closed his eyes.

If you do have power here, help me protect her, Hal...

Rebecca barely even saw the others as she passed them, making their way upstairs to be told her sorry tale. She might have told them herself, only... She didn't have it in her. She bemoaned the loss of the numbness; it was far better than this crushing devastation that left her hollow. It was beyond grief, beyond heartbreak, beyond anything she'd ever felt before.

Just make it to your rooms. Then you can fall apart.

She wasn't entirely sure what she'd expected when Liam had dragged her back. Perhaps a calm, somewhat rational conversation, during which he'd realise there were no choices left for either of them. She had to leave. He had to let her go.

Perhaps, yes, somewhere in the love-addled, still-hopeful part of her heart, she'd dreamt there might be a way for them to be...together always. Happy. Instead, she'd got...

My entire world razed.

Bracing herself with a hand to the wall, Rebecca stopped for a moment, forcing herself to breathe through the pain that nearly doubled her over. Everything she'd been so sure of, everything she had believed Liam to be, had been a lie. And, goddamn it all, if she didn't still love him, with every last piece of herself.

It would be so much easier if I didn't. I wish I'd never come here. I wish I'd never set eyes on Thornhallow Hall.

Sniffling, wiping her eyes furiously, refusing to be broken by this—any of this—she forced herself to move.

Just keep moving, always, she told herself ceaselessly as she made it through the final steps to her rooms, where she could finally make a plan.

'Well, this certainly is a delightful surprise,' came the voice Rebecca had prayed never to hear again as she closed the door to her office. It chilled her to the bone, and her stomach turned. 'I couldn't believe it when I discovered where you'd ended up. You've led me on quite the merry chase, my dear.'

Rebecca crushed every single emotion within herself, determined to show him none of it, stood proud, and met his gaze.

There he was, her prince, as dangerous and handsome as ever. Tall and lithe, fine-featured, his appearance was effortlessly but carefully curated. From the perfectly tailored pantaloons, waistcoat and jacket, to the crisp, immaculate linen shirt and intricate cravat. From the tousled yet exquisite strawberry blond curls and immaculately shaved skin, to the selection of little rings on the long, delicate and expertly manicured fingers.

Francis hadn't aged a day. He still had the youthful, innocent air which concealed his dark spirit. Once, he'd reminded her of a fairy; now he reminded her of a fox. The way his mouth curled in a perpetual sneer and his pale green eyes swept across every inch of her, calculating, full of terrible intent… Once, she'd been charmed by the innocent facade. Now she saw only the rancid soul beneath.

Arms crossed, he was lounging in her chair, his lazy,

nonchalant manner in no way dissimulating the ready tension in his body. She knew she could run, scream, call out to the others, but she also knew this was her battle, and hers alone to fight.

And now I have the courage to.

What she'd found here, in Liam's arms, even despite all she knew of him now, what they had shared gave her the fortitude to face anything.

I will tremble before you no more.

'I am not your dear, *my lord*,' Rebecca retorted coldly. 'Nor shall I ever be. I suggest you leave the same way you slithered in here.'

'Now, now, is that the way to greet an old friend?' Francis drawled. 'Besides, I'll be on my way shortly, with no one the wiser, once we've had a little chat.'

'Please do not tarry on my account.'

'I will have what I came for.'

'And what is that?'

'You know very well,' he said, straightening and slowly moving towards her. 'Fifteen years, Rebecca, and nothing has changed, I assure you.'

'Many things have changed.' Rebecca smiled, raising an eyebrow in challenge to his approach. The Viscount stopped, acknowledging her newfound strength with admiration. 'Though one thing has not. I will not be yours. I'm not afraid of you anymore.'

'I see that. And may I say, it serves only to make you more interesting.'

'Losing can be a valuable lesson, my lord.'

'Losing? But I have not lost. This little battle of ours is not over.'

'I think you'll find it is,' Rebecca bit back, her unease growing at his unblemished confidence. 'Nothing you can do will force my compliance. So I bid you farewell. May we never meet again.'

Rebecca moved to open the door, but in a flash Francis had his fingers curled around her arm and pulled her in close to face him. She tried to wrench herself free, but he simply tutted and tightened his grip.

There was triumph in his eyes, and she felt her heart sink.

'We are not finished, Rebecca,' he said.

He was so close she could see every fleck of grey in his watery green eyes. She swallowed hard, trying to conceal any trace of fear he might use against her.

'I'm not angry.' Francis smiled soothingly and her stomach roiled. 'I was, at first, you made a fool of me, but then... I always did love a good hunt, and you've been such excellent sport. I've enjoyed our game. Only now it is at an end. So I suggest you listen, and that you listen well. Will you behave if I release you?'

Rebecca nodded as defiantly as she could, and Francis shot her another sickening smile before letting go of her arm.

God help me, for no amount of courage shall help me now.

'You may not fear for yourself,' Francis said, as though discussing the weather. 'But I think, you would not see others pay the price for your stubbornness. So, my terms are simple. You will come to me by sunset, or I will end the lives of everyone in this house. Including His Lordship. If you run, I will end them. If you are not convincing enough in your farewells, and anyone comes after you, I will end them. Do I make myself clear?'

Rebecca nodded, her voice and fight gone. She didn't doubt for a moment he would make good on his threats, no matter that Liam was an earl. There were always ways.

'Good. Until later, then,' Francis said lightly, sliding past her and out of the office.

Fumbling, Rebecca closed the door, falling against it as she did so, feeling her entire world crumbling around her.

You knew this was how it would end; no use crying about it now.

She had stood tall, faced her enemy, and he'd won. There was nothing more to be done but to accept her fate, and be glad that she'd been granted the chance at such a happy life, for a time at least. Be grateful for her time at Thornhallow, her time with Liam. There was nothing for it but to pack her things and disappear into the air like some sprite. Disappear before anyone could stop her again.

You can do this, Rebecca. You know the price if you do not.

Chapter Twenty-Three

And you would call me a coward, Liam thought as he stared down at the note on Rebecca's desk.

He'd come down here with the others, once he'd told them of Mellors, intent on finding some way to convince Rebecca not to leave again, intent on at least apologising to her for the hurtful things he'd said, only to find her gone.

He hadn't believed it—she had promised she would not go just yet, and still here he was, in rooms empty of all but her scent.

Her scent, her keys and this blasted note.

I am sorry, Liam.

But talking more will not change the fact there is no other way. I will not live another moment in fear, knowing he is circling this house, waiting for a moment to strike.

Forgive me my harsh words. You are the man I thought you were, and more. I hope you find a way to peace, and perhaps some day even happiness.
Rebecca

The note crumpled in his hand as anger, regret and fear pounded through his veins. He dropped himself into her chair and stared unseeing at her desk. He didn't deserve this—any of it. Not her contrition, not her pleas for his own peace and happiness.

He crumpled himself, then, into the piles of paper and ledgers on her desk, the force of all he felt crushing him.

Despite his vow, he had failed her.

Just as he'd failed Hal, and Angus, and Peter, and his mother. As he'd failed everyone in this house, everyone on the estates, and worst of all, himself. Rebecca could never stop running, could never find peace or happiness but for a moment if she was lucky, and yet she wished all that for him.

God...

Yet again, everything she'd said had been nought but the truth. The truth he had so blindly, vehemently, refused to see. He *was* a coward. He *was* running. He *would* become the man he'd feared he was. If he continued down this path he would never have a chance at being the man she'd seen when she looked at him. The man he'd always searched for, always longed to be.

And what the Devil had he been running *to* all this time? All he'd seen for so long, like a shimmering mirage in the distance, had been *freedom*. But after that? He'd never imagined what would come *after that*. He'd never given it second thought, *what* precisely he would do with that freedom once he'd earned it.

'Instead of staying, and fighting to make that world yourself, you would run again.'

No. No more.

Rebecca was right. He had a title, means and *power*. For once in his goddamned life, he would use it for good.

Hope flooded his breast and he rose, giddy, and nearly drunk on it. He had the power to set *her* free, if not himself.

He would go to the magistrate, and discuss her situation with him. They *would* find a way to give her life back to her. He would spend every penny of his fortune, leverage his title for all it was worth. He would stop her running, and so he would, too. He would break Mellors, ensure her safety, and then he would find her, and...

Tell her.

What she did with that freedom—whatever life she wished for—he would offer it to her. He would offer her himself. Whether she wanted him or not would be up to her.

Feeling as if he might burst out of his skin with the promise of what could be, Liam marched out of her office and to the stables.

You will be free, Rebecca. We all will be.

'I hope you find the room to your taste,' Francis purred as he showed her into the disgustingly ornate chamber.

Rebecca was well aware of the Viscount's eyes on her, of their triumphant, gleeful gleam. She wished she could give him a more convincing performance of indifference, but it had taken every ounce of strength she possessed to leave Thornhallow, and write that note.

Those words had been the hardest yet the truest she'd ever written. Her meeting with Fate—*Francis*—had put everything with Liam into perspective. She might not agree with his plans, might have felt betrayed by them— still, she knew *him*. Knew his soul.

Really, it was a miracle she hadn't soaked that note with tears. And now she truly had nothing left. Nothing left to pretend, or to fight. Francis had broken her; he'd won as she'd always known he would. He was far from finished, but the breaking of her body would be nothing compared to the breaking of her spirit.

It doesn't matter anymore. Liam and the others are safe. Liam will live. He will have a chance to begin again.

'If it isn't, I'm amenable to suggestions.'

'I rather expected a dungeon somewhere,' she managed to say. 'Not a guest room in your house.'

'Why ever not?' Francis chuckled, gliding around the room, sliding his fingers across the counterpane and tassels of the bed curtains. 'You *are* my guest. I'm not a monster, Rebecca. Life will be good for you, you'll see.'

'You will, of course, keep your end of the bargain,' she said flatly.

'Of course,' he said smoothly, slinking over to her. 'I'm a man of my word. The people of Thornhallow will not be harmed. I will be good to you, so long as you are good to me.'

A spidery finger toyed with a stray tendril of her hair, before running along the edge of her jaw and neck. Rebecca closed her eyes, unable to bear the look of greedy, possessive lust in his eyes. The smirk at the corner of his lips. The flick of his tongue over his teeth.

'Whatever you wish,' she assented feebly.

'Precisely.' Francis straightened, sought her gaze and kept his eyes locked on hers. 'Mrs Pearson will be up later to prepare a bath and dress you for this evening. Dinner will be at eight. Mind you keep out of trouble until then.'

'Yes, my lord.'

Francis's eyes lingered on her lips, and he hesitated for a moment before he gently brushed his against them. A taste, a sample.

A smile, and then he left. Rebecca made her way slowly further into the room, unsteady, but unwilling to succumb to her weakness. Her feet would carry her, for they must. She would not falter. She would bathe, and dress, and eat dinner, and make conversation, and endure whatever came with grace, and courage, and above all, dignity.

For she had loved, and for a brief, inimitable moment, had felt loved by the best of men.

Chapter Twenty-Four

Liam never made it back from the magistrate's.

He remembered arriving in the village, riding through it to Ford's house, which lay up the hill by the church. Laying out Rebecca's tale, and Mellors's role. He remembered Ford's assurances that *something* could be done. That he would ensure protection for Rebecca if she went to him, and gave a formal statement. From there, they would need to get more advice, and likely they would need resources, and time, to bring charges against Mellors, and ensure they stuck.

He had thanked Ford and rushed back towards Thornhallow, to prepare for his pursuit of Rebecca, but then...

There was nothing but sharp pain and darkness.

Liam's eyes fluttered open at that memory, then shut again almost immediately. The pain which had been but a memory was now very real. His head ached, clouding his mind as he slowly regained full consciousness.

Someone had hit him at the back of the head; he could feel it throbbing.

What the Devil has happened and where the hell am I...? Lying on a floor somewhere...

Somewhere warm and comfortable, that much was true.

He may be on the floor, but he was on what felt like a rich rug.

Liam forced his eyes open and found that he was still surrounded by darkness. Suffocating darkness.

A sack.

Someone had covered his head with a putrid-smelling Hessian sack. And tied his hands—he could feel the burn of rope against his wrists as he tried to move. That hurt, too. In fact, his whole body ached, as though he'd been thrown about like a sack of potatoes. Which he suspected was not far from the truth.

What the hell is this...?

Liam made the mistake of taking a deep breath, in an effort to keep calm and clear his mind, so that he could get himself out of whatever mess he was in. The thin and rancid air caught the back of his throat, and Liam coughed and groaned, gasping desperately for air.

There was a hollow laugh, footsteps, and then the sack was ripped from his head.

Blinking furiously, as the now overwhelming brightness blinded him, Liam welcomed the sweet breaths of fresh air.

'Finally, you're awake,' drawled a familiar voice. 'I was growing bored, and was about to have Rupert here fetch smelling salts.'

'You,' Liam growled, his eyes adjusting and recognising Mellors sitting in the chair before him.

My chair. My library. My house...

So he'd arrived back at Thornhallow after all—only not quite how he'd planned.

'Do you have any idea how grave a mistake you've made? Untie me at once, you disgusting invertebrate.'

'I don't think I will,' Mellors laughed. 'Rupert, go and see that everything is ready.'

Liam heard heavy footsteps lumbering away, out of the library and through the hall.

Good—one less to deal with. Think, man, you need to get out of this...

'You see, Reid, I don't particularly enjoy people meddling in my affairs, and you've been doing just that.'

'Whatever you're planning, I can assure you, you won't get away with it. I've already spoken to Ford. He knows everything.'

'Won't I?' the Viscount asked, his eyes glinting dangerously and his mouth curling into a sardonic smile. 'But I already have. Here you are, at my feet, powerless. Rupert's knots are quite remarkable. As for your rather *pathetic* household, they've been rounded up and secured. Soon you, they and this house will be nothing more than a tragic memory.'

'They aren't a part of this,' Liam snarled, trying with little success to loosen his restraints. 'Let them go.'

'You are hardly in a position to bargain, Reid. They are part of this now, thanks to you. You forced my hand, forced me to come here myself—'

'Whatever your quarrel is with me—'

'Whatever my quarrel is with you? My quarrel is that you presumed to interfere in an affair that has absolutely nothing to do with you,' Mellors whined. 'Fifteen years I've been chasing her, you know. Rebecca was smart, always a step ahead. I dare say, though, the chase was certainly invigorating. Had she not run, well, she would've been just like the others. Nothing.'

The others...

Liam's stomach roiled at the thought of other girls like Rebecca—*how many?*—suffering because of this monster before him. He would get out of this bind, he swore—he'd got out of perhaps not worse but similarly dire circumstances before—and he would see this man hanged as a symbol of what befell those like him.

Justice.

'And then—' the man grinned, fuelling Liam's rage '—just when I begin to grow weary of hunting her across England, she falls straight into my lap. First mistake she ever made, coming back here. I shall ask her about that later...'

Mellors's words penetrated his haze of fury, and Liam's heart stopped beating.

He has her. She didn't leave.

'As for you, well...you should've let it be. Enjoyed the life she bought you.'

'The life she bought you...' He threatened you with my life so you went to him...

The realisation of what she'd done filled him with both inexorable joy and breathtaking heartbreak. He really needed to get out of here. Luckily the bastard was enjoying the sound of his own voice.

'Damn you, Mellors!' Liam cried, beyond caring that his voice betrayed his pain, his fear at all he could lose. 'You will pay for all the ill you have wrought. On Rebecca, on—'

'Oh, do cease your remonstrations,' Mellors sighed, rising to his feet. 'Really is dreadfully boring.'

'Time to go, my lord,' came a voice—Rupert? 'Shouldn't tarry, it'll be taking off now.'

'Excellent, thank you, Rupert, out in a moment,' Mellors called back.

With a sickening grin, he strode to the window, tore down one of the silk curtains, then turned back and stopped by the fireplace. He stoked the fire, slid away the screen, and with a disturbingly overenthusiastic flourish threw one end of the curtain into the fire. It caught immediately, whirling and twisting into a mighty flame.

Mellors laughed and stepped away, before coming to loom over Liam.

'Not that I don't trust Rupert's capabilities, but best to make sure things are done properly. On that note, I really must be going.'

'I don't think so,' came Rebecca's voice. 'Not quite yet.'

The sound of shouts and a creaky wooden cart had torn Rebecca from her daze. Hours she'd sat there at the window in Rochesdale, in the gaudy, stifling room the Viscount had declared her own, staring out onto the dales and fells which only months before had seemed to sing as they welcomed her back into their embrace.

There had been nothing else to do but wait.

It had been meant as a torture—the slow ticking of the gilded clock on the marble mantelpiece, the solitude—time for her dread to grow as the hour of her surrender drew nearer. Yet Rebecca had been grateful for the time to prepare herself. To say her prayers, and find some peace.

And then, she'd heard the noises.

So at odds with the calm silence otherwise permeating the house, they had caught her attention.

She'd slipped quietly from her room, along the corridor, until she'd found a room which overlooked the tradesmen's entrance. From her vantage, she'd seen a couple of brutes driving a cart meet Francis. She'd seen them discussing the covered bundle in the cart—unmistakably a man. Gesturing, they had beckoned the Viscount, and when they'd lifted the blanket…then she had seen the man beneath. And though his head had been covered, she'd known him in an instant.

There had been more shouting, and gesticulating, and

then the brutes had driven off south. Somehow Rebecca had known precisely where they were going. *Thornhallow.*

Francis had returned inside, and she'd slipped back to her room. She'd heard shouts ringing throughout the house. Orders. Preparations. And then, not half an hour later, the sound of a door slamming, and the Viscount riding out.

It was not difficult, since Francis trusted that she would *not* run away, to do just that. To steal into the stables, and lead away a thoroughbred stallion with no one the wiser. Just as it was not difficult to slip into another house, particularly one she had lived and worked in.

No, slipping back into Thornhallow Hall to find her family was no great feat at all.

No, no, no, no... Get out of here, Liam thought, as he rolled over to be sure his mind was not playing tricks on him.

Sure enough, there Rebecca was, standing at the doorway, a pistol pointed at Mellors, another tucked in her belt, the image of a fierce and formidable pirate warrior queen.

It might have been romantic had it not been so terrifying.

'Rebecca, you need to leave, go, before—'

'I'm not going anywhere, Liam,' she said, her eyes never leaving the Viscount as she carefully made her way towards them. 'Step away from him.'

'Be careful with that, my dear.' Mellors smiled derisively, nonetheless doing as he was told, arms raised, careful to seize the opportunity to move away from the fire growing behind him. 'No need for anyone to get hurt.'

'Do not doubt for one second I know how to use this.'

'Rebecca, please, just—'

'Liam, enough,' she said sharply, stopping beside him. Without losing her focus she dropped down and handed him a knife from her pocket, before rising again, the pistol still aimed and at the ready. 'You might've had it all, you know. If only you'd left them alone.'

'In my defence,' Mellors drawled, eyeing the door, 'he went to the magistrate. I was otherwise quite prepared to keep my word.'

'Strangely enough, I believe you.'

'Well, one mustn't dwell… Might I suggest perhaps we adjourn elsewhere? Things are beginning to heat up, if you'll forgive the witticism.'

'How are you doing, Liam?' Rebecca asked, her voice as calm as she appeared, though she hadn't failed to notice the growing flames in the library, nor the smoke drifting in from the hall. 'Time is rather of the essence just now.'

'Almost, there,' he said, finally freeing his hands.

Liam rose, but did so too quickly and stumbled, still dazed from the blow to his head.

Rebecca moved to catch him, but in that second of inattention Mellors seized his chance, and ran for the door. She fired and nicked his arm before he disappeared.

Just as she made to follow there was a tremendous roar and crash in the hall, followed by a scream. Liam grabbed Rebecca's arm, but she shook him off, extracted the other pistol from her belt, and ran after Mellors, determined to end it once and for all.

Struggling to keep steady on his feet, the smoke increasingly hindering his breathing and his sight, he stumbled out after her.

Why did I have to be cursed with the most stubborn woman in the world?

Chapter Twenty-Five

Rebecca reeled back as she burst into the hall, and threw up an arm up to cover her nose and mouth. The hall had turned into a hellscape. Flames licked and climbed every wall, every tapestry, every corner, and dark smoke curled in thick clouds. Beams and floors had crashed down from above, blocking the main entrance and the doors to the other rooms.

Coughing, her eyes stinging, she glimpsed Francis, unconscious, trapped under a smouldering pile of floorboards a few feet away. Time seemed to stop then, as Rebecca hesitated. She could leave him there. Pretend never to have seen him at all. Her nightmare would be over. Justice would be served. She'd heard what he said about *the others*.

That is not justice. That is vengeance.

And though one nightmare might end, another would begin. Her guilt, it would follow her always, and taint the rest of her life.

You don't get to escape so easily.

Tossing away the pistol, Rebecca tore away strips of her petticoat and wrapped her hands as she slid over to where he was.

'Rebecca!' Liam shouted, appearing beside her, wrapping his own hands in his jacket. 'Where are the others?'

'Safe!'

'If the entire edifice was not on the verge of collapse, I would chastise you for this folly!'

'Hurry and you can do so later!' she shouted back, as they both began liberating Mellors.

'He isn't worth it,' Liam grumbled when they had freed him, shaking his prickling hands.

'He isn't worth the price if we don't.'

Liam nodded and grabbed hold of Mellors's arms, dragging him away from the growing inferno the hall had become.

'Together,' Rebecca protested, when he moved to sling the Viscount over his shoulder.

He relented. Only because, loath as he was to admit it, he wasn't at his best, and he knew that if he fell behind, Rebecca would stay.

They each threw one of Mellors's arms around their necks, and dragged him through the house. Together they raced through to the conservatory, the smoke blinding and suffocating, the flames flickering at their clothes and hair, singeing them as they ran.

The rush of air from the conservatory fuelled the fire behind them as they burst in, the flames chasing them as they ran towards the doors to the park.

Just as they thought they might not make it, the doors were there before them. They flew out into the fresh, clean, cold air, gasping for breath, their eyes adjusting to the bright, smokeless surroundings. Onwards they ran still, distancing themselves quickly from the scorching blaze.

It was then that they heard the rumbling, ominous and louder than twenty thunderstorms. They stopped, turned and stared speechless, as the East Tower crumbled, falling in on itself and tumbling down with a mighty roar through the roof.

The blast of hot, smoky air that followed threw them back even further, and Rebecca felt more lost than she had ever before.

'Rebecca,' Liam croaked. 'Are you hurt?'

'No, I'm fine… Are you?' she asked, slowly coming back from the daze she had sunk into.

She'd been so scared, terrified of losing him and the others… She'd done what she'd had to, without succumbing to her emotions, but now they all came crashing down on her.

I could've lost him. I could've lost them all.

'Are you injured?'

'A bump on the head, a bit singed and some sore ribs,' he said, shrugging away as she reached for him. 'Nothing to worry about.'

Rebecca nodded despondently and shifted Mellors's weight on her shoulders, gripping the worm's wrist tightly, lest he rouse and try to slither away. She couldn't blame Liam for wanting nothing more to do with her. He'd just been attacked, kidnapped, nearly murdered, and now his home was burning brightly before their eyes.

All because of her.

'The others will be out on the drive,' she said, pushing away the utter despair which threatened yet again to overwhelm her. 'Lizzie went to get help.'

'Let us deal with this, then,' Liam said fiercely. 'Before the pond scum wakes.'

And so, they began to make their way around the house, keeping a very wide, safe distance, looking like strange demons, singed and sooty, born themselves of the blaze.

Though Rebecca tried her best not to look directly at the destruction she'd wrought upon Thornhallow Hall, she could do little to avoid it as they made their way around. The fire illuminated the landscape, the red-orange light dancing and multiplied tenfold by the frost. Gigantic shadows gesticulated across the land, and the roar of the crumbling house was deafening in the evening's silence.

As for the setting sun, it only emphasised the whole terrible sight.

Perhaps I have died and this is hell... It surely looks, sounds and smells like it.

As best she could, with both her hands still supporting her tormentor, Rebecca furiously wiped away the tears that fell across her cheeks, quickening her pace so they could put an end to all this as soon as possible.

At least Liam was safe. At least she'd made it in time. He could rebuild. Start a new life. He may never forgive her for what she had inflicted upon him and his house, the wreck she'd made of his life. But at least she'd saved him and the others.

Shouts and screams brought her back harshly to reality, and through the cloud of smoke ahead she spotted Mrs Murray and Gregory, rushing towards her.

'Thank the Lord above!' the cook screamed, flapping like a mother hen. 'Mrs Hardwicke! Master!'

Rebecca felt a pang as she watched Mrs Murray's eyes scan them both, noting their injuries with winces of her own, barely able to restrain herself, it seemed, from pulling them into her embrace.

Her eyes narrowed, as did Gregory's, when they realised who hung limply between Liam and Rebecca.

'Is Ford come?' Liam asked rather harshly, marching on towards the drive.

'Yes. He's there by the cart, with Mellors's brutes,' Gregory bit out reproachfully when Mrs Murray seemed near to tears.

Eyes ahead, they marched on towards the magistrate, a tall, rail-thin but fierce-looking man, well into his middle age. They ignored the rest of the staff, who at least had been seen to, covered in blankets and carrying mugs of tea as they were.

The magistrate turned away from Mellors's men, and met them halfway. 'My lord—'

'In a moment,' Liam said, continuing past Ford to drop Mellors by the cart. 'If you would be so kind as to re-strain him.'

Blinking, the magistrate stared for a moment, then came to and did as Liam bade, signalling to a few of the nearby men to keep an eye.

'Fetch Dr Sims,' he instructed one of them. 'My lord—'

Liam raised his hand and turned away, making directly for the immense line of people that wound around the house to the well. Half the village must have been there, passing along buckets of water, attempting to delay the flames' progress, their carts and horses lined up along the drive.

'Enough!' he shouted, turning everyone's heads, stopping them in their tracks. 'Thank you for coming to Thorn-hallow's aide, but that is enough. The house is lost.'

Everyone exchanged looks of confusion and disbelief, most staring at Liam as though he had lost his wits.

Rebecca clenched her jaw when she spotted Bradley, Tim and Mr Brown, who had been leading the effort. The look on their faces said it all: their hope, their home, their world, it was all lost now.

Because of me.

'It's all right, lads,' Bradley said, setting down his bucket. 'Nothing more to be done now. Off you go back home, then.'

Confounded by the mad-looking Earl's behaviour, but

unsure of what else to do, the villagers slowly dropped their buckets, disbanded and began making their way back, grumbling and muttering their confusion as they did.

A few passed by the huddled staff, offering them rooms for the night or hot food. They did not quite know what to say, other than to express their thanks, shocked as they were by the reality of their situation, their imminent future still uncertain.

Right now it seemed all they could do was wait.

Wait and see what would become of them.

Wait, whilst the house which had been their home burned brightly before them, a haunting, fittingly violent end to the house which had for so long been at the centre of so many terrible tales.

'My lord, a word, if you please,' Ford said reproachfully as Liam strode back towards him.

There was a grim expression on his face, though he nonetheless tossed him a blanket. Liam wrapped it eagerly around his shoulders; shock had set in, and he'd begun shivering.

Shock at having been nearly killed, and at the thought that he might never live to right his wrongs, nor see Rebecca again. That she might be subjected to a harrowing future at Mellors's hands because of his failures. And, if he was honest with himself, that she had saved him.

He glanced around for her, found her tucked into the care of the rest of his staff—*family*—and Dr Sims, and felt a little of the weight in his chest lift.

'I have already spoken to your household,' Ford continued, a frown creasing his brow as he studied the oddly calm Earl. 'They have advised they were attacked and bound by two men known to work for Viscount Rochesdale. Those men were eventually subdued and restrained with the help of your housekeeper, whose rather timely arrival ensured the staff's escape. I have also spoken to these men, who have confessed their crimes—though they did make it immutably clear that they were only following orders, and that the Viscount was the one who orchestrated this whole *disaster*.'

Liam nodded, and the magistrate sighed.

'This is to do with what you came to see me about, my lord?'

'Yes. Mellors was here, intent on murdering me and my staff. I think that clarifies our next steps considerably, don't you agree?'

Ford sighed again, heavily, though he nodded grimly after a moment. Arresting and making a case for the conviction of a peer of the realm was not to be treated lightly.

'I only need you to keep him contained until I can make further arrangements,' Liam reassured him. 'I will engage the best legal minds and the fiercest guards. We'll get him to London, and before the House before he can even think to try and weasel his way out of this.'

'I will prepare the battlefield as best I can,' Ford said, resolve in his gaze. 'Speak to Mrs Hardwicke and the other staff about today's events, as well as her personal history with His Lordship over there, and get written statements. I will also ensure I get the confessions from these vermin,' he spat, gesturing towards Mellors's men. 'In writing. We'll ensure you have everything you need to make a case.'

'There have been others,' Liam said gravely.

Ford's jaw ticked as he regarded Liam carefully for a long moment.

'I didn't... I know you, Ford,' he continued, realising what he'd implied. 'You're a good man. An honest man. Not one who would forgo the truth to preserve reputations.'

Ford's gaze softened.

'I mention it only as I hope you can look into the matter. I will hire others, but here...you are trusted. People might talk to you when they might not to a stranger.'

'Of course. I will speak to Mrs Hardwicke first, I think,' Ford said after a moment. 'And then see this refuse removed from your land.'

'Thank you.'

Ford strode off towards Rebecca, Liam following slowly behind. As the magistrate took her aside, Liam wandered over to his staff—*family*—and made his apologies for his earlier behaviour. He'd barely finished before they forewent all propriety and passed him around for embraces, tears flowing generously.

The doctor saw to cleaning up his wounds, and soon he was just as bundled as them all, with tea in hand, and he told them of his talk with Ford, and their plans.

As they digested the news in silence, too amazed to formulate any questions, Liam watched Rebecca discussing matters with the magistrate, as composed as ever despite everything that had happened. She really was an extraordinary woman, his love.

Love.

Yes, that's what it was. The revelation hit him with dizzying strength, and he smiled beatifically, like some witless dunce. How blind, how stubborn he'd been, indeed. Denying the simple, obvious truth; concealing it behind notions of comfort and passion. She had captured his soul the first night he'd found her in the library. Every time he'd been presented with the idea of losing her, he had found himself unable to face it. Why? Because she was his friend? Because he felt he owed her a debt? Because she had breathed life back into him and shared his bed?

What an utter imbecile I have been...

Unwillingly, unwittingly, Rebecca had become part of

him. Her flesh, her being, her soul, woven into his. And he, at every turn, had refused to recognise that. Had refused to see the blatant truth, even as he knew her to be mistress of his heart. He loved her with everything he was. She had awoken him, given him hope of a future he'd thought long-lost.

Rebecca glanced over at him, and a frown appeared on her face before she turned back to Ford. Liam realised he still stood there, smiling like an idiot.

Drat.

What must she think now? He had behaved badly—that much was certain. Even as she'd risked her life to save him, even as they'd escaped with their lives, what had he done but stand there and ask her if she was hurt? No demonstrations of relief, not even any thanks. He had not taken her into his arms, shown her what he felt at that moment, expressed the love that he may not have *known* he felt, but that he most certainly *did* feel. What had he done but recoil from her touch?

True, Mellors had been between them, but really, he should have tossed the sorry excuse of a man to the ground and shown her what was in his heart.

Damnation...

He may have inadvertently broken that which he held most precious.

Again.

There would be much begging in his future.

So long as she is, too.

If the day had taught him anything, it was that he'd already wasted far too much time. Missed far too many opportunities to seize the happiness life had seen fit to offer him.

Ford was extending his hand to Rebecca now. With a

smile, she took it, and then the magistrate was coming back towards him.

Finally, Liam thought, feeling as though he couldn't get back to her quickly enough.

'Mrs Hardwicke and I have had a most promising conversation,' Ford said. 'I have reassured her, I think, that Mellors will never be a threat to her or to anyone else again.'

William Reid, you are an ass.

Thank God Ford, at least, had seen to reassuring her. In all the turmoil, Liam had never quite thought to tell her she would have her life back, if it was the last thing he did.

'Thank you, Ford,' Liam said, offering his hand.

'You and your staff are welcome at Heathfield, for however long is needed. I will leave you now, but I will send word to my wife that we will be expecting guests...?'

'Again, thank you, Ford. Your kindness is very much appreciated. Until later, then.'

'Until later, my lord.'

With that, Ford marched away, mounted his horse and made his way down the drive, followed by the cart bearing a still-unconscious Mellors and his restrained associates.

Liam turned to his little army of staff, all gathered now to watch the continued destruction of their home and livelihood. Their faces bore more sadness and regret at the loss of Thornhallow than he himself could ever feel. For now, he finally felt that he could look towards the future, and hope for happiness.

And there is no more time to waste...

Chapter Twenty-Six

It wasn't long before the fire began to dwindle, and soon Thornhallow Hall crumbled into itself, the flames which only moments before had seemingly touched the sky now giving way to smoking embers and groaning timbers.

The bitter wind howled around them, fanning the seemingly endless destruction, while sweeping the ash and smoke far away into the horizon, a grim mist in the twilight. They all stood there in stunned, shocked silence, watching, waiting. For what, no one really knew.

Liam had told them all of Ford's offer, and they had agreed to accept it. No one preferred the houses of gossips or the rooms at the local pub to the peace and tranquillity of the magistrate's home.

Bradley had left at that news, promising to visit the following morning. They had all agreed to make their way to Heathfield, that there was nothing more to be done at Thornhallow, and yet no one had moved.

It was as if they needed to see the final end of the house, to see it through its last moments. Not until they had could they leave, could they even begin to think of asking the master what would become of them all.

All except for Rebecca.

After Liam had joined them again she'd slipped away, on the pretext of checking on the horses—not that anyone had paid her much attention. She hadn't been able to bear to stand among them, she who had cost them everything.

Rebecca stroked Callie's neck, and thought back to her first day here, to her first view of Thornhallow. She remembered the dread and foreboding she'd felt that day, and wondered if this devastation was what she'd been warned of.

All this had come to pass because of her. Liam and the others had nearly lost their lives, because of her. Because of her weakness, her inability to muster her strength when she'd had the chance to run from them all.

'God forgive me,' she whispered to the air, tears pricking her eyes again.

'Don't,' Liam said fiercely, appearing beside her. 'This isn't your fault. You have nothing to be forgiven for.'

'Of course I do,' she croaked, shaking her head and moving away from Calliope. The last thing she needed was for the poor mare to get upset. 'I brought this on you. On all of you. On Thornhallow.'

'Rebecca, look at me. Please,' he said, slipping his bandaged hand gently in hers and coming to stand before her. 'You are not responsible for the wrath and ill-doings of that vermin. We are all alive and safe.'

'And your home is nothing but ash!'

'It's not my home,' he said softly.

He lifted his hand to cup her cheek, and for the life of her she couldn't move away.

'You know that. It was only ever a house. I dreamed for years of burning that pile of rocks to the ground, and now it is done. Even though you brought life back to it for a short while, it would never have been enough. Thornhallow held only sorrow, and pain. I'm glad it's gone.'

'You're upset, Liam, you don't know what you're saying—'

'I have never been more certain of anything in my life, Rebecca,' he said with a ferocious smile, pulling her closer to him. '*You* are my home now.'

'What? N-no, Liam,' Rebecca stuttered, gently pushing away.

'Yes,' he promised, holding on to her as tightly as he dared. 'I did not have the courage to admit it before, and I am sorry. I did not have the courage for many things,' he admitted.

Rebecca sagged slightly. 'Liam, what I said, I'm sorry—'

'Why?' He laughed softly. 'You were right. Again. I was a fool, trying to convince myself abandoning the title would free me. Give me a chance at being the man I always longed to be. It wouldn't have,' he said quietly, stroking her cheek again, even though she still refused to meet his gaze. 'It would've made me the man I always feared I was. The man I want to be, I am with you. I am free with you. I'm staying, Rebecca, and before you say it, not because of you, but thanks to you. And if you will have me—'

'No, Liam, *that* is impossible.'

'Why? Why is it so impossible?'

'You know why. You are an earl, and I...I'm a servant. Some things, just cannot be.'

'They can if you fight for them to be.' He smiled, bending a little to catch her gaze. Finally he snared those eyes that saw so much, and in which he saw his own soul reflected. 'You challenged me to build the world I wanted to see, and I intend to. That begins with having a partner by my side whom I love, and respect, and who is, in every way, my match.'

Rebecca opened her mouth, but words were not quickly forthcoming, so Liam forged on, determined to lay himself bare before her one last time.

If she refused him then, so be it. But he would not let her doubts, her fears, society's expectations, make the decision for her.

'It will not be easy,' he warned, admitting that he was not so blind as to think it would be a simple happily-ever-after for them. 'There will be talk, and scandal, that is for sure—particularly since I intend for Mellors's trial to be very public indeed. Doors will close, and I doubt we shall ever be invited to the more respectable houses. But I have a title, and a fortune, and what good are they if I cannot do as I please? Besides, I am the Disappeared Earl, so who knows? It might just add to my renown.'

Rebecca let loose a half-sob, half-laugh, and Liam grinned.

'I can, and will, weather anything so long as you are by my side, helping me build the life I dream of, for us, and for the world. I cannot see a future without you in it. You brought me back to life, Rebecca, with your stubbornness, and heart, and understanding, and relentlessness. Do not abandon me now.'

'I… Liam, I,' Rebecca stuttered, suddenly aware of their growing audience, the rest of the staff having slowly made their way over. 'You don't know what you're saying.'

'Look at me, not them,' he ordered gruffly. 'Do you love me?'

'Oh, God,' she sighed, the starkness and suddenness of the question flustering her. 'I, that isn't important—'

'Like hell it isn't. Do you love me—yes or no?'

'Of course I do,' she blurted out before she could censor herself. 'With all my heart.'

'Good. Because I love you, and that is the only important thing. Now, I know you've only just been given your life and freedom back. I know you said you did not see yourself settling, taking a husband, relinquishing your independence. But know I would never ask that. All I ask is that you be free with me. Let us rebuild this place, and build a life, together. However you wish, as my wife, as my companion, as my partner—I care not, so long as you're with me.'

Fifteen years of running.

From everything. Family, home, love, connection.

And here, before the smouldering remains of Thornhallow Hall, the man she had inadvertently fallen in love with was declaring his love to her.

Everything about this was impossible. And yet, here he was, asking her to share a life, to be his. Offering her the world, a life of love.

Rebecca felt the stares of the staff, and turned to them, expecting to see disapproval, judgement and dismay. Instead, she found them all smiling—all save Mrs Murray, who was crying unmistakable tears of joy. Thomas nodded, and that was all the approval she needed to bless her and Liam's unholy union.

'Yes,' she said, grinning like an overly excited schoolgirl as she leapt up, throwing her arms around his neck. 'Yes.'

Smiling, Liam grabbed hold of her and twirled her around, raining kisses upon her cheeks, brows and lips. Both were dizzy by the time he finally stopped and set her once again upon the ground, entwining his hand with hers as they turned back to their family.

'I suppose we should all make our way to Heathfield,' Liam said. He, too, was unable to stop grinning. 'We have much to discuss and much to decide.'

The bedraggled yet hopeful band of Thornhallow Hall's staff nodded in unison, and with candles to light their way, and the horses in tow, they all began the long walk to Heathfield. Not one of them turned back to look at the glowing pile of ash.

Though Liam and Rebecca both said silent farewells to the ghost of Thornhallow Hall—the ghost that did not exist, but which they knew had dwelled there.

By the time they arrived at Heathfield, some two hours later, all their hearts were full of joy and hope as they celebrated a new day, sitting together at Ford's table.

Epilogue

Thornhallow Estate, four months later

'If I didn't love this hat so, I would eat it,' Spencer said wryly as he joined Liam beneath the shade of the largest of five tents peppered across the hunting lodge's lawn.

They had been erected to house the Earl and Countess of Thornhallow's wedding breakfast. Well, more of a village fete than a breakfast, really, but Rebecca had insisted on inviting the whole village.

Liam wasn't sure if it was the refreshments, curiosity or the fact that the lodge was well away from the ruins of the old house, but most had actually come.

'You made her your countess.' Spencer grinned, sipping his champagne. 'And I have never seen one to rival her.'

Spencer raised his glass in a toast, and Liam followed suit, his eyes following his friend's to where his bride stood smiling amidst a rather eclectic group, half local gentry, half ladies from the village, all united in their admiration of her gown, it seemed.

Not that Liam could blame them. She was glorious, shining brighter than the May sunshine, and none could resist.

Though to him, it mattered not whether she was adorned in a mint tulle and silk gown with a coronet of flowers, or the drabbest wool, really. She was all he ever saw. And though the fashionable wardrobe he'd been thrilled to lavish upon her had eased her way into people's homes, it was her kind and determined spirit that had eased her way into their hearts.

Life had not been easy since the fire. News of Thornhallow's destruction had spread like a blaze itself, along with that of Mellors's arrest, and Liam and Rebecca's engagement. The truth of the matter had been distorted in a hundred different ways, and they had faced more scrutiny and judgement than Liam could have imagined when they'd gone to London.

But together, they'd weathered the worst of the storm, Rebecca's fortitude and determination to rise above it all, slowly gaining them more and more support.

Despite the scandal of it, Mellors's shockingly expedient trial had been cathartic for them all, and helped quash most of the disgusting gossip.

In the end, he'd been convicted and sent to Van Diemen's Land. Between the testimony regarding the attempt on Liam's life, that of the five other women he'd found who agreed to speak, and the public outcry against the Viscount—the newspapers all having seized upon the affair with gusto—the House had been reluctant to drag on the proceedings, and been forced to ensure not only that Mellors was *dealt* with, but properly punished.

Liam still had men searching for any others who had suffered Mellors's perfidy, and he would do right by them as best he could, just as he had with those he'd found.

On Spencer's urging, he and Rebecca had remained in London awhile after the trial, and though they had not been *welcomed* into society, they had been *accepted* at some choice events of the Season, and they'd even made some acquaintances that in time may prove to be friends.

Liam knew Spencer and the Dowager Marchioness— much to her own dismay—had paved the way for them, just as the pair had worked their connections in the House to secure Mellors's conviction, and he was beyond grateful.

Just as he was grateful to have his friend by his side in church today.

Without him, Liam wasn't entirely sure he would have been able to stand there and not spout nonsense once Rebecca appeared.

'Have I thanked you yet?' Liam asked, turning back to Spencer.

'A million times,' he laughed. 'But I shan't begrudge you a million more.'

'Thank you,' Liam said, offering his hand. 'Truly.'

'My pleasure.' He nodded, taking it. 'Your life has kept mine from being ghastly dull.'

Liam was about to press his friend about the bitterness in his voice when his wife appeared before them, radiant, rendering him speechless.

'I apologise for the interruption.'

She smiled, making his heart skip a beat. *My wife...*

'Only I was hoping to steal my husband for a moment.'

'By all means,' Spencer said graciously, literally bowing out. 'Freddie has initiated a game of bowls and I find myself in need of thrashing him.'

Rebecca chuckled as Spencer wandered off to do just that, and Liam couldn't stop himself from sliding a hand into hers and tugging her close.

She didn't even chide him for the scandalous move— not that she had much time before he lowered his lips to hers and ensured she felt every ounce of the love he felt today, and every day. It seemed to grow, and he wondered if in time, he might simply expire, his body unable to contain it any longer.

After a long moment she pulled away, a slight flush in her cheeks, her eyes twinkling with mischief and desire. 'I have something for you,' she said softly, smoothing the lapels of his jacket.

'Will I like this surprise?' he asked, grinning, his hands travelling to places suggestive of what he wished her surprise might be.

'I hope so.'

The seriousness in her voice, the earnestness in her eyes sobered him, and he nodded, slipping his hand into hers.

'Lead the way, my love.'

Rebecca did just that, leading her husband across the lawn, throwing smiles at those who greeted them and wished them well.

She might have waited until later to do this, but she really wanted to know sooner rather than later if he liked his gift. And, in truth, she wanted a moment alone with Liam. It seemed they'd only had snatched moments here and there, between everything that had happened in London, and then once they'd returned here.

The staff, despite being offered their own homes and allowances, had decided to stay on, and worked miracles while they were away, fixing up the old hunting lodge at the edge of the estate. But as for the estate itself, there had still been so much to be done, even though she and Liam had spent days with Leonards, planning out a shockingly modern future for the Earldom.

And, of course, there was the construction of a new Thornhallow Hall to oversee, not far from the site of the old one, much simpler and smaller, but worthy of an earl and his countess nonetheless.

Ducking through the lodge, careful to avoid being stopped by anyone, Rebecca led Liam to the sunroom. He frowned, likely a little disappointed not to be led up-stairs to their bedchamber, but she smiled and tugged him onwards. He watched every move she made as she un-locked the door and led him inside, towards the windows on the far side.

There, on the sill, sat her gift.

Liam froze when he saw them and she looked over at him anxiously, unable, for the first time in a while, to read him.

'Are those…?'

'Yes,' she breathed, searching his face for any clue as to his feelings. Only, he was as still and stoic as she'd ever seen him, giving nothing away. 'Gregory helped me save them,' she said, looking back towards the two pots of roses. Barely more than seedlings, but resilient.

Such a silly idea.

'I thought, we could plant one when the house is com-pleted, and perhaps the other, with your mother, and Hal,' she rambled on. 'Do you—?'

I think that is a yes, then, Rebecca thought, her heart lifting as she melted into Liam's fiery kiss.

Any, every doubt she'd ever had seemed to melt away when he touched her. She wasn't sure what would have become of her if she hadn't had him these past months. If she hadn't ever found him at all.

Liam finally released her from his spell, though his hands still cradled her face. That light that had ensnared her from the first was there, as magnetic and transfixing as always. He told her often how she'd helped him through the darkness, but so had he. He'd given her things she had never dared dream of. Love, a home, family. The latter of which they were hoping to grow in the coming months.

A small smile appeared on her lips then, as she imagined it all.

'It's perfect,' Liam said, and she reminded herself that he spoke of the gift, not of the image in her mind.

Though it is that, too.

'She would have loved you,' he whispered, his fingers idly rubbing the ring beneath her glove. His mother's. 'And Hal, too.'

Nodding, she turned her head and kissed his palm, unable to say anything.

They stood there a long while, simply basking in each other's presence, and in the memory of those they'd lost, but who would remain with them always. They remained there until rowdy shouts and the sounds of a fiddle and flutes brought them back to the day.

Then, rather than do as she knew he wished to, sweep her upstairs, Liam led her back outside to their celebration, where they danced and laughed and sang well into the balmy night.

Then and only then did he carry his wife upstairs, and as he did, Rebecca knew that never would she regret having become the housekeeper of Thornhallow Hall.

For she had found Liam.

And with him a life of love.

* * * * *